THIS ISN'T WHAT I ORDERED

But It Rarely Ever Is

V V Edwards

Ordering information: quantity sales and special discounts are available on quantity purchases by corporations, associations, and others. for details, contact the publisher at Info@Amazonbookpublishingcenter.com.

The information contained within this book is strictly for informational purposes. the material may include information, products, or services by third parties. As such, the author and publisher do not assume responsibility or liability for any third-party material or opinions. the publisher is not responsible for websites (or their content) that are not owned by the publisher. readers are advised to do their own due diligence when it comes to making decisions.

Amazon Book Publishing Center works with authors, and aspiring authors, who have a story to tell and a brand to build. Do you have a book idea you would like us to consider publishing? Please visit Amazonbookpublishing-center.com for more information.

Table Of Contents

Dedication

To my sister Nora Henslin, who thought this would be a great distraction, It was Sis. Thank you for being supportive through this journey and thank you for being a part of this story. I can only hope the reading keeps you entertained and that I made you proud.

To my dearest friend Marshawn Ford-Rush, Your belief in me never faltered, and your words of encouragement daily have seen me through to the end but really only the beginning. I hope that others have a friend as positive and fierce as you are with our friendship. I will forever be grateful to you for never doubting me.

To Mr. Salvatore. Thank you, Sir.

To all my Kitty's, thank you for your patience. I really wasn't ignoring you. All the Darlin's in the book are a reflection of you. Meow.

To my Chelsea, I hope you enjoy my story because "It Is What It Is." Thank you for all the positive vibes and the long talks as we rode from one end of Texas to the next.

To everyone who thought I had a knack for putting pen to paper, You were right, and I salute you!

This is also dedicated to all those who want to do something with their life that they can be proud of. Never let life get in the way of your dreams. It's never too late.

Preface

From childhood to maturity, writing has been a way for me to define my existence. The written word allows a thought, a memory or a place in time, whether fact or fiction, to come alive on paper.

Applying pen to paper to express a story is done to draw in the reader, opening their mind to places and events that may have a hint of a real-world in it, all the while allowing them to visualize what they are reading.

My intent in writing this book is to take you, the reader, on a journey where you can visualize what is happening, feel what the character feels and let it touch you in a way much the same as a good movie does after watching it.

My inspiration comes from a lifetime of trips to the library to get one and then another book, taking it home, reading it and becoming emotionally moved by its content. I saw what was happening, felt how the character felt and related excerpts of the story to my life. I laughed and cried, and in reading this book, I only hope you will, too.

"Some Old, Some New
Some Sad But True
To Dream Is Real For Those Who Feel
The Sting Of Life In Fact Or Fiction
Is Often Just A Mere Contradiction..."

V V Edwards

Chapter One

Another failed date. What is the problem, or is it just me? I get all excited when I meet someone, and then, Boom, they grab a piece of ass and fade into the woodwork. Was it something I said or did or didn't do? Maybe I'm too needy? Maybe I'm not good enough. Oh God, seriously? All I really ever wanted was a warm body next to me in bed and someone to have a conversation with. Was that too much to ask for? Evidently, for Vivian, it was.

Flopping down on the sofa, Vivian looked around her comfy apartment and wondered when it all started. Was it when she was prepubescent? When? It would all become painfully relevant as the years passed. Right now, though, Henry, her cat, just wanted attention and didn't care much about her dating life. Although she had another early morning ahead of her, she was definitely far from ready to lay down alone again, so she padded to the kitchen for a late night snack. Henry followed closely behind her, hoping for a treat of his own to pacify him till morning. For years, Vivian relied on food to provide her the comfort she longed for. She was by no means overweight, but she was always on one new diet after the other. The thought of the word obese being etched on her chart at the doctor's office made her cringe.

She eyed the takeout container and remembered the date that garnered these leftovers. The food was much tastier than the company she had kept that night. She had found his profile online, and as with so many before him, he really didn't match up to the description she had been given. Why lie? You know you're going to get busted. Vivian had had only one true love in her life, and he had never lied, so she supposed that the bar was set too high for most men to obtain, and she was left with whatever was available. Pitiful.

Relationships had always been something she dreamed of but, in reality, never came to fruition. Maybe it was the baggage she constantly carried with her for years. I guess to know her, one would have to go back to the beginning. Almost as a chronology of the men who had been a part of who she became and the life she would lead. She sat down on her sofa, pulled her cat closer and began to reflect.

She was born as the fifties ended in a small town where everyone literally knew everyone. You couldn't piss without the neighbors talking about it the next day. Her father drank, and her mother stood by and watched her father drink. Her siblings were older than her, and her early recollection of life was grim, to say the least. They had next to nothing, and whatever was left, her father drank away. He was the first man in her life and not the last to throw her away when things got serious. Vivian always wondered how a father could leave a child, his child, for someone else to take care of, but that was exactly what he had done to her and her siblings. She would not know or care to know why for many years. No memory, no pain. I guess she was better off for not knowing. Anyway, not knowing him made his story a short one. Vivian had no idea that the ghost would come back to try to haunt her. Damn, why cant sleeping dogs just lie.

Vivian realized the evening had long since turned into the early hours of the morning, and she knew she wouldn't be worth a shit at the office if she didn't get some shut-eye, so she turned down the lights and let the thoughts of the past rest as she called it a night. They would keep for another day, and as she lay her head to rest on her soft pillows, she soon drifted into a deep sleep, clear of the thoughts that weighed on her in the light of the day.

Vivian awoke to Henry softly making biscuits on her cheek. She loved this time of the day. The sun awaking and reaching through the drapes, soft hues on the walls, calling her to the new day. Henry snuggled next to her as if he knew she needed his loving touch, and he purred his gratitude for the love she gave him. She dreaded going to work. Although she loved her job, the thought of having to deal with her boss gave her the creeps; however, the aroma of the coffee brewing in the kitchen drew her from her bed into the bathroom to wash the sleep from her face and then into the kitchen for her morning fix of caffeine. An hour later, she was dressed and ready to hit the road. Luckily for her, she was not really that far from the office, and as she pulled into her space, she pulled up her big girl panties and prepared for another day with Derrell. She plunged into her work, pretending not to notice the penetrating stare coming from the office adjacent to hers. He always made her feel uneasy whenever he would speak with her about any assignment they were working on. Too close, her personal space in jeopardy of being invaded, he would lean in as if he and she were involved in a private conversation, and although they weren't, he liked to give the rest of the office staff the illusion that they were. Yuk! Vivian always feared that the crap that was tucked into the corners of his lips would escape and find its way to her desk or, worse yet, her face. Yuk!

By the end of the day, Vivian was ready for a quick drink with a couple of the girls, then home early as she had disciplined herself to do after many hungover mornings. Derrell always looked worse through bloodshot eyes. Steve's was a neighborhood tavern that had been in business as long as the neighborhood that was built around it. It wasn't much to look at, but the bar was clean, they served great drinks, and nobody bothered you while you were there. Vivian and the girls grabbed a table close to the back, out of the way of the happy hour crowd that flooded the bar. Plus, it afforded them a bird's eye view of everyone coming in. Jamie and Lulu were Vivian's closest friends. She trusted them, which, for her, was an oddity. It was low-key busy, but they got their drinks quickly. The jukebox was playing great songs from the 70s, and they began to unwind after another very long day. They were all in agreement that Derrell was a real piece of work and, if they weren't making good money, would have bounced a long time ago. They playfully teased Vivian about her "boyfriend" which sent the three of them into a fit of laughter at the thought of it.

As the bar filled with patrons, Vivian decided this was her cue to head for the safety of her apartment. She despised crowds. The closeness, pushing and vying for a better position in the room always made her feel suffocated and always left her searching for an exit and breathing room. She bid her friends farewell and stepped out into the cool evening. She opted to walk the short distance to her place, not concerned at all that the daylight had faded, and it was now dark. Her neighborhood was quaint and well-established, and the sidewalks were lined with brightly lit rows of lights. It also helped her feel at ease knowing the can of mace was tucked into her purse, just in case.

She unlocked the apartment door, knowing Henry was already waiting on the other side to greet her. It was a good feeling even though he was on four legs, hairy, and pooped in a litter box. The joy he gave her was like a warm blanket on a cold winter day. So after their daily ritual, Vivian changed out of her work garb into comfortable lounge pants and her favorite Yankees t-shirt, grabbed a drink to pair with the sandwich she had ordered from the bar and sat down for a quiet evening. Alone. Again. She ate in silence, and her mind drifted once again to her childhood, the place she was certain started it all.

Vivian stood in the kitchen of her "new parents" house, not knowing or understanding. She was a baby, really. The new dad looked stern, not friendly or loving. Not the wrap his arms around her, good feeling type of guy. Do I call him daddy, father, dad, sir? Vivian clung to her sister, Lyla. She felt safe with her. She felt protected by her. She would know what they were supposed to call him. Everything Lyla said was right in Vivian's world. Vivian followed her around like a puppy, always looking to her for reassurance. Lyla had always taken care of her and her brother, and she was very protective of them, even now when she should have been able to relax and be the child she had never been. She was so much older than her years. The trauma she had suffered at the hands of her parents was unspeakable for a child her age. She would hover over the new mom, watching her every move. "Don't hold her like that, she doesn't like to be bathed like that, she doesn't eat that kind of food," she would repeat over and over until the new mom did her best to assure her that Vivian would be alright and she didn't have to worry anymore. Her sister, Lyla, through the years, would always worry about her and her brother. It was comforting to know that no matter what, she would know what to do.

Even as a small child, she feared the new dad. She couldn't put her finger on the reason, she just knew she was. It wasn't the type of fear one feels when they've experienced something scary. He wasn't scary at all. He actually was a handsome man with jet black hair styled in the traditional 60's crew cut, medium build and fit. It was the look that he gave her. She felt that when he looked at her, it was through eyes that really didn't like what he saw. He never really interacted with Vivian or the rest of the kids except Babs. He loved her. She was his pride and joy, never doing anything wrong in his eyes. She was the reason Vivian believes to this day, that he didn't like her. Vivian remembered him one day telling her that she was trouble. Trouble? Vivian always did whatever it took to steer clear of him, so she didn't really know what that meant. He always provided for them and took them all on summer vacation, picnics at the lake, where he would sit in his lounge chair smoking cigarettes with his eyes hidden behind his Foster Grants. She guessed he tried his best, but there was always something missing. Something that every child cherished and held on deeply to in their memories, forever. Love. Affection. A hug when something hurt. A pat on the back for a good grade, a kind, encouraging word when something was tough. Yes, Vivian did not have that memory. It must have been tougher for him to have children that weren't his own than he ever admitted to. She guessed he did his best.

Vivian was a shy, tomboyish girl growing up. She would rather have played outside with her brothers and his friends than sew with her mom. She didn't like to be dressed up in girly clothes. Shorts, t-shirts and jeans were her preferred garb. She had naturally curly hair, so her mother kept it cut short. She wanted so badly to have long flowing hair like her sisters, but nope, she had curls for days. Ugh! The dad thought it was out of line for her to play with boys and yelled at her about it all the time. The boys in the neighborhood didn't mind because Vivian was at an age where she started wearing bras, and you know how that goes. Boys to men, they all thought alike. Her dad was never home at night, and on the weekends, he found things for the kids to do as he sat in his easy chair in front of the television, trying his best to ignore the noise around him. He wasn't a happy man, and he was not really kind to Vivian's mother. When she got sick and was hospitalized, he dutifully visited her, but by then, he had a side chick he would stop to visit on his way home. He tried to cover it up by saying she was doing his laundry for him, but Vivian knew. On one occasion, he took her there with him but made her swear she wouldn't mention it. By then, Vivian was a teenager, and the thought of her father with another woman sickened her. Why couldn't he be like the other dads? Why didn't he want to be home with his kids? Why did he fool around on Mom? She had gone with him to visit her mother, and they stayed with family for the night. Vivian was assigned to a cot in the back bedroom, and while her father was out, she remembered a man, not an uncle as he claimed he was, just a man, crept into where she lay, and the rest is still blocked to this day from her memory. Her father asked her, however, where she had gotten the necklace that had suddenly appeared around her neck and when she told him that her uncle had given it to her, her father became furious. He fired so many questions at her. She didn't know the answers or what to say. He blamed her. She must have done something. She hadn't. She swore she hadn't, but he looked at her with such contempt that she felt as if maybe she had. Again, he had no comfort for what he might have known happened but would never say. He wasn't an Uncle, and after that, life with her father was strained, to say the least.

When Vivian's mother passed away, her dad checked out, but that, to a teenager, was pure bliss. Vivian rebelled. She was attractive with a cute figure and big boobs, and the eyes of most boys and men fell upon her as she walked the halls of her school. The bad boys welcomed her to hang with them, and the jocks secretly made their moves, never noticeably but just the same. She playfully flirted, not knowing that in doing so, she was inviting something she knew nothing about.

Chapter Two

Vivian fell asleep that night troubled. She hadn't wanted to remember the events of the past, but as her therapist of many years always told her, "In order to move forward, you have to relive the past, work through it, then move on." All that money she was paying him, and that was the best he had? It was bullshit in her opinion. More like tucking it away and never trying to analyze it. She tossed and turned all night, and by morning, she had resigned herself to not fighting it, so she got up and made coffee, as ready for the day as possible. Weekends were always relaxing for her. No late evenings at work, no incessant blatherings from the office gossip and no Derrell. She dressed in a cute sun dress and sandals and tied her long hair, yes, long hair, back in a ponytail and headed out to the farmers market, a place she liked because it had everything she needed without having to make multiple stops, which was something she disliked more than anything. She wasn't able to handle the crowds of people milling around, touching everything, kids screaming and crying. They probably didn't want to be there either but had no choice.

The farmers' market had a rainbow of brightly colored arrangements of flowers, fresh fruits and vegetables, smoked meats, and freshly caught fish, and it just felt good being there. It was a sunny day, not too hot, perfect for shopping. She had never been able to do that in the past, always having to do things for others, putting her life on the back burner. Always making room in the square for someone else to stand in. Her whole life had been like that until she had decided no more. It was cleansing for her, and she didn't feel bad for saying no. She shopped at her leisure and made several purchases that would brighten her already lovely place. A large bouquet of Gerber daisies, her favorite, a lovely scarf that she could either drape or hang as wall art, her very favorite cheese, smoked salmon, a few hand-painted tiles to line her wall in the kitchen and her favorite Rolling Stone magazine. She eyed a cute little toy for Henry stuffed with catnip, his addiction. Having exhausted her shopping list, she walked the short distance to the center where starving artists were painting or playing music. Other shoppers had gathered to take in the sights and sounds and just hang out for awhile. It was a relaxing day, and Vivian was absorbed in the atmosphere, so she didn't notice the person who had seated himself next to her, not close but near enough for her to catch the faint aroma of Polo Black, a scent that was tattooed in her memory forever. Don't ask. That could be a story of its own.

She glanced over, and he smiled, she smiled back and, for some reason, she wasn't sure of, said hello. He was tall, had dark hair and a well-groomed mustache and beard, something Vivian was quite fond of. He had a nice build, not the workout-every-day build, but a hard-working man type of build. He worked construction, lived in the city and was single. His name was Jack Wilson. Their conversation was light and refreshing, not uncomfortable for her at all. She felt at ease talking to him. When the sun began to move westward, Vivian got up to leave, and he asked for her number. She wasn't in the habit of giving her number out and often had given her fair share of fake numbers, but there was something about him, so they traded numbers and went their separate ways.

When she arrived home, Henry was quite put out with being left to fend for himself all day, but in reality, he had basked in the sun and slept for the better part of the afternoon. Vivian prepared a light dinner and settled in for a quiet evening with her new mag and a bottle of Moscato, her favorite adult beverage. She watched, amused, as Henry played with his new toy, quite pleased that he had not been forgotten. Vivian loved cats. She always had. They had minds of their own and needed no one but, at the same time, wanted love on their own terms, of course. She relaxed on the vintage sofa she had found one day while out with her thrifting buddy, and as she sipped her wine, she looked at the card Jack had given her. Wilson Construction was embossed in bold letters across the top with the usual address for the business office, phone number, and a sketch of a skyscraper shadowed the background. It was classy but not overbearing. Halfway into the bottle of wine and feeling good, her mind wandered to an earlier time when another construction worker would enter and exit her life, stage left.

Vivian was in high school and not very popular, but she did have a friend she could confide in, and it seemed that every time she got into trouble, so did Lilith. They were cutting gym class, hated by both of them due to the stick-thin girls that were relentless in their pursuit of making the two girls' lives a living hell, and they both agreed that checking out the workers that had been hired to build the new addition to the school would be more entertaining than sweating with a bunch of bitches. What harm could it do? If they had only known the drama that would ensue as a result of their innocent curiosity. Nate and Butch were buddies, and the girls had seen them together in the hallways before being careful not to look too hard or long at the teens under the watchful eye of the school's principle. When they saw the girls come across the construction site, they smiled, knowing that the two girls were there to see them.

Now it was the seventies and was a time when men were regarded as the powerful sex and women and young women should always behave like ladies, prim and proper, keeping their legs crossed at all times for God's sake, but Vivian's hormones were all over the place, and all she could think of was getting into some heavy petting with someone that was more mature than the sloppy high school boys. No silly relationship, no future for them, just a whole lot of kissing and touching, or so she thought. They had already met up with the guys a few times, so they retired to their own secluded areas behind the curtain in the auditorium that afforded them some privacy. Immediately, Nate was all over Vivian, kissing her deeply, taking her breath away. They touched each other in places that lit a fire in their souls and between Vivian's legs, but she was afraid because although she was no longer a virgin, an event so unceremonious that it was not worth mentioning, she had heard the horror stories regarding teen pregnancy and the stigma that came along with it so as soon as Nate's hand made its way to her jeans, she pushed away, catching her breath. She blamed the untimely end on the lateness of the hour and having to return to classes before they were missed. She called for Lilith, who came out from behind the curtain looking disheveled, and they hurried back across the walkway to finish the day. She told Lilith about Nick's intentions, and for the first time since their friendship had formed, Lilith gave her shit for not going "all the way." "You're a cock tease," she said, and Vivian, not wanting to fall from grace with her only friend, silently decided that she would give in to Nate's desire, sadly, just to impress Lilith.

From that point until the dreadful day that ended it all, Vivian and Nick broke all the rules. Her father was never home, having engaged in his own disgusting relationship with Mary, the town drunk, so she really had a lot of free time to do whatever she wanted without having to explain where she was after school. Nate always picked her up on the corner, and they went at it in his station wagon like sex was going out of style. The parking lot of the local McDonald's was one of their favorite spots to hide out, neck like crazy and not give a damn who saw them. Months passed, and everything was perfect until the night when Nate decided to drop her off at home because it was dark, and he wanted to make sure she got there safely. They sat in the driveway, making out like teenagers. Well, one of them actually was when headlights shone through the fogged-over back window. Vivian's father was not supposed to be home until later, so she wasn't really too concerned. Big mistake, BIG! The door swung open, and there stood her father, pissed as hell and ready to kick some ass. Vivian flew from the car and ran into the house, afraid of what was to come in the aftermath of the scene that had just unfolded. She could hear shouting and threats from her father. The local police were mentioned something about statutory rape. Oh God, would he really call the police? After what seemed like hours, Nate pulled out of the drive and sped off, and Vivian's father stood out at the edge of the driveway, wondering how in the hell he had been burdened with this and how he would deal with this now that his wife, Vivian's mother had passed and he was left to deal with the uncomfortable.

Vivian tiptoed around her father for weeks after that, grounded, of course, and she was confused by the cold shoulder she received every time Nate crossed her path. The school principal had been notified by not only Vivian's father but Lilith's as well. The principal feigned not knowing anything at all and should have won an award for acting shocked and appalled by the whole incident, but she knew. Nick and Bill were removed from the site, and Vivian never saw him again. The whole sordid affair ran rampant through the halls of SS High, and the constant barrage of name-calling was relentless. Vivian's father took her to PP and had them put her on the pill. That was his solution to the issue. Case closed, no talking about it, ever. It was a nightmare, and Vivian felt so alone. She overheard her father talking one day, and it was sad to know what he really thought of her, his daughter, the child that he had raised as his own. It was heartbreaking and had an enormous effect on Vivian's young, impressionable mind. Thoughts raced in her head, and she tried her best to rationalize what to do to make it better, how to fix whatever was broken. How to get her father to stop looking at her through the eyes of a stranger. She mulled it over and over, and one night, while everyone slept, Vivian did what she thought was best. She wrote her father a letter, and she left her home. Little did she know that it would be forever. Damned McDonald's could never get her order right anyway.

Chapter Three

Vivian polished off the bottle, certain that it would be alright because she hadn't planned to drive anywhere that night and didn't have to work the next day, so she was pleasantly buzzed and in a great mood when the phone rang. She lowered the sounds of BB King and picked up the phone, corded and the cutest antique style on the planet. She had to be one of the few left that still had a dial-up line, and she loved it. She always thought the act of dialing each number was sexy as hell, plus a good slam down when she was pissed was truly classic. It surprised her to hear a male voice on the other end of the line, but it was music to her ears. She hadn't expected Jack to call that soon or to really call at all. That's how it usually was for her. She tried to act casual, but her heart raced as they casually talked about the rest of the day and what the remainder of the evening looked like for both of them. She didn't share with him what she had planned on doing once the Moscato really kicked in, which was to turn the lights down to a soft amber glow, light some candles and draw a hot bath, which Vivian loved to take in her claw foot tub. She liked to climb in and wait for the warmth of the water to ease the day from her body. The heat was so damn soothing and relaxing that, for some reason, she felt turned on. The water alerted her senses, and she touched herself softly so as not to rush things. This was the only time she ever felt at ease sexually. No judgment, no show to put on, no letdown at the end of the evening. Just raw heat between her legs. She would climb from the tub, rub down with oil to soften her skin, then retire to her bedroom, door closed (Henry staring at her was alarming and kind of creepy), and finish what she started in the tub. It was a ritual that satisfied

her desire for a meaningful sexual relationship that, for some reason, always escaped her.

She was so lost in the lustful thought that she barely heard Jack's
voice until he snapped her back to reality by asking if she would like
to meet him for a drink at Steve's. She agreed, and a half hour later,
she entered the crowded bar not really sure why she was excited, but
happy to explore her options anyway. Jack had chosen a table towards
the middle of the floor, which was now separated so that the pop-up
dance floor would bring couples together with the slow grind of blues
and seventies music. They drank and danced and fell out into the night
to catch a breath of fresh air. He stood close but not too close; he lit
her cigarette, and she waited for the usual lecture of its hazards that
surprisingly never came. The quiet of the evening was not uncomfortable, with no expectation of no-nonsense conversation that, at the end
of the day, really meant nothing. Just peaceful and relaxed. They talked
some more, drank way too much, and danced the night away, and soon
it was last call. She could vaguely hear Rich's famous, "Yall don't have
to go home, but ya can't stay here" message, and they, along with others, crept out into the late night.

Very few people of the opposite sex knew where Vivian lived, and
she liked it that way. Her home was her sanctuary, and it would take a
special person to be invited up. So far, Jack was nice but not yet someone she wanted to share her space with, even if only for a nightcap. Besides, her head was spinning a bit too much to be totally aware of her
surroundings, something she prided herself on. They walked the short
distance to her walk up, and before she had a chance to say anything,
he leaned in and kissed her lightly on the lips. It wasn't the nasty, wet,
all-tongue type of kiss she loathed. How the hell was that anywhere
near sexy? His kiss was soft, smooth and not rushed. He moved away
from her politely and waited until she unlocked the door and was safely inside. It had been a lovely night, and as she stripped off her clothes,
her mind drifted to the man she had just spent the evening with. She
was too buzzed to put on sleeping attire, and as she climbed between

the cool sheets, she thought that she also wouldn't mind if he crawled between her legs. With a giggle, Vivian drifted off to sleep with her last thought. Not a bad way to end an evening.

Overthinking it was a problem that plagued Vivian repeatedly through the years. It was as if she saw a beautiful flower, and instead of picking one, she grabbed the whole patch. Call it insecurity or low self-esteem, whatever label fits, but whatever the case may be, it was always detrimental to her personal and professional life. Zero to one hundred, balls to the wall, plunge in head first, Vivian. It was a wonder that she had managed as well as she had so far. She sat at her desk and mulled over why she hadn't heard from Jack in almost a week, and her mood darkened. She had sent the complimentary "had a great time" text followed by a voicemail a few days later, then another text and, oh shit, another text or two. Oh well, whatever. Derrell was out of town on business, thankfully, so the mood of the office was relaxed. Vivian could tuck herself away in her office while her thoughts drifted back to another time several years earlier when she had obsessed over a casual relationship that she regretted much too much later. Oh, and the sandwich from the night before was not what she had ordered again.

Chapter Four

1976 had been a tumultuous year for Vivian. She had fled the confines of her father's home shortly after her sixteenth birthday and was basically living on the streets of New York, her only comfort was the period when she was taken in and sheltered in the arms of Angels. They treated her kindly, made sure she went to school, protected and kept her as safe as they would have their own child. Her father caught wind of her location, and a short time later, he tracked her down there, had her arrested as a juvenile runaway, and Vivian went to jail. She had been housed in a small town jail until she was assigned a probation officer and released. Her only visitor had been her sister, Lyla. Time passed, and Vivian, a rebellious teen, abided by the terms of her probation but never returned home. As it were, she lived out her time with her probation officer's family. Shortly before her eighteenth birthday, she ran again and sought refuge in Arizona with her sister, always her refuge in a storm.

Vivian was on her own and feeling quite grown up with her new-found employment at the pizza shop on one of the busiest streets in Phoenix. She was young, built like nobody's business and had a way about her that oozed sexuality. Vivian caught the eye of many of her male patrons. Two were Dan and Skip, who became regulars shortly thereafter and flirted with Vivian on a regular basis. Vivian loved the attention and was not surprised when Dan asked her for a date. She accepted, of course, I mean, come on, he was tall, dark-haired and handsome with equally dark eyes and was quite the smooth talker. Had Vivian known then what she learned later, she would have turned and run as quickly in the other direction as she could, but she was young and inexperienced with regard to affairs of the heart and in her quest for the love she had longed for since her childhood she plunged forward, assholes to elbows as her granddaddy used to say.

It was dark in the room when she regained consciousness. Shit, Nate had choked her out again. Vivian lay on the floor trying to piece it all together, wondering when it all went wrong and why she hadn't noticed the warning signs. This man who had been so kind and gentle had changed. The same man who welcomed her into his home even after she went just a little cray cray and pushed herself into his life, never taking into consideration that maybe, just maybe, it was not really HIS plan. She had been almost obsessive after the first time she had spent the night. Vivian had gone to the store, filled a cart with food and supplies, and pushed the cart all the way to his place, and by the time he had returned from work, she had transformed his bachelor pad into a love nest. Why hadn't she paid attention to the look on his face? He had never said a word. She did everything to keep him close and within her grasp. She was afraid if she stopped for one minute, the fairy tale she had created would vanish like a thief in the night, and in her never-ending quest for love, she ignored the reality of things.

Vivian recalled that she and Dan never fought in the beginning. They drank and laughed, smoked and laughed, had passion-filled sex, and life was good. She never once realized that as long as things went his way, it was perfect. The subtle tell-tale signals went unnoticed. The stale mood if she wanted to stay in for the evening, the little remarks when they were in a group, and she didn't pay enough attention to his needs, all the behaviors she now, as an adult, would steer clear of. Vivian recalled with great clarity the first time he raised a hand to her, and it had frightened her, but sadly, it was not enough to send her packing. He had begged for her forgiveness, and she fell for it like a dumb ass. He didn't mean it. It was her fault. She should have left well enough alone. Foolish rationalizations on her part. He promised never to do it again, and she believed him. It was a long time before it happened again, but when it did, Vivian packed a bag, grabbed her hidden stash of cash and left, swearing she would never look back.

She hid out long enough for the bruises to fade, went back to work and tried so damn hard to put him behind her. A bit of the liveliness she was always so proud of vanished a little. She was quieter, more guarded. She didn't date. She stayed holed up in her room, crying herself to sleep every night. Vivian was afraid. She was always afraid. She didn't tell her sister Lyla because she would have killed his ass. Joe, the owner of the pizza place, saw the faded bruises but never asked questions. Instead, he did all he could to keep her busy, make her laugh at his ridiculous jokes, and never once addressed the elephant in the room. Vivian hadn't seen Dan for months, but his friend had come in to eat several times, feeling it necessary to let her in on how Dan was doing, although she never asked. It was obvious to her that Dan had only shared his recollection of the events leading up to her departure by the tone with which he used when speaking to her. She listened attentively and pretended not to care, but deep down, she did. She had fallen in love with him, and like a fool and like so many other women in domestic violence situations, she missed him despite what he had done. She longed for the strong arms that held her tight, the warmth of his lips on hers, so it was no surprise that when he came into the shop, her heart skipped a beat, and a small smile crossed her face.

Now, don't get it twisted, Vivian did not rush back to him. She did not move back in as he had suggested, but they began seeing each other again. He didn't know where she lived, and she felt secure with that knowledge. It was her safety net. Fast forward four years later, a stint in the Air Force, four years of getting her ass beat on a regular and Vivian was being served with divorce papers because Dan was seeing another woman and didn't want to go through a lengthy military trial where all his dirty laundry and deeds would be exposed. After the hell he put her through, the papers were as welcome as a cool breeze on a warm summer day. Vivian signed the papers without as much as a blink of an eye and never looked back. The trash had taken itself. Years later, she would come to learn that Dan had remarried another Vivian, seriously, no bullshit, and sadly she suffered the same abuse as Vivian had, only much worse. As Vivian reflected, she felt a cold chill run up her back.

Some ghosts never leave but instead float around in the back of the mind just far enough out of reach. Meatballs and bad Memories never went well together anyway.

Chapter Five

Vivian had all but forgotten about Jack. I mean, after all, he never did call her back, so when she exited the train on her way to meet a client, she was taken by surprise when he called out to her from the platform. Never knowing what to say under these circumstances, Vivian played it cool so that he would not know how excited she really was to see him again. Some people you can go a lifetime not missing, and then there are those that stay in your mind like a jingle you hear on the radio. Jack, for whatever reason, was that jingle. It wasn't really because of the time she had known him, as that was very brief, but more so the impression he had left. Vivian had felt relaxed and comfortable with him, a feeling she did not know all that often. They spoke as if no time had lapsed between them and agreed that they should hang out later that night. Vivian agreed, and as she left for her meeting, there was a spring in her step. Throughout the meeting and the hours after, Vivian's mind drifted to Jack. Where had he been? What had he been doing, not even sending a word? Always suspicious, she went over and over it in her mind so that by the end of the day, she was in a pissy mood. The girls told her she was a fool to jump right back in, not knowing who this guy really was, and although they were right, she still wanted to see him. She had just enough time for a shower, a little play time with Henry, and then out the door to meet Jack down the street at Steve's.

While she waited for him to arrive, she grew weary from the day and wished she hadn't left the comfort of her apartment. Why was she always so quick to jump? Why was she always so eager? Why did every encounter have to be a long-lasting fairy tale in her mind? Why couldn't it be just a chance meeting, some heavy-duty sex, and I'll see ya later kind of thing? If she had been honest with herself, she would have been able to see it for what it was. A longing to be loved. The desire to be needed by someone. A feeling that had been lost to Vivian for a very long time, maybe her whole life. Well, shit, now she really wished she could just leave and leave is what she did but not before telling Steve that if Jack asked, she had left, claiming not to be feeling well and extending her apologies. She hurried home to the refuge of her place. Here, she was brave, bold and courageous. Here, she didn't care if she left Jack high and dry. It was her right, dammit, and she could do whatever she wanted, or so it seemed, here in her place. Vivian had, her whole life, been tough, everything she said she meant and challenged those that confronted her with a screw you type of attitude. She had always been what one would call a badass, so why, in her relationships with men, could she not exhibit the same mentality? I'm just an old softy, that's why, she told her furry friend as she snuggled closer to him, who, by the way, had been very happy to have the company of his favorite person unexpectedly.

She suddenly felt a chill run through her bones, although the night was quite pleasant. It was the same cold, chilling feeling she always got when she remembered "him." She wrapped a blanket a little tighter around her. Fatigue from the day lulled Vivian into a semi-sleep, and she drifted back to the 70s, the most thunderous of all her years.

She was living in the Bronx with Hector, a very handsome Hispanic man older than her and well-versed in the areas of desire and sex. He had come into her life at a party in the neighborhood, and after their first encounter, they were inseparable. She moved into his one-bedroom apartment, and day after day, night after night, he wove his magic. Their sex was fueled like wood to a fire, raging hot. Latin lovers were always passionate, and he did not disappoint. He would go to work each morning, and she would wait for his return, always ready for a night filled with passion. Vivian was only seventeen. Naive in so many ways but willing to believe she was a woman, she did her best to prove that to him in every way possible. He loved that about her and whispered in her ear, breath hot on her neck, always acutely aware of his touch and its effect on her. She felt that she loved him, but was it really love or was she taken in by his strength and the power he had over her. Whatever it was, she loved it. They smoked weed together and drank cold duck on the front stoop of the building, and it was on one of those occasions that she was introduced to his friend Tito. He frightened Vivian from the moment their eyes met, and she did everything she could to never be alone with him. She often expressed her concerns to Hector, but he assured her that his long-time friend was harmless and that she could trust him. Still, Vivian made sure she was never anywhere he was if Hector was not around.

It was July and very hot in the city. The apartment was sweltering, and Vivian decided to go to the corner store for a cool drink and a couple of singles(loose cigarettes). She loved that about New York. Where else could you go and buy just a few smokes and not the whole pack if you didn't want to? She headed back to the block and wasn't ready to return to the heat of the apartment, so she sat in front of the building, unaware that across the street, Tito was lurking in the shadows, staring in her direction. Vivian did not notice him until she stood up to go inside, and then he was there pushing his way into the foyer with her, leering at her like a hungry animal. His smile was insincere and crooked, and the sense she felt was fear. She tried to hurry to the safety of the apartment, but he blocked her, asking why she was in such a hurry and why she couldn't just talk for a few minutes. He came closer, and she backed away, stumbling on the steps as she made every attempt to distance herself from him.

Then it happened. At the same moment that Vivian saw the pistol, it was already too late. He had it out and positioned it in the small of her back. His voice was menacing as he forced her into the apartment and closer to the room she shared with her man. He smelled of liquor, and she knew he was drunk. She had seen the shift in his mood before when they all partied together, so she knew she was in danger and there was nobody there to help her. He pushed her into the bedroom and locked the door. Vivian pleaded with him not to hurt her and warned that Hector would be home soon as if knowing this would change what was about to happen. His laugh was like a growl. Vivian felt as if she were in the midst of a nightmare that she couldn't wake up from. He punched her in the face and ordered her to take off her clothes, all the while holding the gun on her. He was bigger than her, and she knew she could not fight him without being hurt, but she tried and that just fueled his disgusting desire. Vivian was crying after being hit so many times. She tasted her own blood, and she was sure she would be dead before the end of the day. He told her repeatedly that he would, in fact, kill her when he was done with her. He forced her down on the bed she had made love to Hector in so many times, knowing she would never again be able to lay down in it and feel safe. Vivian was brutally raped over and over for what seemed like hours. Every inch of her body was in pain, and as she prayed for it to end and for God to have mercy on her, the gun jammed just as he pointed it and pulled the trigger. In that instance, it was over, but was it really? Somehow, Vivian knew that if she lived to be eighty, it would live on in her soul.

She must have lost consciousness because when she came to, he was pulling on his pants and the last thing he said before he left was that if she told anyone, he would find her and finish the job, then he stormed out of the room. Vivian didn't move for fear he would hear her and come back. She lay deadly still until the day turned to night. She saw the streetlights come on and knew that Hector would be returning from work soon. She gingerly stood up, and as she did, her profile appeared in the mirror. Dried blood was caked to her lips, her clothes were torn, and she was afraid of the person she saw staring back at her. Vivian tried to clean herself up but wasn't doing a very good job. Her hands were trembling so badly that she could not control them. Suddenly, she heard the door to the apartment close and footsteps on the floor coming closer and closer. Had he returned? Instinctively, she ducked behind the door, not daring to breathe. She heard the voice that had always brought a smile to her face, but tonight, as he opened the door, she was not smiling. Tears streamed down her face as he took in the scene. When the deadly silence broke, he rifled off so many questions, and all Vivian wanted was for him to hold her. She said as much, and he wrapped her in his arms, and the couple stood frozen in time. Something inside her made her acutely aware that although he was holding her, it wasn't the same as so many times before. It is often said that in situations such as this, men may initially want to back away from the reality of things, not wanting to deal with the idea of someone they are intimate with having been sexually assaulted. They want to blame someone and, at times, may inadvertently direct it towards their loved one.

Vivian tried her best to rehash the whole attack, and it was painful. She blamed him for bringing Tito around, knowing how she felt about him. He blamed her for not being more cautious. Hector never believed that his friend could or would do something like this. "Not in a million years," he stated. Bullshit! Vivian shrieked. He was always leering at her like she was an item on a menu. Was there doubt in his mind? What did he mean by what he was saying? Did he believe her? Why was he defending his friend? Vivian shut down. Call it self-preservation or simply exhaustion. All she wanted to do was what she should never have done, and that was to take a shower and try her best to wash away the assault. Hector never asked if she wanted to seek medical attention or if he should call the police, and many years too late, she wished she had. Why hadn't he done that immediately? He thought it best for her to shower and put it behind her. Maybe to make him feel better because it sure wouldn't change things for her. She excused herself, went into the bathroom, closed the door and waited for the water to get hot before stepping in. She scrubbed her skin until it was red, but it didn't feel clean. Would she ever? She cried not only for herself but for all the women before her who had suffered an attack of this nature. She must have been wailing because Hector came to the door and asked her if she was alright and if he could do anything. No, she was not alright, and what she needed was for him to go find Tito and kill him. Yes, kill him. She wanted him dead.

The bruises were already prevalent, and she knew they would be worse the next day but not as bruised as her heart. Her whole frame felt weighted down, and as she wrapped the towel around herself and opened the door, she was shocked to see an empty room. Hector was gone. To where she did not know and honestly did not care. This was no time to consider his feelings. Really. No time at all. Vivian needed a friend. Someone who would feel as bad for her as she felt for herself. She didn't really have any friends, and that saddened her as well. She was alone. Why would he leave without saying a word at a time like this? Screw him and everyone else! She took a couple of Tylenol to help with her pounding headache and lay down on the sofa. She wouldn't sleep that night, but she needed to rest. Vivian must have dozed off at some point, though, because when she opened her eyes, Hector was there, staring down at her with a contemptuous look on his face. She asked him where he had been, and the beginning of the end of them began. He had gone to find Tito, to kick his ass for betraying their friendship in the worst way possible. By the time he did find him, he was enraged as visions of Vivian blinded him. Tito had seen him coming and began to formulate the lie. He wove a tale so unbelievable that anyone who didn't know Vivian might believe what he was saying. He told his friend that there had been no assault. Rather, what had transpired was Vivian's doing. She was the aggressor, she had come on to him, she initiated the sexual encounter, and when Tito threatened to expose her, she flew into a panicked rage, and he had merely defended himself against HER attack on him. He swore he would never jeopardize their friendship if it was someone who REALLY was committed, but he said that she was not that person. He reminded Hector of their lifelong friendship, of the many years their families hung out together. Did he really think that Tito would be willing to throw that all away over a girl? Hours later, Hector left, his friendship intact. The lie believed. How could she do this? How had he not seen the type of woman she was? His anger was now redirected towards Vivian, and all he wanted was for her to be gone. Gone from the apartment, gone from his life. Vivian just sat there, numb, not knowing what to say or do as she listened to the lie. She refused to defend herself. She had done nothing wrong, and if he wanted to believe that piece of shit, then she would walk away. She felt attacked once again, but this time, it would be at the hands of someone she had shared her heart with.

She didn't cry as she walked down the steps of their building. She didn't look back. She had, but one regret and that was the time she had wasted with a man she had thought would be by her side and protect her. She would not be broken by him or anyone. The first bricks of the wall she would surround herself with fell into place. There would be no turning back from here. It was not only the end of them but the end of her innocence, and as she walked down the street, she longed for a friendly face, a safe harbor in the storm, something or someone who could wipe the trauma from her mind. It would be years later that she reconciled that her love affair with alcohol and drugs began that day.

As she looked down at her plate at the corner diner, what should have been the number three was actually the number four. Dammit. Not what she ordered, again.

Chapter Six

What the hell was that?? A loud noise from Vivian's hallway startled her awake. She got up, realizing that it was morning and that she had slept through the entire evening. Books were sprawled everywhere, and Henry sat indignantly in the very middle of the mess with a look that was familiar to Vivian. The "I'm starving" look she always got when he felt too much time had passed between meals. The books would wait, and she padded into the kitchen to satisfy her feline friend's needs. The aroma of freshly brewed coffee was appealing to her senses. She loved Auto Brew. It was a must-have for her. She loved her morning coffee, sitting by the window in her favorite chair. Alone time was something Vivian treasured. She loved it. It was a time when she could gather her thoughts, organize her schedule for the week, do some reading and enjoy time with Henry. As she nestled in her chair, she noticed the light on her answering machine flashing, indicating that she had at least one message. It, like the books, could wait.

Several hours later, Vivian, dressed for the day, checked her voicemail and heard Jack's voice on the other end wishing her a quick recovery and to give him a call when she was back on her feet. And also a message from the girls suggesting a weekend getaway, which actually sounded like a great idea. It was a gray day in the South, but to Vivian, it was the perfect day for a walk along the boulevard, maybe a stop by the cafe for an iced coffee, a snack, and just to relax. After all, it was Sunday. At the last minute, she picked up the phone and dialed Jack's number. She left a voicemail, so she left a message relaying her plans, and if he was not busy, maybe he could join her. It was her way of making up for ditching him the night before. She gathered her purse, took one last look in the mirror, reassured Henry that she would not be gone for the eternity he always imagined and headed out the door. A light mist filled the air, and Vivian was glad she remembered to grab her rain jacket at the last minute.

After a bit of window shopping, Vivian decided on a hot drink from one of her favorite coffee shops. The staff knew her, and before she got to the counter, her order was being prepared just as she liked it. Joe, the owner, was very friendly and always had a smile on his work worn face. It was part of the reason she always came to this particular shop. His kindness reminded Vivian of an old friend she had once had who had passed away tragically from a terrible accident. The thought of him brought the mist from outside to her eyes. Vivian quickly refocused her attention on a tiny dog in a sweater embossed with the name Butch on it. She smiled to herself as she sipped her drink and lazed the day away. She caught up on a few emails and briefly scrolled through her social media account, not wanting to waste too much time there, a promise she had made to herself one evening after realizing she had spent three plus hours watching reels and listening to a comedian on a popular video app. Vivian was about to leave the shop when she saw him. Jack was across the street headed her way. Her pulse quickened just a little at the sight of him. He smiled when he saw her, and the rest of the day was spent walking, talking and catching up. She admitted she had not been sick the night before but, in fact, had grown weary and felt she would not be good company, so she had left. She had always had a bit of an attitude if she was tired or hungry, and rather than subject him to that, she had just gone home. Jack was understanding and let her know there was no apology necessary. Hmm...okay. Cool points for Jack. They chatted about their jobs, and she clued him in about her boss and the fact that he was disgusting. Vivian didn't like to be mean, but in his case, it was unavoidable. Jack chuckled as she described Derrell's behavior, imagining the poor guy's tormented soul over Vivian. He had obviously never met the guy but knew he was no match for Vivian. She had a strong sense about her. He wanted to know more about her but knew somehow that it would take time. He was intrigued by her, but she didn't strike him as the type that would just open up her life. It would take patience on his part, and for some reason unknown to him, he was willing to take all the time she needed.

Jack had come from a hard-working middle-class family, born and raised to work for what they had and never take life for granted. He was the only male in a family of six girls which helped him to understand the female psyche. When Jack was older, his father began to teach him about the family business, wanting Jack to follow in his footsteps. His father had a successful construction company, which he had worked long hours to build. Jack was proud of him for being able to juggle work and family and never missing an evening meal. Jack inherited that same work ethic in the now-expanded Williams Construction. Jack worked hard and played even harder. He was dubbed a ladies' man, but in private, he had never really committed to anyone seriously. He liked the thought of it, but in reality, he was all about having fun and playing the field. That was until he met Vivian. Could she be the one he might have a go at a serious relationship with? He had only been in her company a few times, but he thought about her more than he should have. She wasn't like other chicks. Whoa, buddy!!! Calm your ass down. You just met the girl. Don't get into something you can't get out of later, a voice inside his head reminded him.

Vivian laughed at something, and his thoughts snapped back to her. She wondered where his head was at as they sat in silence. He apologized for the distraction, but Vivian knew all too well what distraction was all about. Her thoughts took her back in time whenever something reminded her of the past, so there was no apology necessary. They decided to go to dinner, and Vivian was pleased that he wanted to spend more time with her. Jack's car was parked down the street from the coffee shop, so Vivian accepted the short ride to her place so that she could freshen up. She also wanted to check in on Henry, who by now would be ravenous, in his mind, of course. Jack had wanted to wait, but Vivian let him know she would meet him at The Pub, a trending bistro in the city, at seven, making up an excuse that she had an errand to run before dinner just so she could drive her own car to meet him. Jack didn't think twice about it and stated that he would see her at seven.

Henry was right at her feet the moment she opened the door, so before she began to get herself ready for the evening, she treated her feline friend to a delightful dish of salmon she had purchased from the market, specially blended for Henry's pallet. He cooed his appreciation as he dove in while Vivian ran a bath with her favorite scented oil added. She had plenty of time before she was to meet Jack, so she relaxed in the tub, blues playing on her record player, the only way to listen to blues and a little prescribed medicinal spirits to smooth out any rough edges. Vivian didn't smoke pot on a regular anymore, but for years, she sometimes would feel on the verge of a panic attack, so her MD had given her a script for marijuana, to be used only when necessary, of course. It helped her to breathe a little deeper in those moments when, for no reason at all, she would, well, panic. It saved her from extra sessions with her therapist, so hey, why not. With the combination of the weed and the steamy tub, Vivian felt her body relax and her head clear, and it was a good feeling. Not at all like the feeling she had for the better part of the eighties. Those were very troubling, even dangerous times for Vivian. She reflected now as she often did in the solitude of her apartment.

After the assault, Vivian (Liz) wanted to escape to someplace far from the city and its inhabitants. She really believed that if she left NY, everything that had happened to her would not follow her, but that she would be able to start over, a fresh start and all. Like miraculously, the sadness and hollow feeling she had would just hang tight in the city. Yeah, okay. Vivian withdrew all of her money from the bank, took the subway to Port Authority and purchased a one-way ticket to Florida. She had family there and thought the reconnection would be just what she needed. I mean, after all, families in tough times are stuck together, right? She took a seat at the back of the bus so that she could smoke. Did they really think that the last three rows would keep the remaining passengers safe? It was early morning, still dark outside, so there were plenty of available seats. Vivian had one bag with her, the rest of her belongings stowed under the bus, and as she sat down, she breathed heavily. Call it a sigh of relief of sorts, or what have you. Her friend from the bodega had given her some pills for the ride, stating they would help make the trip more bearable. Vivian had never done drugs. She smoked some weed but never anything heavy. She was afraid of them, and that fear would save her life on more than one occasion in the future. As the bus rolled out of the terminal, Vivian contemplated what lay ahead of her. She knew her father had moved his bitch of a girlfriend and her kids down to a small town on the far outskirts of Tampa, and of course, Babs had tagged along, not wanting to be left out. Her two brothers had places of their own. One big happy family...Bullshit.

Vivian drifted off to sleep, lulled there by the humming sound and motion of the bus. When she opened her eyes, she could see that several of the seats had been filled with weary travelers, some with children. Thankfully, the seat next to her was still vacant. Where were they? How far had they traveled? She stared out the window for telltale signs that would give her a clue to their location. Vivian had napped through Maryland and learned from a conversation she overheard that they were now traveling through Virginia. Immediately, John Denver's hit Country Roads played over and over again in her head. Ugh!! She hated that. Did anyone really know why that happens? The only advantage of taking a bus to your destination was enjoying the journey on the way. Virginia was beautiful. The picturesque landscape was postcard perfection. As they pulled into the rest stop and the passengers hurried to disembark, Vivian took a deep breath and filled her lungs with the clean, fresh air New York had always lacked. It was cool but not cold; the skies were clear, and the view of the mountains was breathtaking. She made a mental note to come back here when she had more than the hour they had before moving on. Even the restaurant was cute. Old fashioned, diner-style, she loved that, with good food. She sat at the counter and ordered one of her favorite road trip breakfasts. While she was waiting for her food, she thumbed through the postcards and memorabilia with everything Virginia engraved on it. She settled on the salt and pepper shakers. Her meal was delicious, and before she re-boarded, she grabbed some snacks to tide her over until the next stop, went to the ladies room to freshen up and then grabbed a quick smoke at a picnic table.

When the bus lumbered out of the parking lot, Vivian settled in with her favorite rag, Rolling Stone, oblivious to the passengers around her and the children fussing at having to stay in their seats, a nearly impossible task for a child. She embarked on a great story about a famous rock star caught in a hotel with someone other than his wife, and the time passed. From time to time, she would gaze out the window as they passed through small towns, the townspeople looking, wondering in silence where the passers-by were headed. Kids were on their bikes, waving and trying their best to ride faster than the bus as the bus rolled by. It made Vivian smile, reminding her of her childhood and a much more innocent time.

She relaxed and thought about what lay ahead in Florida. She had briefly spoken to her father while she was at the diner, the first time in years, and he seemed genuinely happy that she was coming. Yes, she could stay with him, but there would be ground rules, of course. Shit why did there always have to be a caveat with him? He could have just left it at see you soon but hey, his house, his rules as always. Vivian was excited at the thought of seeing her brothers. It had been a long time for them. After her mother's death, everyone seemed in a big hurry to leave. Mom was the glue that held it all together. I guess they figured there was nothing left with her gone. One brother went into the Navy, and the other to the Army. Her sister was already living with her friend and their family. Babs was away at college, and for Vivian, it was out of sight, out of mind. Vivian's oldest sister wanted her to go with her, but their father had other ideas, and so it goes. Vivian was not quite sure why they all decided to land in Florida. Maybe they wanted a second chance at the whole family thing that they had missed out on growing up. Maybe she was hopeful as well. Whatever the reason, she looked forward to their reunion.

Somewhere between Virginia and the Carolinas, Vivian dozed off. It wasn't a deep sleep but one just enough to shake some of the long ride off her bones. The little pill she had given her made her head feel light and carefree. It was nothing heavy, and Vivian liked its pleasant effect. A little voice in her head reminded her not to like the feeling too much. Vivian wasn't worried. She had only taken one the entire trip. The bus pulled off the highway into a little roadside station where passengers who didn't have a major bus station could get on. Vivian got off and stretched her legs, sat down outside to catch some fresh air and smoke a cigarette. She thought of the oxymoron and laughed to herself. She glimpsed two very attractive men boarding the bus, and her curiosity got the better of her, so she re-boarded early to check out the eye candy. She spotted them a couple of rows from where she was sitting. Nice! She nodded in their direction and took her seat pretending not to notice that one of the men was checking her out as she did. Vivian had been around quite a few men in her young life, brothers, friends, coworkers, and she knew that buddies chatted it up just as much, if not more, than chicks, so she noticed how quiet the two new travelers were. She had always marveled at the nonchalant ease with which men would converse, which was one of the reasons Vivian had always felt more at ease around the opposite sex. There was no fuss, no hating on the other person, not much gossip. Sports, fishing, more sports (a topic she loved), chicks and surprisingly, their moms. She wondered in silence why they, two young guys, sat rather stoically, watching the other passengers return to their seats.

Vivian's very active imagination began to get the better of her once again, and she formulated their story in her head. Maybe they were undercover cops on assignment staking out one of the passengers, or then again, maybe they were criminals escaping by bus from a crime they had just committed. Oh, okay, Vivian, slow it down. Maybe they were just passengers, tired from traveling. Even though the latter was probably the case, she liked her options better. Way more intrigue and mystery. It was late afternoon, and everyone was either napping or involved in ways with which to pass the time. It would be a few hours before their next stop and dinner break. Vivian didn't mind the mode of travel or the endless humming of the bus tires. She didn't mind being alone. There was a difference between being alone and being lonely.

She plugged her earphones int o her transistor radio, tuned it into a classic rock station and leaned back in her seat. The music of the seventies was the best music ever created. She prided herself in knowing all the words to all the songs. Music was her escape from all things in the real world. She thought of herself as that of a hippie. Muslin blouses, bell bottom jeans, a peace sign dangling from a leather chain around her neck. Yep, she was a hippie. Her luggage was proof of that, and she was sure her father would hate it. He was retired military buzz cut and all. He had earned a silver star and displayed it proudly, as she recalled. His buddies would come to the house and talk for hours about their service to their country. Her brothers had served in the late seventies, and she was always worried about them being overseas, but thankfully they made it back home. The sounds of Stevie Ray Vaughn filled her soul, and Vivian sank deeper into her seat. Deeper...

Chapter Seven

Holy shit! Vivian sputtered water and bolted upright in the tub. She had sunk so deeply into her bathtub that she damn near drowned. Freaking weed! She sat there for a moment, trying to even out her breathing and catch her breath. Henry had been sitting on the bench she had put in the bathroom, staring at her, eyes wide. When she bolted up out of the water, she had scared one of his nine lives right out of him, and he took off like a bat outta hell. Right then and there, she vowed to never again smoke weed in the tub. Whoever said weed wasn't fatal was full of crap. The water had grown cold, and Vivian got out of the tub, wrinkly and running late. By the time she had put the finishing touches to what she was wearing, it was almost seven. Oh well, she would just have to be late. She did call Jack's cell to tell him she was going to be just that and that she would see him soon.

The Pub was located in the heart of the city, and although it was Sunday, there was a very good crowd. She let the hostess know she was meeting someone, and she knew right away that it was Jack because he had left details of her arrival at the door. They weaved their way through the restaurant where Jack was seated. He had already ordered a drink for her and smiled as she seated herself. They had a lovely dinner. Their conversation was light and smooth. Vivian thought that it was perfect, maybe too perfect. Why did she always assume something bad was going to happen? Why couldn't she ever just relax and enjoy the company of a very pleasant man? She wanted to, but her mind would not. Freaking ghosts...

The restaurant had a second level with live music, and after dinner, Jack asked if she felt like going up for a while. She agreed, and they headed up just as the band started playing a great blues tune. Vivian was feeling good after the cocktails she had at dinner. Not drunk but feeling good. Jack asked her to dance, and they moved across the dance floor, his hand on the small of her back, close but not too tight, his breath warm on her neck. It felt nice. The scent of the cologne he was wearing smelled amazing. It would remain long after he left her. A few cocktails later, Vivian was feeling buzzed. Damn, she had driven to the restaurant and now wondered how she would make the return trip. Jack offered her a lift, and she accepted, partially because she didn't want their time to end and partially because she didn't want to wait for a cab. It was late, and the drivers always made her feel uneasy. Jack secured her car and promised to give her a lift in the morning before work to pick it up. She hated leaving it there. Twenty minutes later, they were parked in front of her building. She thanked him for a great night and proceeded to fall out of the car as she opened the door. She burst into hysterical laughter to cover being completely mortified and thought she would pee her pants for sure if she didn't get it under control. Jack was in a panic, thinking she had hurt herself for sure. He ran to the other side of the car, where Vivian still lay sprawled out. "Damn, Vivian, are you alright?" She assured him she was as he quickly helped her to her feet.

A few moments later, they were at the door to her apartment. She fumbled in her purse for her keys and invited Jack for a cup of coffee before he hit the road. Vivian didn't have too many visitors. Her closest friends, maybe, but that was it. Her place was her place, so Jack was pleased by the offer and by what he saw upon entering. Everything was in its place but cozy at the same time. While Vivian was making an attempt at coffee in the kitchen, he decided to try to make friends with Henry, who, in true form, ignored him. Vivian was his person, and he didn't care much for strangers. He strolled into the kitchen, knowing he would be able to get a late night snack, and he was right. Vivian carried the two cups of coffee to the table and sat down next to Jack on the sofa. It was late, and work would come too early for her. She was deep in thought when Jack leaned in and kissed her softly. She was surprised only for a moment. She kissed him back. Kissing was sexy to her. It was intimate, an expression of how someone felt about the other person. He didn't grab at her and try anything inappropriate. When she drew back for some air, he took it as a sign to say his goodbyes. Vivian had an idea and ran it by Jack. He agreed. She lay in bed thinking of the kiss and how it made her feel as she dozed off. Jack spent the night on Vivian's sofa. We all know that a lot of men would have been like, screw this. I'm outta here if what Vivian proposed to Jack had been offered to them, but Vivian was almost certain that Jack was not like most men. As a matter of fact, he thought it was a great idea given the late hour and the number of miles he would have to travel to come back and take her to retrieve her car. He liked being close to her, and if it wasn't in her bedroom, then the sofa was the next best thing. For now. The next morning, they had a quick cup of coffee. Jack didn't live by a time clock, so he really was in no hurry, but Vivian, who was nursing a mild hangover, did so, so he moved on her timeline. Twenty minutes later, but not before a quick shower, she was in her car and on her way to work.

Vivian prided herself in rarely missing work. Otherwise, she would have loved spending the day with Jack as he had suggested. She had a lot of work to do and was behind on a project, so there was no way she could or would play hooky. Her client, a very wealthy businessman and his wife were remodeling their home and needed a reliable interior decorator. Vivian was their choice. Having worked so many dead-end jobs, she was happy to finally be in one that she loved. It was her true calling, and she was really good at it. Derrell was always right there breathing down her neck, suggesting items that just would not go. She was never sure how he had gotten his position, but she was pretty sure it was because of his daddy's money.

She slid unnoticed into her office and dove into her work. Several hours later, Jamie and Lulu flopped down on the sofa in Vivian's of-fice, ready to discuss where they would go for lunch and would she please explain where she was all weekend that they could not reach her. She eyed them coyly, dying to spill the details of her time with

Jack. The girls loved a juicy story, and if Vivian could not be reached, it had to be good. They decided on Valley's because they all knew Derrell would never step foot in there. It was a little too upscale for him. Strange how he always managed to show up wherever they lunched. Freaking stalker... Ten minutes later, they were out the door, and after a short walk, they were seated at Valleys, an eatery that was visually pleasing to the palette, with a menu much the same. Vivian, always on a diet, ordered a Greek salad and iced tea while her lunch dates, who were model thin, ordered the house burgers complete with a side of house fries and cokes to drink. While they waited for their food, Vivian dished the details of her time with Jack, ending with his sleepover. Jamie shrieked with delight, but Lulu was a little more reserved, only because she saw herself as Vivian's great protector. She knew Vivian's story, and although she was truly happy for her, she would be keeping a watchful eye on Jack. Their lunch arrived, and they dove in, continuing their chat as they ate. Vivian caved and took a small bite of Jamie's burger. "You are not fat, girl, I would kill for your figure," Jamie stated matter of factly. After lunch, they discussed the girl's weekend trip, and all agreed that it was a done deal. They would work out the details later in the week.

After lunch, Vivian had to make a trip to her client's home to go over some patterns she had picked out for the drapes. The drive was beautiful, and she opened the sunroof, welcoming a cool breeze as her companion for the trip. She arrived a short while later, and her client was thrilled to see her, as always. They had a relaxed relationship, and as they mulled over ideas for the drapes and the sofa fabric samples she had brought with her, they talked about the upcoming road trip the girls were planning. Mimi (of course, that's her name, why wouldn't it be) suggested they use her summer place. "You simply must, darling," she stated emphatically. She and her husband were temporarily living in the city while the work was being done and were not using the house, so it was theirs if they wanted it. She made Vivian promise to text her decision, and if they decided to accept her offer, she would have her driver courier the keys to Vivian's office. One usually never turned down an offer from Mimi. It just wasn't heard of. On her return trip, Vivian called Lulu's line, telling her to meet her in her office and to bring Jamie with her. She needed thirty minutes but would see them shortly. Back at the office, she could see the girls heading her way, and her excitement at the news bubbled over, and she couldn't wait to let the girls in on it. There were no finer friends than these two, and she couldn't think of anyone else she would rather spend a long weekend with. Well, maybe one other person, as her thoughts went to Jack. When she told the girls the news, they could barely contain themselves. Everyone knew Mimi came from old southern money and married into money. They didn't care. The entire office loved her. She was that sweet and kind. It was decided within ten minutes that they would take her up on her generous offer, and while Vivian texted her, she had to laugh at their excitement. Kids at Christmas. None of them could remain focused as they continued working through the end of the day. Adventures always had that effect on people. The unknown of what lies ahead and the thrill of it all.

After work, the girls wanted to grab a quick cocktail at Steve's, but Vivian was worn out from traveling the whole day. She really just wanted to grab a bite to eat and relax. They begged she caved as always, and a short while later, they were seated at the bar ordering their favorite spirits. Vivian vowed to only have one, a condition of her coming along. She played it smart and ordered some food to go so she would have an easy out when she was ready to leave. They all talked some more about the trip, and their excitement spilled over like a glass too full of champagne. They were all single, and the only arrangements that would have to be made would be made by Vivian. She had a regular lady who looked after Henry when she had to go out of town, so she was not worried at all. Henry loved going to her place. He had made friends with her tabby Stuart and was quite comfortable being left behind. They agreed to leave early on Thursday. Thankfully, off time was done electronically and approved by HR, so she did not have to explain to Derrell why she needed the time off. It was none of his business anyway. She had a friend in HR, so the approval was a cinch.

She parlayed hers with approval for Jamie and Lulu. It was a done deal within hours. They would not have to return until Tuesday because, of course, everyone needs the day after a long weekend to get their shit together. If this trip proved to be anything like their trips from the past, they would all need the extra day. Vivian finished her beer, gave her friends a hug, grabbed her food and headed out the door. She always loved the walk from Steve's. The shops were lit for the evening, the sights and sounds pleased her. She started to hum a song she had stuck in her head that had been playing at the bar, and before she knew it, she was singing loudly. People walked by averting their eyes, pretending not to stare at the crazy lady. Vivian didn't care at all. She just kept right on singing.

Chapter Eight

Vivian felt a tap on her shoulder that startled her back to the realization that she was still on the bus. She yanked her headset off and turned her attention to the person who had interrupted REO Speedwagon's Time for Me to Fly. She turned her head upward, and there stood one of the two guys. "You were singing out loud," he stated with a grin that turned into a laugh. "Very loud!" It was then that Vivian noticed for the first time that many of the passengers were looking her way, and she felt her face flush with embarrassment. She was mortified, to say the least, but he seemed amused by it all. If she could have crawled under the seat, she would have. She started to say she was sorry, but he cut her off, stating that nobody should ever apologize for anything and returned to his seat without another word. She heard him and his friend talking, and she was certain it was about her. Oh well, big deal. She tried to rationalize her undoing. So she was singing a bit too loud on a bus traveling down the road filled with passengers. Yeah, okay, it was a typical Vivian move for sure. Good Lord, just let me off this bus right now, she thought. The remainder of the ride before the stop for dinner was a quiet one for Vivian. She wasn't about to make a fool of herself again, that was for sure. They stopped for the dinner break, and Vivian damned near broke her neck, trying to exit as quickly as possible. Some of the passengers made comments directed towards her, in good humor, of course. Kids who have no filter were less discrete.

She found a table towards the back of the restaurant so she could disappear from prying eyes, but to her surprise, the two men from the bus found their way to her table and asked if they could join her. Sure, she replied. I mean, they were drop-dead cute, and who was she to say no. She promised not to burst into song, and they all laughed about the whole thing. Vivian learned that the two men, Skip and Dave, had just returned from a second tour in Iraq and were headed to Georgia to hang with Skip's girlfriend Constance, a southern belle with a daddy who had more money than Buffet. Her parents were out of the country, and she had their home to herself indefinitely. They spoke very little about Iraq, and when they did, they had a very distant look on their faces as they described their time there. Their whole body language was a sign that she would be more than happy to talk about anything else with them unless they brought it up. She noticed they didn't eat much but helped themselves to several beers and stashed a few for the ride. There was something about them that made her curious to learn more, and she hoped they could continue their conversation once they reboarded. As it turned out, three passengers had reached their destination, so there were empty seats right across from her, which Skip and Dave hustled to occupy before anyone else could claim them. As they all settled in for the evening's ride, the three picked up the conversation where it had started at the restaurant.

They talked about everything, their hometowns, their families, relationships, everything from A to Z. Vivian, when asked, explained her reason for heading South, minus the assault, of course. She left it at needing a change of pace, new scenery, and to see her family. Dave and Skip were impressed to learn she had lived in the city by herself. "A city that big with all those people must have been hard on a young chick," Dave said. If he only knew just how tough it really had been for her. It was very late, and Vivian was road weary and ready to settle down for a nap. The guys were still wide awake. She mentioned as much, and they looked at each other with a question in their eyes. After silent agreement, they explained the reason for their perpetual sleeplessness. They both had done something called MDA. It was like uppers but much stronger. Vivian was aware of the drug but had never thought of trying it. She had heard all the stories about people who did speed and what happened as a result. She didn't want to sound like a prude, so she pretended to know more about it than she really did. They offered her some, and even though she knew she should say no, she accepted their offer. A decision that would prove to haunt Vivian for many years to come. They gave her a small amount because of her size, in addition to knowing the dangers of taking too much. A short while later, the effects of the drug took over her senses. She felt heavy but light, awake but in a fog; everything around her was brighter than it should be. She heard a ringing sound and realized it was in her ears. Ever paranoid, she wondered if she had done too much and if an overdose was imminent. Her new friends assured her that she was quite alright and to relax and enjoy the buzz. Why do I feel so uninhibited, she thought. Once Vivian relaxed, she found the high to be a pleasant experience. That should have sent up a warning flag, but it had quite the opposite effect for Vivian. She was an all-or-nothing type of person, zero to one hundred, with an addictive personality. If she liked something, she really liked it and tended to overindulge. That was bad, very bad.

They all stayed up for the rest of the night, and Vivian could not recall one single thing or what they had talked about, but somewhere near dawn, the boys asked her if she was in a hurry to continue on to Florida or if would she like to stop off in Georgia and party a little with them. Normally, Vivian would have replied with a no thank you, but she was having too much fun, and the boys were really very sweet. Plus, she would not be the only female and was, in fact, in no real hurry to get to Florida. Constance would be meeting them in Atlanta, and Skip was sure she would not mind. To be sure, he would give her a call at the next stop. Suddenly, Vivian could barely contain herself and felt the need for more room. The confines of the bus, coupled with the drugs, were suffocating, and she was relieved when the driver announced they would be stopping for breakfast shortly. They pulled off the highway and into a nearly deserted restaurant. She wasn't ready to make a decision just yet, so she went inside and forced herself to eat something. She was never good at making decisions on an empty stomach, and this was no exception, high or not.

While she waited for her order to arrive, she went to the ladies room and freshened up a bit. Bus travel was hard on personal hygiene, but she did her best at taking a gypsy bath. She washed the smell of the long ride off her body and felt much better, with the exception of her shaking hands. Damn, she was really buzzing. Her pupils were black as night. Yep, she was freaking high. She hoped the food would calm things down, although she was not really hungry at all. Side effect, she remarked to herself. What else could it be? The guys were nowhere to be seen, so she ate her meal alone, and it was good. It did help to calm things down a little. She sat outside afterward and smoked like a feign, which she never did. She saw the two men come out of the little bar across the street and figured they had drank their evening meal. Skip shouted out to Vivian that Constance had been called and it was al-right with her if they brought a guest along with them.

They were not far from the Georgia line, and although Vivian had not verbally committed, she had already made up her mind. What the hell? Why not stop off for a while, party a little, then head out to Florida. Had she known what lay ahead, she would have stayed her ass on the bus. She sat still in her seat, trying to calm her heartbeat. She plugged in her headset. Music would soothe her soul, free her mind and help her to think more clearly. Keep your head together, Vivian. Stay in the game. Don't get caught up in something you can't control. Why did the waitress give her white toast instead of rye? It wasn't what she ordered. Damn...

Chapter Nine

Have you ever noticed when you have something planned for the weekend that, the week seems to drag its ass? Vivian and the girls thought Thursday would never come, and they tried to keep busy, but all three of them were already in vacation mode, and there was a lot of paper shuffling, emptying email boxes and tidying up in an effort to kill time. The courier had delivered the keys on Tuesday as promised, she had met with Jack for lunch on Wednesday, and he was genuinely excited for the girls when he learned of their impending trip, although secretly, he was sure he would miss Vivian. She promised him a date when she returned, anywhere he wanted to go. His choice. They sealed the deal with a deep kiss that left Vivian breathless. Something to remember him by, she surmised. Thursday!! Yes!!! Finally, it arrived and not a minute too soon. Derrell was on the verge of a meltdown again and was doing his level best to put a wrench in their plans, but Vivian wasn't about to fall for his crap. She had worked with him too long to not see what shit he was up to. Any time anyone planned something, he always, without fail, tried to keep it from happening. They had all dubbed him the "fun hater." Vivian knew it wasn't nice, but sometimes... Anyway, despite all of his attempts to thwart her trip with the girls, four o'clock finally came, Out of Office switched on, Voicemail set and a wave in Derrell's direction as they disappeared through the door as if they had never been standing there a minute sooner.

Vivian and the girls jumped in the rental and went down the road. Vivian had dropped Henry off that morning before work, and he barely noticed her leaving in his excitement to see Stuart. They greeted each other much in the same way two friends would, minus the butt-sniffing. Vivian often times swore he was someone she knew in a past life.

She would miss him more than he would her. As they headed toward the highway, sunglasses on, sunroof wide open, the wind in their hair, music blasting from the radio cranking out the sounds, Vivian felt free. She was always at her best when she was relaxed with no stress and no revisiting days gone by. Just her with her besties and the open road. Mimi's summer home was about 40 minutes from the city, and the girls decided at the halfway point to make a quick pit-stop at a little roadside store to pick up a few extras. They were all sure that the house was well stocked, but a girl had to have her favorites, so they pulled in, grabbed a few things and resumed their travel. GPS kept them on track, and sometime later, they pulled off the highway onto a private road that would lead them to their destination. They pulled up to a gate, and Vivian punched in the code. The gates opened, welcoming them to the well-manicured property. It was a summer place, but they could already imagine how gorgeous it would be. They could make out the sound of the waves crashing on the beach beyond the house, and they felt like school girls giggling with excitement.

As Mimi's home came into view, the girls were in awe of its beauty. It was big but not gaudy. Classy, just like its owner. The French doors to the entryway were made of stained glass, and it took another code to open them. Security was everything for the rich. Looking around, Vivian could understand why. The three girls scattered as they entered the foyer, trying their best to take it all in. Three bedrooms on the main floor, all with a breathtaking view of the beach and all with a private bath to complete the suite. After they settled on which room they would occupy, they went to the kitchen to unload what they had brought with them. In fashion, the fridge was well stocked with everything they could ever want to eat and the adjacent bar was equally stocked with refreshing fixings for adult spirits. A note from Mimi was attached to the fridge, welcoming them and inviting them to make themselves at home and enjoy whatever she had. "Don't be shy y'all." My home is your home. Enjoy and have a fabulous weekend. Ciao, Mimi.

Vivian was a beer drinker. Always the same beer, never switching up to follow the trends. She couldn't handle the buzz of hard liquor and didn't really like the person she was when she drank it. She grabbed a few beers and ice for the cooler while the girls mixed up drinks for themselves, and they hurried to their rooms to change into beachwear, grabbing towels and a large blanket on their way out. It was a private beach, but there were plenty of weekenders in the surrounding houses. It was nice to be alone but not at the beach. Hard-bodied men were playing sand volleyball while well-oiled girls cheered them on from the sidelines. The girls already had tans and agreed that suntan lotion and sand did not mix. The three of them were all about sunscreen, however. They stretched out their blankets, covering a wide area for relaxing, set up their chairs, and then headed for the water. It was refreshing, and the girls swam until their legs and arms felt like rubber. It was the perfect way to unwind, and they were all so glad they had decided to take this trip. Vivian was a sunglass fanatic, literally having a pair for every occasion. She had purchased a few pairs for her girlfriends, and they each donned a pair with appreciation for her thinking of them. Suddenly, out of nowhere, a ball came their way and landed at Vivian's feet. One of the players came rushing over, making sure he did not kick sand in their direction, reached down with a glance at the beauties in front of him and introduced himself. His name was Tim, and he was adorable. Lulu struck up a conversation with him right away, and they learned that he and his friends were there for the weekend, staying in the guest house of one of the guy's parents. His buddies were yelling at him to return to the game, and just as he was about to resume playing, he asked the girls if they wanted to play a game with them. Lulu, of course, said yes right away. Not wanting to be left out and quite enjoying the view of Tim's friends, Jamie said yes as well. Vivian resisted and watched from the sidelines, trying her best to be a good sport and cheer them on. She sat down near the game players, and as she laid back and relaxed on a beach recliner, her mind drifted back to another game she was involved in many years prior that was not as much fun and at the end of play, no one was a winner.

Vivian, Skip and Dave exited the bus in Atlanta. Finally, it had been a long trip, and Vivian was glad to be on solid ground again. As promised, Constance greeted them as they exited the bus. They all hugged one another, and Vivian felt a little awkward until Constance wrapped her in a bear hug a few moments later. From that moment on until the day it all fell to pieces, Vivian and her new friend would be inseparable. Constance was born and raised in Georgia and was as sweet as a Georgia peach. If one looked at her, they would never have dreamed she would keep the company of wild, reckless men such as Skip and Dave. She obviously knew they partied, and she was definitely on board with whatever they had in mind. They all jumped in her car, a convertible Mercedes, and headed to her parent's home. It was a beautiful southern home with two winding staircases leading up to the bedrooms where they put their belongings before heading to the enormous family room equipped with a pool table, arcade games and a huge theater screen style television which was tuned in to MTV, a very popular music television channel. Right away, Vivian noticed that one of the tables in the corner was set up with a mirror, a glass of what appeared to be water, a spoon, a belt and a bag of needles. Being naive, Vivian thought Constance was a diabetic, and this was set up in case she had an attack. She couldn't have been more wrong.

The first stick and rush of the drugs entering Vivian's bloodstream was like nothing she had ever experienced. It was almost indescribable, but it was as if someone lifted her up and sat her down on a cloud. She felt weightless, outside of her own body, all control was lost, and she was not her own. She fell madly in love with the feeling, and still unknown to her to this day, she could not remember saying yes when she was asked if she wanted to try the drug this way. Surely, she would have said no, but she must have said yes, but in her mind, she just did not remember. All she wanted from that day on was to get high. She learned quickly how to inject herself, rationalizing that if she had control of this little corner of her life, she would remain safe from any harm. It was her new lover. Money was no object, and there was a steady flow of drugs coming into the house on a regular basis. People came and went, some stayed and partied, offering drugs as compensation for being there. Nobody that lived in the house had to work, having an income of their own. Vivian had her own money as well, having saved just about every cent she earned while living in New York. In a brief moment of clarity, she had stolen away for a little while and set aside a large portion of her cash for safe keeping knowing in the back of her drug-riddled mind that she would one day leave and head to her dads, and she would rather die than to show up broke. The rest was to be spent as she liked. Thank God Constance was there looking after the group because had she not been, there would have been no showering, eating or resting. As it was, all of that was hard for all of them because of the drugs. The drugs kept them always very near to the table, and the table offered them a plethora of supply. Why leave it? The table was the epicenter and controlled everything.

Vivian was growing thin. She noticed how much when she took a shower and viewed her reflection in the mirror. For some reason, she didn't care. The fat girl was getting skinny. Nobody would ever tease her again. This would be her justification for continuing to use. One day, about a month or so into things, Constance suggested they get out of the house for a while. She had realized it had been a month, and none of them had seen the light of day, always keeping the drapes closed so that no one could see into the house from the street. Had it been a month, Vivian pondered. She loved being outside and was shocked to learn it had been that long. The thought of this saddened her. Skip and Dave had no intention of leaving as they dove further into the depths with which the drugs took them. It was an escape from all reality for the two men. Something one could only imagine had they not been a part of active wartime. Dave and Vivian had become an item primarily because there was no one else. It was a terrible way to en-tangle themselves in a relationship because when they weren't hitting up, they barely spoke, but once the drugs flowed, they couldn't keep their hands off of each other. The sex was amazing, euphoric in some ways. Out-of-body sensations fueled by zero inhibitions fueled their time in bed. Vivian did whatever Dave asked of her without question.

As long as it felt good, why not. Dave said he would not go out with them when Vivian asked. "You go, babe," he mumbled. He would be there when she got back. Well, no shit! Where else would he be. Skip said much the same to Constance, and both of the girls were a little irritated by their responses.

Thank God for Vivian's love of sunglasses because she truly believed had she not put them on just before leaving, she truly would have gone blind. As it were, it still put a strain on her vision while adjusting. The Georgia heat hit them dead in the face, and they almost turned back, but instead, they forged ahead, long-sleeved in ninety-degree heat. Track marks were hidden. They moved through the store after a short drive, collecting the bare necessities. They barely noticed the stares coming their way from shoppers at the upscale grocery store. One never talked about what one did behind closed doors, and they knew Constance and her family were from very old southern money and didn't dare say a word in an effort to keep their standing in the high society circles. Silently, they were firm in their belief that this was unacceptable and just would not do. After grabbing a small amount of food, hygiene supplies and alcohol, they checked out and left the prying eyes behind. Screw them! It really wasn't all that serious. But was it? They decided on some fast food and thought maybe if the guys smelled it, they would eat. Nothing really looked good, but they ordered anyway and dove into the fries on the way back to the house. They were heaven! The girls had decided on a swim after eating and hoped the guys would join them. The sun's rays and the heat of the day brought them out of the haze they were shielded under, and they needed the natural vitamins the sun offered. Skip and Dave were jamming to a music video when the two girls returned, not at the table, surprisingly. They welcomed the idea of food and a swim. After eating, the girls changed into swimsuits and the guys into shorts and for a while, they felt a semblance of normalcy returning.

The cool water felt good on their pale skin. The sun kissed their bodies as they relaxed on the deck chairs. They all agreed that it was just what was needed. Vivian looked at the track marks on her arms, and for the first time since her arrival, she was ashamed. She was frightened at what she saw and vowed to slow down. She said as much to the small group, and although they sat quietly while she spoke, they all silently thought the same. They'd be dead soon if they didn't. Accidents always happen in the drug world, and none of them wanted that to happen to the other, so they formed a pact to party a little less if they could manage to control that. It was a fool's dream, however. The power of the drugs was much stronger than they were, and within a month's time, they all were right back into it as if they had never agreed otherwise. Constance and Vivian had touched base with their family shortly after Vivian's arrival just to save face, and just as Vivian had figured, her father reacted negatively. He seemed to enjoy being unkind, unlike her friend's parents, who seemed genuinely happy that she had friends to keep her company. Everybody's family was always nicer to their kids. Vivian was used to that. She pretended everything was fine after her call, even lying to her new friend by telling her that her dad was disappointed that she was going to delay her move for a bit but that he understood how young people were. Bullshit! He didn't give a damn about her. What mattered was that her delay inconvenienced him.

Another drug-fueled month passed, and it was but a blur to Vivian. The tension in the air was getting thick, and small things began to annoy each one of them. They picked at each other, even trying to lecture the other if they were partying too much without the others. Vivian caught a cold, and getting sick was probably just what she needed in order to take a break if that sounds logical at all. They were pissed at her for being sick. Instead of concern, there was anger at the thought of her having to go to the doctors or, even worse, the hospital. "You better not get us busted, Viv," Skip remarked. Dave had checked out, so her being ill didn't matter one way or the other to him as long as there was no bullshit because of it. Constance was the only one who kept her head about her and did her best to nurse Vivian back to health. Despite her efforts, it wasn't working. Vivian's temperature soared, she was vomiting profusely, and her head pounded like someone had crawled inside and was playing drums. Her friend was concerned, and after arguing with Skip and Dave, she called on their family's private physician. He was paid well to scoot whatever he saw under the rug, and he had seen his share of strange goings on in the world of the elite. A half-hour after her call, he came through a side entrance with his medical bag. He was directed to Vivian's room, and as soon as he saw her, his face became etched with concern for her welfare. She was pale and withdrawn. She had a high fever, but her skin was cold and clammy. He told Constance he would have to know everything in order to properly treat Vivian. Despite the protests from Skip and Dave, she came clean with the doctor and told him everything. A half-hour later, he exited the room and informed the group that he would be staying, something he almost never did. He had started an IV with fluids to help with Vivian's dehydration and hopefully to reduce her fever. He applied cold packs to her armpits as well. He had seen the tracks on her arms but knew from past experience that his words would fall on deaf ears if he said anything, so he didn't bother to lecture on the dangers of shooting up. His job was to make sure he left the residence without a corpse. That was what he was paid for, and that's all he would do here, as he had done in so many other homes in this area. The secrets exhausted him.

It was a long night, and for the first time in months, nobody got high. None of them realized just how serious Vivian's illness really was, and they became frightened for her safe return to health. Constance stayed by her side throughout the night, and the men chain-smoked out on the deck. They had a couple of stiff drinks to get them through it all. Vivian's high fever had her talking out of her head, and through one of her rants, Constance learned of her rape in bits and pieces. She saw Vivian in a completely different light after that. How courageous and strong she must have been to carry that weight on her shoulders, never mentioning the recent attack in all these months, pretending that everything was alright in her life. How alone she must have felt. It saddened her, and she instantly felt the need to protect her new friend from any further harm. She would talk to Vivian and encourage her to continue on to Florida as soon as she felt strong enough to do so. She shouldn't be here. The drugs were just masking her pain, and Connie feared that if she stayed longer, it would not end well. Sometime in the early hours of the morning, Vivian's fever broke, and by later that morning, some color had returned to her deathlike pallor. The doctor felt comfortable with leaving her in Constance's care and left strict orders to be followed. He would return at the end of the day to check on her condition, and as he pulled out of the driveway, he hoped she would be alright with her companions.

A week or so later, Vivian was back on her feet and feeling much better than she had in a long time. She barely remembered being sick or why it started, but she had an idea it was from a dirty batch of speed someone had dropped off. She knew the rules and never said a thing, but by the time she had recovered, all traces of the drugs were gone from the table, and the house was actually bright and sun-filled. The guys were still getting high but not in her presence, and she was okay with that. Dave had moved into his own room, and normally, that would have bothered Vivian, but she welcomed the solitude. Constance made her eat when she could, gave her the meds the doctor had prescribed and gave her extra vitamins to help her along in her recovery. She never mentioned what she had heard to Vivian. Vivian was grateful to her for helping her through her illness. She was back to her old self finally and wanted to go out and do something. Connie and she had decided to go visit an old friend of the family, but the guys begged off, claiming it would be a drag for them. They dressed to go out, left some cash on the table for the guys and off they went. The evening was interesting. The family friend was a guy Constance had seen before Skip's return. Constance swore her to secrecy, and it not being any of Vivian's business, the secret was theirs. He offered the girls a line of some coke he had, and although Vivian knew she had just returned to health, he did the line anyway. Constance and her friend disappeared into his bedroom for a while, and sometime later, they reappeared, and she was ready to go. Vivian was, too. On the drive back to the house, they talked about the friend. Vivian assured her she was no one to judge someone else, and they enjoyed the rest of the ride to the house. As they came around a corner, the police were there directing traffic. It was at a standstill, and an officer came to the window to let them know it would be a while before they could pass because there had been a terrible accident involving a car and a motorcycle. Connie froze in her seat. Skip and Dave had bikes. They had gone riding a couple of times, and the girls always worried that they were too high to stay alert. She and Vivian got out of the car and walked toward the scene of the accident, afraid of what they might see, but there was Skip lying in the street, not moving, lifeless, or so it seemed. Dave was nowhere to be seen, but they both knew that they would never let the other ride alone. They looked up the street, and the other bike came into view wrapped around a pole, the bike mangled, its rider also on the ground. Vivian would never forget the blood-curdling screams she heard coming from Dave. As she got closer, she could see that Dave had serious injuries but something much worse. His lower leg was missing, and the medics were working to keep him from bleeding to death as they rushed him into one of the ambulances and towards the hospital. Skip was transported in the other with his own very critical injuries. Constance and Vivian ran into each other's arms and stood holding on for dear life before going back to the car and rushing to the hospital behind a police escort. Oh my God! How could this have happened? Apparently, a drunk driver had rounded the corner at a high rate of speed, in the wrong lane and ran head-on into the bikers. He, of course, was not injured and was transported to jail. This night would be the beginning of the end of the road for all of them. Weeks later, Vivian would leave for Florida, Skip would stay with Constance to recover from his broken pelvis, and Dave would be taken to his parent's home in Wisconsin to begin his rehab journey without his natural leg. None of them would ever have thought in a million years that things would end this way, but it had nonetheless and for better or worse, Vivian believed it was a sign from God.

It was a tearful goodbye for the two women as Vivian prepared to board the bus. So much had happened in such a short time, but they felt they would always remember their time together. Everyone says they will never forget someone they met and spent time with, but as Vivian boarded the bus, there were tears in her eyes because although their time had been short, it had left an imprint on Vivian's heart that would last a lifetime. Even when the years passed, Constance would come to mind, but none of them would ever see the others again.

Vivian was exhausted mentally and physically, and as the bus lumbered out of the station, she laid her head back, thinking of what was ahead of her in Florida. As she tried to sleep, thoughts swirled through her mind. Why was her life so crazy? Would it always be full of turmoil and despair? Would things ever get easier for her? She was only eighteen, and she had already been through more than her share of shit. Questions left unanswered, Vivian would sleep straight through the Georgia/Florida line.

Chapter Ten

"You're asking for a sunburn in places you shouldn't have a sunburn," a voice in the distance stated. She blocked the sun with her hand, and there stood Lulu, looking down at her while she lay sprawled in the sand. What the hell? When she drifted off, she swore she was sitting in the beach chair. How in the world had she ended ass up in a most unbecoming position? Mortified, she gathered herself and sat upright, looking as if she knew what was up all along. Lulu knew better. She had seen that look before. It always happened when Vivian remembered. "Aw, come on, girl, who gives a rat's ass anyway? They're all playing the game, so I doubt anybody noticed. Vivian knew it was her sweet attempt at making her feel less uncomfortable, and she loved her for that. Vivian grabbed a beer for herself and her friend, and they sat in silence, watching the waves crash onto the beach. "I had the strangest dream, she confided to her friend. She summarized, and Lulu listened, never saying a word about it. She just nodded at the appropriate moments and figured quietly that Vivian's dreams were the best therapy she could have, a less invasive way of dealing with the pain of her past and a lot less expensive.

Jamie came rushing up to where the girls sat, breathless from several rounds of play. She was the youngest of the three, and Vivian adored her free spirit. "Let's take one last dip before we go back to the house!" She must have been reading her two friends' minds, and they all ran into the water to cool off one last time for the day. As they headed toward the house, they bid the volleyball players goodbye and promised to see them at the bonfire later on in the weekend. It was a tradition, and they were not about to break it. Plus, it was said to be the event of the season and not just any bonfire. There would be food catered to and offered by the other beach guests, a band to dance the night away with, fireworks and, of course, the bonfire, which was pulled together by the parents, mostly the dads. It was their time to bond as men and feel their youth again for a little while.

The girls passed the gigantic pool at Mimi's, and all swore they would be poolside the next day. Just the girls relaxing and sharing the details of each other's lives outside the office. They rinsed off in the outdoor shower made specifically to avoid bringing sand into the house, then retired to their rooms to shower and change for dinner. Of course, they would check their cell phones as well. A girl cannot go the entire weekend without checking even though they had made a pact to leave them behind for most of the time. Vivian had two calls from Jack and a voicemail simply stating he hoped they were having a great time, and right before the message ended, he added, miss you. Vivian didn't really know how to accept affection for what it was, always thinking there might be a joker in the deck and for a split second, her mind let her think that it really had only been a day and that Jack added this as an afterthought. Dammit, couldn't it just be that she really did miss her? Whatever...

The three girls worked to put dinner together. Music was playing, and the atmosphere was pleasant. After the steaks were prepped and ready for the grill, they all grabbed a cocktail and headed for the large patio that faced the pool and the beach. The sun was nearing the western sky, and it was a gorgeous sight. Lulu manned the grill while Vivian and Jamie set the table and fixed the sides to pair with their steaks. They tossed a salad of chilled shrimp with cocktail sauce, and 20 minutes later, they were ready to eat. The mealtime conversation was light, and the girls agreed that a good flick in the theater room was a perfect way to spend the rest of the evening. They hurried to clear the table and clean up, then headed to the large family room to watch the movie they had agreed upon. The snacks and drinks were piled up on the table, and the girls settled in. After the movie, they said goodnight and headed to their rooms to rest. They were all tired from the day and were certain they would sleep well. Vivian hated to sleep with clothing on. Just a light tee shirt suited her. She drew back the covers and crawled in, sinking into the plush mattress as if she were lying on a bed of feathers. She was asleep almost as soon as her head hit the pillows, and for the first time in a very long time, Vivian would sleep through the night with no nightmares to haunt her.

Being an early riser has its advantages. She caught the sun as it awakened and welcomed the earth to another day. She had the first cup of coffee that was already brewing when she awoke. Mornings were her favorite time of the day. As she sipped her coffee, she was surprised to see an email from Maggie, her cat sitter. She opened it to see several photos of Henry and Stuart enjoying each other's company. She missed him. She sent a quick thank you reply and turned off her phone, keeping within the promise of the pact. The other two girls straggled in a short time later, grabbing a coffee and joining her on the patio. Not ready to fill up on breakfast, they grabbed a muffin from the basket on the table that Mimi had left as a welcoming gift and, in a short time, were headed out the door to the village only a couple of miles away. They drove Mimi's enormous golf cart in keeping with the custom of the beach community. There were still a few cars on the road, but most of the residents got from point A to point B using this mode of transportation. What the hell! When in Rome... It was more fun anyway, plus the view of the surrounding neighborhoods and homes was stunning.

They arrived in the quaint village just as most shops were opening their doors for the day. Shop owners were busy setting out their wares, knowing the weekenders would be eager to spend time and money, and there was no time to waste. Eye-catching garments, jewelry, scarves, sun umbrellas, and much more, as far as the eye could see, were being readied for the day's onslaught of shoppers. Vivian loved shopping for items that were unique and would suit the decor in her already eclectic apartment. She adored black-and-white art that contained a splash of color. She often used scarves as backdrops in strategically placed areas throughout her rooms. Some were hanging, some draped casually on the back of a chair, wherever it drew the most charm to the space. The three girls shopped for their favorites and may have spent just a little too much money, but they came prepared to spend and didn't concern themselves with the cost. They decided midday to grab a bite to eat at an adorable cafe that offered a variety of familiar menu items, nothing fancy but done just right. Vivian was talked into foregoing her diet, and she agreed to splurge for the weekend. She ordered a club sandwich, her favorite, with a side of coleslaw and a huge dill pill. She had to have the homemade potato chips because she just could not and would not even think of eating a sandwich of any type without chips. For Vivian, it was unheard of. She recalled a cold winter day, putting together a sandwich to pair with her soup and discovering she had not one chip in her cupboards. She put the sandwich in the fridge, donned her winter garb and trudged through the almost barren streets to the corner mart for her beloved chips. The things a girl will go through to have what she wants.

After lunch, they parked the golf cart and walked off some of their meal as they shopped. They decided on henna tattoos, Vivian being the only one of them to have a real one (her NY Yankees logo), and the artist did such a fabulous job that you would have to look close to notice it wasn't permanent. Jamie rode right above the cut of her low-rider jeans, and she exclaimed with delight that it would be an excellent conversation piece on the beach. Sweet Jamie, always planning ahead. Lulu got an arm chain that was embossed with tiny jewels that glittered in the sun, and Vivian's was similar to the Cheshire cat from Alice and Wonderland, the movie. She loved the color teal, and it was perfect against her already-tanned skin. When their feet grew tired, they copped a seat on one of the many benches that lined the sidewalks and watched the passersby. They giggled so hard Lulu almost peed when two men wearing speedos and muscle shirts, sipping something from a flask, walked by holding hands while two toy poodles rested in their arms, dressed to the nines for their outing. It probably wasn't nice to laugh, but it was one of those moments where even though they knew they shouldn't, they just could not help it. The lifestyles of the rich afforded them the luxury of doing and being whatever they wanted, and to hell with anyone that didn't like it. Kudos to them for keeping it real.

It had been a wonderful day, and when the girls were all shopped out, they decided it was time for a dip in the pool and happy hour. They hauled their purchases onto the cart and headed back, returning a wave each time a passerby waved at them. Pool time was relaxing and cleared away what little fatigue they had from their excursion. They talked about their purchases and how lovely all of the shops had been. "Why don't we go down to the beach later and make smores," Vivian commented. We can watch the sunset if we get down there in time. "That sounds like an excellent idea," Jamie and Lulu chimed in. After dinner, they packed up a cooler and headed for the beach. Others had decided to catch the view as well and were camped out on blankets as the sun began its nightly spiral toward the West. It was breathtaking, and from their vantage point, they felt they could almost reach out and grasp the end of the day. Each section of the beach had its own fire pit stocked with logs, so the girls made a fire and dove into making smores. It had been years, and the girls felt like kids again. How funny it is that in trying so hard to be a grown-up, we forget what it's like to be a child.

The three friends ate, drank cocktails and sang along with the songs playing on the radio, although none of them could carry a tune. They lay back and gazed at the stars so clearly outlined in the sky. They were having the time of their lives, and their bond as friends grew deeper with every passing moment. Jamie was the comedian, always telling great jokes, and she was the life of every party she attended. She had Vivian and Lulu rolling with laughter, and the buzz they had from their drinks was attributed to their uncontrollable, side-splitting howls. Thankfully, they were far enough apart from the others on the beach that their laughs were all their own. Sometime after two o'clock in the morning, Vivian, Lulu and Jamie wove their way back to the house and fell into bed, sleeping fitfully and fulfilled from the day's events.

They would all need their sleep if they were going to be fresh for the upcoming bonfire extravaganza.

Vivian woke up to a bit of a headache, shit, a hangover was more like it. Just how much had they drunk? She showered and donned a pair of scrubs and her favorite tee-shirt and headed to the kitchen for some much-needed coffee. She knew if she felt this bad, then Jamie and Lulu would as well, so she mixed together a pitcher of Bloody Marys and laid out a tray of garnishes for the drinks. Chilled glasses awaited the other two house guests. Just a little hair of the dog to make things right again. She set out everything: bagels, cream cheese and lox to pair with the cocktails. She downed two Tylenol, and by the time her friends awakened, she felt just a little better. They had showered but still looked a bit under the weather. They looked at each other and cracked up laughing. "Damn, aren't we a freaking mess?" They welcomed the inviting Bloody Marys, and the food helped to absorb whatever was left of the booze. None of them noticed the cooler hanging upside down from one of the statues and an empty bottle in the cherub's hand until they were cleaning up the table, which, of course, sent them into hysterics. Thankfully, Vivian had the mindset to disarm the security cameras as soon as she got up, or she might have had some explaining to do later. Mimi was as cool as they came, but Vivian didn't want to come off as disrespectful of her kindness.

They had a few hours before the festivities started, so they did some cleaning inside and out. They wanted to leave the home as clean as it was when they arrived and didn't want to have to do so the morning they were to leave. There was no better way to express one's appreciation for the generosity of a friend. After a run to the liquor store, they restocked the bar, wiped down everything in sight, ran the vacuum, changed the sheets and then, thank God, their tasks were complete. From what they had heard in passing, everyone normally slept on the beach the night of the bonfire. The girls had no idea just how fabulous it would actually be, and they were filled with excitement and anticipation. They selected their outfits carefully, each of them having exquisite taste in dressing to complement their figures and personalities. The outfits they chose would enable them to transition from day to evening with very little fuss.

Jamie chose a leaf green midriff tee top with small daisies embroidered into the hem. Her Capri pants were a pale green with a zipper that ran up her hip to her waist. A cute little white belt and crisp white deck shoes completed the ensemble. Her hair was done in a ponytail, and her makeup was flawless. None of the girls would need much in the way of makeup as the sun had kissed their skin, giving them the perfect shade of blush for any occasion. Her friend was so petite and adorable that everything she wore looked fabulous.

Lulu's outfit consisted of brown cuffed skinny jeans that fit like a glove on her slender body. She had paired them with a loose-fitting tan muslin blouse with capped sleeves and a beautiful rope chain with a tiny rose attached at the base. She had seen it in town the day before and had to have it. Opened-toe mule skin sandals with a strap at the heel were the perfect selection. She decided to leave her waist-length raven hair loose, her signature look that drew many an eye whenever she walked by. She looked stunning.

A teal shift dress that fell just a bit above the knee with a plunging neckline, hidden pockets and a zipper with a jeweled silver loop that ran down the back to the base of her buttocks was the perfect choice for Vivian. Her henna tattoo was the only accessory she needed. She wasn't really into jewelry, but in her case, there was no need for any with this look. The dress said it all. Her sandals were sensible but classy and strapped up the leg just enough to give her just a little height. Vivian was only five foot three, but she had "legs for days," as some of her friends had commented. She wore a high braided ponytail that met the end of the zipper on her dress. She chose this look because her hair and humidity were not friends, and this was a perfect way to keep it under control. It showcased her profile beautifully. Vivian looked at her reflection in the mirror and was pleased with what she saw.

The weather forecast would have the temps in the low eighties for the day and close to sixty for the remainder of the evening, so the girls made sure to tuck something warm to wear once the sunset. The girls took the golf cart, a much easier way to make their way down the beach to the pavilion where the food and drinks were housed. As it came into view, the girls were stunned beyond words. The building, usually open, was covered with a beautiful white and blue striped canopy and secured to the sand with large anchors, fitting for a beach-themed party. It was reminiscent of the sail on a boat and was simply lovely. Lights were strung from corner to corner, encasing the tent. They would provide the perfect lighting later in the evening. The band had set up shop close by and had begun playing tunes that would appeal to all age groups. They sounded really good, and the girl's mood switched to party mode. The path that lined the way to the pavilion was lined with large buckets of wildflowers with a lighted chain-linked fence put into place so that part-goers could not stray from the path and bust their ass in the dark.

Quite a few people had already arrived and were at the bar being served whatever was pleasing to their palate. The girls ordered something light. It would be a long day, and they wanted to pace themselves. The fragrant smells of delicious appetizers hung in the air, luring them for a brief moment in their direction. There were tables casually set and a dance floor in another area, complete with a disco ball. Jamie thought it was a bit much and had not seen a disco ball in ages, but to Vivian, it was perfect. Later, Jamie would be under that ball dancing her ass off, loving it. Caterers were arriving with tray after tray of food that had been ordered by the guests. The girl's contribution was a large charcuterie tray filled with an assortment of meats, cheeses, fruit and nuts with rows of toasted bread and crackers. A separate tray housed the condiments they had ordered to pair with the tray. Italian olives, varieties of pickles, several flavors of mustard and many other selections were all neatly arranged, and the girls were impressed with their offerings.

Outside, some of the men were manning an open pit that smelled like a slice of heaven. It was customary for the hosts to provide a portion of the meat, and they caught a glimpse of the rows of chicken, burgers, gourmet franks and several large briskets that, when cooked, would be kept piping hot in the outdoor oven brought in just for the gathering. While the girls were checking out the grills, the men were busy checking them out. The girls were flattered by the howls and whistling their way. They giggled, knowing their advances were harmless. They innocently flirted right back, and the men puffed up like roosters in the hen house. Up and down the beach, there were private cabanas ranging in size as far as the eye could see. The girls looked at each other and said "sleeping quarters" at the same time. A young lady was seated at a table with what looked like tickets and a registration book, so the girls asked what it was all about. "Oh, these are cabana assignments," She stated brightly. The girls had registered as invited guests the day of their arrival, so they gave her the address of the house and the girl gave them a ticket for their cabana. "Oh, how cool is that," Lulu exclaimed! The girl pointed in the direction that would lead them to their spot, and they removed their shoes and headed down the beach. It wasn't that long before they reached the cabana, and the girls squealed with delight when they saw how adorable it was. Three beds, a small table with a wash bin with towels neatly placed on it. Lights in the shape of lanterns completed the look. Security had been hired for the entire day and evening, so there would be little concern for theft. There was a box with a lock and key attached, and they assumed it was for any personal items they would not want to just leave out. An ice chest for drinks sat in the corner with ice already in it and a note that read, "We'll fill it for you!" They had thought of everything, and the girls loved it. Back out on the beach, they passed by several booths where activities were already taking place.

Throughout the day, they visited many of those booths, having the time of their lives. Jamie broke off from the group to join the volleyball players. She had worn her bikini under her clothes, as did the others, and they left her in good hands, noticing that Red paid special attention to their friend, and the other girls fawned over her newly acquired tattoo. Vivian stopped at the roulette table and tried her luck playing her favorite numbers. She was not a winner, but it was fun anyway. There were booths where purchases could be made, and the girls decided it was better to spend their money and not lose it, so they shopped just a little. Vivian spied the cutest toy for her furry friend and several bags of natural cat treats, and she swooped them up, knowing Henry would be expecting rewards for being left behind. She also found a handsome date book and, for no particular reason, picked it up for Jack. The girls danced into the evening, ate way too much food and helped themselves to the endless flow of cocktails from the bar. The fireworks were about to begin, and Lulu thought it would be a good idea to find Jamie so they could all watch them together. She had gone off to mingle some more with the younger crowd.

They canvased the food tent, the area surrounding the bonfire pit, but Jamie was nowhere to be seen. Dammit, where in the hell was she? As they headed further down the beach, Red hurried by them, trying to go unnoticed, but Lulu stopped him dead in his tracks and asked him when the last time it was that he had seen Jamie was. He was nervous for some reason, and Vivian felt a bad feeling run through her. Suddenly, they saw Jamie coming towards them with a bloody lip and a torn bikini top. She cried out to them, and for a moment, time stopped. Lulu had a sense of mind enough not to take her eyes off Red and flagged down security as they passed. They ran to Jamie, and she, of course, was beside herself, trying to explain what had happened. They tried their best to comfort her. Vivian went to their cabana, grabbed the sweatshirt Jamie had brought along, and gave it to her friend.

Security detained Red until the local sheriff arrived to take over. He was very kind to Jamie as he began to question her. She explained that she had had a little too much to drink and decided to get some fresh air when she ran into Red. Yes, she knew him from the beach. No, he was not her boyfriend. He had said he would walk with her, and that is when things went wrong. He tried to put the moves on her, but she insisted that he stop. He did not, and when she tried to get away from him, he slapped her and grabbed her in an effort to subdue her. She screamed, and only then did he let her go. No, she was not hurt, and aside from the puffy lip, she was sure she did not need medical attention. She was shaken up, and her friends assured the sheriff they would take it from there. Jamie asked that charges for assault be filed and gave him her information in the city if and when she was needed for anything else. As they walked with her past Red, Lulu spat in his face and called him something a good catholic girl would never repeat. After all she had just been through, Jamie insisted they all see the fireworks and end the evening on a good note. "Freaking Red is not going to ruin our trip, that bastard," she stated emphatically. They hugged her tightly, all thankful that she hadn't been hurt or worse. Vivian cringed at the thought and, for a moment, felt as if she may be sick. Lulu saw the look and grabbed her hand in silent support. She was the only friend that Vivian had confided in, and she would take it to her grave.

The fireworks were larger than life and stunning, and as the last barrage lit the sky, someone threw a match in the pit, and the fire lit up the sky. It was amazing, like nothing they had ever seen before. Everyone gathered around the fire and drank, laughed and enjoyed the rest of the evening. It was very late when they made their way back to their sleeping quarters, plates of food piled high, a few cokes in their grasp. They were all in good spirits when they finished their snacks and crawled into bed. Vivian was the last to turn in, brushing her teeth first then, as she was about to turn off the lights, she heard Jamie crying softly. She went to her and held her until she fell asleep. Feeling worked up from the evening, Vivian decided to sit on the beach for awhile to unwind. It was quiet, and she lay back, cleared her mind and focused on the sound of the waves. She drifted in and out in time with the waves. Their sound called to her, and she was lulled further into a restless slumber. When she awoke, she retired to her tent so that she would rest before their return to the city. The trip was over, and she was glad they would be back home in the morning.

They all woke up early, packed up their things and headed back to the house to get the rest of their belongings together, pack the car and do a last-minute check of everything in the house. They left Mimi a note, not sure when she would get it, along with a beautiful crystal wind chime as their way of saying thank you. Fifty minutes later, they were back in the city, and all three of them were elated to be in familiar surroundings once again. Vivian stopped to pick up Henry, who pretended for just a moment to be put out with her. When she unlocked the door to the apartment and unpacked her stuff, his mood changed when he saw what she had brought home for him. She took a hot shower and ordered in, knowing she would be staying home for the night. Jack called, and she promised to see him the next day. They chatted for a few minutes before her food arrived. When the buzzer rang, it was her cue to end the call, and they said their goodbyes. She found a gift bag for Jack's gift, wrapped it in white tissue paper and attached a card she signed with just her name. She curled up on the sofa and ate her Chinese food. Combination Egg Fu Young, fried rice, an egg roll and steamed dumplings. Yum! She would munch on the leftovers for days. It was good to be home. After she was filled, she put the rest in the fridge and crawled onto the sofa where Henry lay napping contently. He purred loudly as she touched him, stretching out for her to pet his tummy. She pulled the soft blanket over both of them, turned on the television, and tried her best to watch her favorite true crime show, but she knew she would be asleep in minutes. People always slept better in their own beds. As she drifted off to sleep, somehow, she swore she could hear the sounds from the beach and the waves rolling in and out, serenading her, caressing her with a peaceful whisper. She was asleep in no time, and her dreams returned her to the day the bus rolled into the station. She had made it to Florida. She was over four months late, but better late than never, she always said.

Chapter Eleven

Normally, a trip to Florida would have been somewhere Vivian would have chosen as a vacation destination; however, when getting off the bus, she felt a sense of dread that loomed over her like a storm cloud on a rainy day. She looked around the bus station as if there would be a familiar face waving in her direction. Why? Dad had already told her that she would have to catch a cab because he had other things to do, and after all, she was late arriving. Very late. She went to the ticket counter to inquire about a cab but heard her name being called as she made her way through the crowded station. She ignored it at first, thinking that there must be another Vivian, but as she closed in on the counter, she heard her name again. She turned around, and there stood her brother smiling from ear to ear. Frank was her only biological brother, and she loved him dearly. He was a little OCD about certain things, but hey, who isn't? His childhood was not a walk in the park by any stretch, and he, along with Vivian and Lyla, struggled to come to grips with it all even years later, but they had each other, and that was all they needed. Vivian was moved to tears as they embraced. He grabbed her bags and left the station. "So how pissed is Dad really?" she asked. Frank looked over at her from the driver's seat and answered, "How pissed should he be?" Dammit. Vivian hated questions answered with a question. "Come on, bro, give me a straight answer, will ya!" She learned that her father had been worried at first when he learned that she would not be getting off the bus, but his worry quickly turned to his typical reactive behavior, and just the thought of not being able to control the situation had him fuming. Her brother assured her that he had moved past his initial reaction and was his same old self again. Like that would be so much better, Vivian thought.

Vivian wanted to freshen up but thought better of it, and as they turned into the driveway of her father's place, her stomach began to turn. Her brother had noticed how small she was, and it worried him. She had always carried a little extra weight, but now she hinged on the skinny side, and it left him to wonder why. He, of course, would never ask. Their father, however, would notice right away, and he would not be shy about voicing his opinion about her weight loss. Frank led them to the front door and knocked, which seemed strange to Vivian. Who knocks on the door at their parent's house? Dad's masculine voice cut through the air letting them know that the door was open and to come in. When he saw that it was them, brother and sister, he seemed surprised. Vivian liked the thought of strength in numbers and was so glad her brother was there. "Well, I see you finally decided to grace us with your presence," he stated flatly. She would have loved a hug and a greeting befitting a father and his daughter, but she knew it was not to be. Rather than feed the fire, Vivian nodded in agreement and changed the subject immediately, commenting on the house her dad and his "girlfriend" had rented, saying how lovely it was. It was truly a smooth move, and Vivian had become an expert over the years at calming the waters when it came to her father. He jumped up and gave her the grand tour. It was actually a very nice place, nestled in a wooded area with a lovely back porch, which he, with no fanfare, announced as her room. He, of course, went over the "rules" of the house, and she half heard them and mostly ignored them. Screw the rules, she thought to herself. Mary stood next to Vivian's dad the whole time, looking at the young woman through bloodshot eyes, but never said a word. Smart woman... Vivian hated her, and she never really hated anyone. This woman was everything her mother wasn't, and she loathed being in the same room with her. Bitch. Vivian's brother cut through the thickness in the air by suggesting they all go get something to eat. Their father agreed, and it wasn't until hours later that she actually had a chance to catch her breath and finally relax. She tried to unpack her things but was so road weary she decided it could wait until the morning. The Florida room was quite comfortable, with soft lighting that bounced off the room in soft hues. The bed was not large but was comfortable. There was a door that led to the kitchen and to one of the bathrooms that would be hers to use as well. She quietly moved through the kitchen to the bathroom to take a well-needed shower. Vivian didn't want a confrontation on her first night there. She just wasn't ready for that. Although she knew it was inevitable, she prayed it would also wait till morning. It did.

Despite being exhausted, Vivian tossed and turned pretty much of the night, and her sleep was riddled with snippets of reality and make-believe nightmares that felt so real that when she woke and muffled a scream, she felt as if it continued. Damn, the nightmares were back. She sat at the edge of bed for a moment, reached in her purse for her cigarettes and stepped out the back door for a smoke. Her father smoked but had not mentioned whether it was permitted in the house or not, so she puffed outside in the early hours of the morning, trying to make sense of what she had just dreamed. Oh hell, why beat it to death? Her father's voice startled her, and she turned quickly, butting out the smoke. "You're up early. Were you smoking a cigarette?" No, Dad, it was angel dust, she thought to herself, pissed that he thought it was anything but a cigarette. "Yes, Dad, it was a cigarette, I didn't wake you up, did I?" Her father had always been an early riser and the years since she last saw him hadn't changed that. "Breakfast at seven, you look like you haven't eaten right in awhile." There it was, the door opening to that discussion, which she hoped wouldn't happen. Before he could remind her, she field-stripped her cigarette and saw that he had been watching, kind of impressed that she had remembered. Was that a grin she glimpsed?

After they ate, she grabbed the ads and began looking for a job because there was no way she was gonna be trapped at the house and although she still had the money she stashed while in Georgia, she needed to be invisible as much as she possibly could and quickly. She circled a few possibilities, got up from the table and resumed emptying her belongings into a dresser she swore had been in her childhood home. Vivian was nearly finished a couple of hours later; her dress clothes hung in a very beautiful wardrobe, and all but a few items left in her luggage had been organized in the dresser. Her favorite magazines were placed on the night table next to her bed. She had set up a table she found in the shed and grabbed a couple of chairs to complete the look. Vivian had an eye for design, and in no time, the room had gone from bland to a relaxing place she could call her own. She was about to stash her bag under the bed when she felt something that was hidden in her front pocket. Just in Case, it was written on the front of the package she pulled out. Oh God! She knew what it was before she even opened it. She didn't want to know and tucked it away so well that even a drug-sniffing dog would not find it. Shit! All she needed was for her father to find it, and the shit would hit the fan, that was for damn sure.

She cleaned up a little and was just finishing up when she heard the sound of her brother's car. He had agreed to take her around to the places she had circled in the paper. The town was small, but it had more than its share of drinking establishments, and Benny's was hiring a bartender. It would not have been her father's choice by any means, but Vivian was still young, and she thought it would be a way of meeting people her age, and she sure as hell wasn't going to flip burgers at BK. She walked out twenty minutes later, her position secured, and she felt great. The only dark spot in an otherwise good day was going back to the house and telling her dad. To her surprise, he was not as upset as she had thought he would be. Maybe he didn't want to be a hypocrite. Mary drank a lot every day, beer being her coffee, so how could he possibly judge Vivian for only working at a bar? It was only part-time anyway, and she had also landed a job as an office assistant where she would be working mornings. She had covered her ass so that she wouldn't have to fall under the watchful eye of her dad very often, and she was proud that her plan had come together so easily.

In the weeks that followed Vivian was thriving at her new jobs, loving Benny's and the crowd that frequented the place. They were a mix of the townspeople, husbands trying to escape their wives, a few rednecks and bikers, more so on the weekends when there was a band. She was good at her job and made really decent money. The guys loved her, and the chicks loved to hate her. Jealous bitches. She made a rule not to drink while on duty even though Mike, the owner (I know, the bar's name was Benny's), had told her it was alright if she had one or two if a customer wanted to buy. She did enjoy a couple of hits on a joint whenever she would step out for a break, but Vivian knew she could handle it. It was better to have a clear head, plus she didn't like drinking and driving home after she closed up for the night. The cops were cool, a few stopping in after shift, but she just couldn't stop thinking of Dave and what he had suffered at the hands of a drunk driver. It was actually a cop who helped her find the car she lovingly named Stella. Nothing fancy, but it was sound and ran like a dream.

Her time at home was brief, and Vivian was okay with that. Her father, on one occasion, when they were actually home at the same time, asked her how long she planned on staying with them. She really hadn't given it much thought before he asked, but it made sense that they would expect her to move out eventually. He and Mary had been on the outs more since her arrival, and he must have thought it was because of her. Screw her! It almost made Vivian want to stay longer just to piss her off even more, but Vivian didn't want her father to have to deal with an angry drunk which, from what her brother had told her, he hated more than anything. Nobody likes a drunk when they are not drinking, and her dad didn't drink, never had, and it always made Vivian wonder just what the appeal was with this woman. Anyway, Mary's daughter Nancy had her own place not far from Benny's, with three bedrooms and two baths. and had mentioned the spare room to Vivian a few times and said if she wanted out, she could move in there for a reasonable fee. Until that moment, she had not thought about it, but it seemed like a good time to pursue the offer further. She made a mental note to ask Nancy the next time she saw her. She told her father she would start looking without mentioning Nancy to him. She was sure if she had, then Mary would get in her business, and that was a bad idea for her.

Five weeks later, Vivian was loading the last of her things into the rental truck bound for Nancys. She had seen her at Segway, a supermarket in town, and the room was still available, so she took it. Neither of the girls mentioned it until the day before the move. Nancy knew her mother could be a bitch about things, and they agreed it would be better to wait until the last minute to tell them both of the plans. Mary was fuming by the time the last boxes went on the truck, glaring hatefully at everyone but at Vivian in particular. She had been on a bender and made it nearly impossible for everyone to get anything done. She made a nasty-handed remark to Vivian's dad, and Vivian felt her temper rising and had had enough. Why not go out with a bang. She jumped up, slapped Mary in the face and told her in a voice that may not have been her own that if she ever spoke to him like that again, she was getting an ass whooping. Straight up! The room was deadly quiet, no one saying a word, maybe even a little afraid to breathe. Vivian's dad broke the silence and ordered her out of the house and to not come back until she was ready to apologize. Ha! It would be a cold day in hell before she did that. Screw her and him. They could have each other. She did apologize to Nancy, but she just laughed and told her she would have done the same thing if she were Vivian. Nancy and her mom had a tenuous relationship, and the less time she spent around her, the better they got along. "Oh shit, hang on a minute. I forgot something in the house," Vivian nearly shrieked. She went in the back way and grabbed the bundle she had stashed and nearly forgot. Dammit, Vivian, that would have been your ass, she muttered to herself. Funny how even though she never touched it, she never got rid of it either. She had plenty of opportunity to flush the dope, but she just couldn't. Her stomach cramped up, and she knew the feeling well. She needed to keep busy, and as she left her fathers, she prayed she would stay busy enough to keep away from it just awhile longer. Maybe even long enough to be able to dump it. She just wasn't strong enough yet and needed more time. She felt like such a coward.

For the rest of the day and into the evening, Vivian unpacked and got situated at her new place. Nancy worked nights, so Vivian had the place to herself. Sometime between stacking books and hanging her favorite artwork, she grew hungry and decided to order a pizza. Sitting on the patio, she got her first real glimpse of her surroundings. The complex was cute but sat adjacent to the projects, almost as if there were a dividing line between white people and people of color. She watched a little girl approach. She was adorable and had the most beautiful eyes. Her name, as she announced herself, was Felicia Barnes, and she lived across the street with her brothers, mamma and daddy. And did Vivian want to be friends? How innocent and unclouded were the eyes of this child. "Sure, we can be friends, but I think someone might be looking for you," Vivian stated as a tall, well-built man moved in their direction. Felicia jumped up and down with excitement, exclaiming very proudly that he was her brother William. Well, William sure was handsome, that's for damn sure, and Vivian wouldn't have minded if he wanted to be friends as well. It had been awhile since she had been with anyone, and her hormones were all over the place. William said hello, introduced himself and promptly told Felicia she had better get her butt home before momma took a switch to her behind.

He stayed behind long enough to learn that Vivian had just moved in, she was, in fact, single, which he found hard to believe and that she bartended at Benny's. Her pizza arrived, and William was about to leave when Vivian asked if he would like to join her. She hated eating alone and welcomed the company. He stayed, they ate and drank a few beers and got to know each other better. William was in the Army and was home on leave. He was stationed in Pensacola, not too far from home and was able to come home more frequently than his buddies. His voice was hypnotic, and he looked her in the eyes when he talked. He had great teeth and a sweet smile. Vivian was entranced. She had dated outside her race but had never dated a person of color before. In the South, in the early eighties, it was still very much frowned upon, but Vivian never did like to bow down to the norm that society set. She had always felt that people date people, but she had been raised by someone who believed that white people date white people and the rest dated whoever they wanted as long as it wasn't white people. He was the reason her sister didn't marry the real love of her life. Her sister was weak, though, and didn't stand up for what she believed in. She ended her relationship because their father did not approve of her choice. Another reason she and Vivian did not get along was that she had no spine, and that was one thing Vivian prided herself on. No matter what the outcome was, she always stayed true to what she believed, and nobody could muddy the waters she swam in. She took an instant liking to William, and in the weeks ahead, they grew closer. He had a great sense of humor, which Vivian found sexy. He gave her a peaceful, easy feeling whenever they were together, which had become quite often. She met Mr. and Mrs. Barnes. He was a very serious man, but she was warm, kind and loved anyone who liked her children. She knew right away that Vivian liked her son, and she warned her to be careful. She reminded her that getting involved with a black man in the South would most likely cause problems. Vivian respected her but, at the same time, didn't see the trouble that lay ahead of her. Sex with William was amazing. He was passionate and took his time with Vivian, making sure her needs were met before his. They had sex every chance they got, anywhere they could, and Vivian couldn't get enough of him. She missed him when he was away during the week and couldn't wait for Friday when he would come see her. Some weekends, he had duty and couldn't get away, so she drove to the base to see him.

One evening, as Vivian was leaving work, she was confronted by a very large woman and her friends in the parking lot. Vivian didn't have to close the bar, so had stayed awhile and had a few drinks. Her guard had been down which never usually ever happened, no thanks to Tito. She didn't have time to reach in her purse for Kenny before the women ganged up on her, and punches flew so quickly she almost got her ass beat. Luckily, a few chicks from the bar came out and evened the score and just as the fight was ending, the biggest of the women told Vivian she had better keep her hands off William because he was her man and if Vivian didn't want her ass beat she better stay in her lane. Vivian was speechless. How could this even be true? Was it true, or was it a black woman not wanting a white woman in her world? Vivian was so confused, and as she drove home, she knew she would have to see William, and she wanted the truth. Dammit, why was this happening? Vivian cleaned up when she got home, and she really didn't look as bad as she thought she would for all the punches she had received. Chicken shit bitch anyway, couldn't fight a fair fight. Vivian was sure she would have knocked her ass out had it been one on one. She was no stranger to fighting to protect herself. Living on the streets had taught her that. Lying down on her bed, thoughts reeled through her mind. She heard pounding on the door and was worried that the woman had found out where she lived and was coming for her. She jumped up, ready to kick some ass.

Chapter Twelve

William stood at the door with a pissed off look on his face. His mother had told him what happened. Word traveled fast in the projects, and upon hearing, he had rushed out to see Vivian. What happened was inevitable. Monique, his ex, was the type of woman who, although proud of her race, was also not accepting of white girls "stealing their men," which was how she saw it. He knew it was only a matter of time before she caught wind of his relationship with Vivian, and she would start some shit when she did. Vivian stood in the doorway, not saying much as he tried his best to apologize and make sense of things. All Vivian knew was what Monique had said. "Her man." Had William lied about being single? That's all she wanted to know. She could deal with Monique later if she had to. Trust and honesty meant everything to her, and if he lied, then what else had he lied about. Vivian was not good with giving the benefit of the doubt or second chances. She felt that if one could not keep their shit together enough to avoid bad situations that involved her, then why let it repeat itself at a later time.

Although she believed what William was saying, she knew it would be better if she backed away. She wasn't ready for another messed up situation, and this was indeed messed up. "I'm not gonna look over my shoulder every time I turn around," she stated flatly, feeling very sad that she would have to be the one to end what might have been a great relationship. She just didn't want the drama in her life. He pleaded with her not to call it quits, but she had made up her mind. She explained that Monique would always be a problem, and she didn't feel that her problem should be Vivian's. Some things just cannot be changed with time. As William left looking dejected, Vivian felt sad but knew she had made the right decision. Nancy came home a short time later, and Vivian filled her in on the details. Nancy wished she would have been there to help Vivian, but what was done was done, and she encouraged her friend to close that chapter and move on.

Vivian sat in her bedroom, and the package in the closet came to her mind. It would be a friend, make her feel better, make all her troubles disappear. A little bit would not hurt if she was careful. She consoled herself with these rationalizations, although she knew it was nothing but trouble. She didn't care. She wanted to feel happy. She took a little hit of the coke, and her worries melted away. One hit led to another, and sometime later, she fooled herself into believing she was all right again. She liked the way the drug made her feel, and it was a familiar reminder of a simpler stitch in time. Or so she thought. She went to work that night high as a kite, and Mike knew something was different. He had seen it too many times before, and he warned Vivian to keep her shit in check, or he would bounce her ass out the door. She loved her job and promised Mike she would.

In the days ahead, Vivian did coke as much and as often as she could but was careful not to let it interfere with her job. She hid out in her room, afraid Nancy would notice. Little did she know Nancy had her figured out but chose not to get involved. Vivian was headed in a downward spiral, and the people who had gotten to know her all knew she was in trouble. Vivian didn't care. She had it under control. She could handle it. It wasn't a problem. All bullshit. It became all too clear how much of a problem it was when she realized her hefty package had diminished, and she was on the verge of running out. Panic set in as it always did when the demand was bigger than the supply. Now, she was met with a new problem. She had to find a connection. There were plenty of people that hung out at Benny's that she could hook up with, but she didn't want Mike to get wind of it and can her. She needed the job because she needed to keep money coming in to pay rent and to buy more drugs in that order. It was funny in a perverse way that a drug user always had the resources to buy drugs but struggled to maintain the basic necessities. Vivian knew a guy who knew a guy, and she put out feelers on the down low. It didn't take long before she got the hookup, and for a while, all was right again in Vivian's world.

Her friends started to notice she was spending more time with some of the less desirable patrons at Benny's and less time with them, and they didn't like it, but Vivian was not a child. She knew the score or was supposed to anyway. It was like watching an accident happen. It was obviously in real time, but it always looked like it was in slow motion to the observer. Most people will watch you crash and talk about it later instead of stepping up like a real friend would. Vivian was crashing, and there was nobody to stop it from happening. But hey, Vivian didn't care, so why should they? It was 1982, and there was a lot more to worry about than a drug addict, even if it was Vivian. The United States was in a severe recession, and times were tough for people in the real world. Her addiction was not a priority.

In a moment of weakness, Vivian lets William back into her life. She had missed him and hoped he would fix whatever was going on in her head. It was a bad move. Between the sex, they argued a lot. Just about everything irritated Vivian, and William couldn't understand what had changed. They had never fought before, but now it was almost as if she wanted to have it out with him whenever she got the chance. Maybe she was blaming him for her reintroduction to coke. She found it easier to blame him than to accept accountability for her choices. During one of their debates, she informed him that she had decided to move out of Florida. It took him by surprise, but it made perfect sense to her. She never saw her father because she refused to apologize to the bitch. Nobody wanted to hang out with her at work anymore, and she felt very alone. Misery loved company, and Vivian was miserable, but it had less to do with the people around her than the real problem. She would have to work hard to save the money she would need to move, but she was determined to accomplish what she set out to do. Too bad she couldn't have the same strength and conviction when it came to drugs. Oh well, she thought. One thing at a time.

For the next six months, Vivian kept her nose clean (pardon the pun) and worked every hour she could and then some so that she could put together the funds she would need to make the trip out of Florida. She went from part-time to full-time at both jobs and busted her ass regardless of how tired she was or how badly she wanted to do dope. She called her father and told him she was leaving, and he seemed relieved. He had heard the rumors of Vivian's drug problem and did not want any part of it. It was easier for him to wash his hands of it and her once again. Nancy knew she would be losing not only a roommate but a friend, and she was going to miss Vivian. Frank thought it was best for his sister to get out before it went from bad to worse, although he had loved being so close to her. Babs was thrilled because she would have their father to herself again, and Vivian's move suited her just fine. Selfish bitch. Even after her last split with William, Vivian remained close to Mrs. Barnes, and they spoke every day. They prayed together, and the older woman reminded Vivian that problems had a way of following someone and that Vivian could not run away from them. She would have to take them with her and deal with them. Vivian knew she was right and hoped the fresh start would get her back on track. Just one time in her life, she hoped it would get easier for her. Was that asking too much?

The weekend before her departure she had a yard sale, keeping only her very favorites that she just could not live without. Vivian was used to leaving material things behind and, for the most part, didn't feel a loss. She had left a lifetime of possessions behind many times. She had accumulated quite a few very nice items, and she was sure her sale would bring in some nice cash. At the end of the first day, she had made quite a bit of money and was pleased with her success. The next day went much the same, and by day's end, she had sold just a bout everything with only a few items left on the tables. She decided to donate them to her favorite charity organization, and by Sunday, she had wrapped things up. Vivian was leaving after work the following Saturday, well, early Sunday morning, and there was still so much to do. She had yet to make a decision on where she was headed until one night when Nancy came into the bar with a map of the United States, laid it on the bar and told Vivian to close her eyes, and wherever her finger landed, that's where she would go, dammit. There was only one rule. She would only be allowed one do-over, just in case. Vivian loved the idea, just in case the first place was a shit hole! Everyone gathered around to watch as she closed her eyes, twirled her finger in the air and put it down on the map. It was a dud. There was no way in hell she was going to Bismark, North Dakota. "Last chance!" Nancy yelled to her. Vivian prayed it would be somewhere nice but really didn't care. Home is how you made it, not where you made it. Someone played a drum roll on the bar, and she repeated her steps. Vivian opened her eyes to a city in Nebraska. She had never been to the Midwest and didn't hate her choice. One of the guys yelled The Cornhusker State, another chanting Go Big Red. She had no idea what they were talking about, but she would find out soon enough. "Nebraska it is then!" she exclaimed.

Vivian decided that she would fly to Nebraska instead of traveling cross country as she had coming to Florida. She sure as hell wasn't quite prepared for another journey just yet and felt it would be in her best interest to get where she was going via the quickest route. Nancy had offered to ship the remainder of her stuff once she got there. She had secured a cute apartment in an area surrounded by a beautiful park, and by all appearances, it was just what she was looking for. The home was quite large and had been converted to apartments, hers being on the main floor with a large screened-in front porch, adding to its charm. She imagined what she could do with it and was excited about the challenge.

Sunday morning arrived, with only Nancy seeing her to the airport. She hadn't heard a word from her father but really wasn't surprised. She had seen Frank the night before, and although he was sad to see her go, he was happy if she was. As they called her flight, she hugged Nancy and, for a moment, felt as if she couldn't let go. She told herself she wasn't running away and that this was right. It felt right, so why was she so anxious? Nancy gave her a pep talk and told her to get her ass on the plane and to keep in touch. As she boarded the plane, she hoped and prayed that this would be her last move for a while and that the days ahead would be good. She deserved a break. She wanted her future to be something she could be proud of. Vivian was afraid of flying, so she immediately diverted her attention to the movie that was offered as part of her flight, and shortly after take-off, she was fast asleep. When she opened them again, she would be in Nebraska. "Go Big Red."

Chapter Thirteen

After the trip, Vivian was so busy with work that she barely had time to socialize at all. She was putting the finishing touches on the remodel at Mimi's and had taken on a new project that would take her out of town more than she liked, but the money was well worth the travel. She and Jack had seen each other on several occasions and had settled into a comfortable relationship. Everyday Jack was all business, but in the bedroom, Jack was quite a different person. He was amazing and made Vivian feel things she had never felt before. Their first time together was not what she had expected. He totally dominated her, leaving her breathless with every move he made. His hands worked expertly, touching her in places that made her cry out for more. His kiss was passion-filled, and she couldn't get enough. He made her do things she had only read about, and she loved it. She had always been shy about sex and a man seeing her naked, but he wanted to, and she let down her guard and was rewarded in the most sensual way she swore she would never get enough of. Their bodies locked together as one, touching, kissing, raw heat between them. They were both exhausted in the aftermath of their lovemaking and as they showered together, she held on to the moment, hoping it would never end. Every time they were together alone, the sex just got better and more intense. He reminded her of a man she used to know that she would swear to this day resembled Brad Pitt, and the short time she spent with him was one for the record books.

When they were together with their friends, he was everything she had hoped for. He was attentive to her needs and sweet to her friends, and they all had a great time together. Jamie and Lulu were smitten with him and approved of their relationship one hundred percent. Even Henry, who didn't like too many people, liked Jack. Could everything really be this perfect? Was he the one she was looking for even though she had not been looking? Jack thought Vivian was everything. When he looked at her from across the room, she was the only one he saw. He knew she had gone through a lot in her life, and until she opened up to him, he would leave it alone. He just wanted to enjoy their time together, and he did. Vivian and Jack went on weekend trips, sometimes alone, sometimes with their friends. Vivian insisted that Henry join them because even though he was "just a cat" as some of her friends had said, he was the love of her life, and Jack agreed. Jack's home was exactly as she had envisioned. Masculine, with deep, rich tones but very modern, built to fit his taste. Vivian felt comfortable when they spent time there, which was quite often. It afforded them the extra space to move around without getting in each other's way. Jack knew Vivian loved her alone time, so he had put together a separate space just for her. Of course, he let her decorate it because she had an expert eye for design, and the end result was nothing short of stunning. They were getting along well, very well, and Vivian, for some reason, still waited for the proverbial shoe to drop. She desperately wanted just to relax and enjoy the man, but years of rejection and letdowns always kept her on guard. There was something about Jack that she just couldn't put her finger on. He was perfect but not too perfect, compassionate and understanding, but she felt there was a side of him that was a mystery to her.

His construction company had taken off and was doing quite well, and he was out of town a few days a week. Normally, Vivian would relish alone time, but for some reason, she felt uneasy about his time away. It seemed silly because he was a very successful businessman, and it required hands-on dedication. He never really talked much about his trips because, as he had said, the details would bore her. Vivian talked to the girls about it, and they both agreed that she was reading too much into it and to relax and just try to trust the guy. She wanted to, but she couldn't, and as time went on, she became suspicious of just what he was doing while he was away. When she mentioned it to a couple of his friends, they acted oddly guarded in their answers. If there was nothing to hide, then why all the 'hush-hush" whenever she even tried to find out more details about Jack and his work. Jack noticed that Vivian was acting funny and asked her if she was alright. She wanted to come right out and ask him what the hell the big secret was about his job and why his friends never wanted to talk much about it, but she pretended everything was alright and blamed her mood on her new project.

It was a cold and rainy day, and Vivian and Henry were cuddled up on Jack's sofa watching a television. Jack was out of town on business, so there was really nothing to do. Vivian snooped. She normally was not that type of person, but for weeks, she had been distracted, and it had everything to do with Jack. She went into his office and looked around for clues. She laughed to herself when she thought about the word clue as if she were a sleuth on the trail of some big story. She was at his desk when she noticed a stack of papers in a box, so she did the only thing she could do. There were several papers that looked official, military or some type of government correspondence. She didn't really understand much of what they said, but they were very formal. Vivian felt a little guilty for prying into Jack's business, and she tucked the papers away, vowing not to invade his privacy again. Ha! Right! She could tell herself that all day, but she knew there was no way in hell she would not look. She couldn't help it. She had to find out if he was up to something that he wasn't willing to tell her. In the hours before Jack returned, Vivian thought about the papers she had seen. Thoughts of espionage, special forces, and SEAL teams ran through her mind. Oh my God, Vivian! Calm your ass down. You are really getting ahead of yourself, she thought out loud. She was really tapped out by the time Jack turned into the driveway, and all Vivian could do was nervously fidget as he opened the door.

Jack was always happy to see Vivian, and he loved having her in the house when he got home. She added life to his normally boring evenings of TV dinners, but she was acting strange. "What have you been up to?" he asked. Vivian had just about spit her drink across the room when she heard his question. Did he know she had been snooping? She quickly regained control of her senses and nonchalantly responded, "Oh, not much." She hated lying, and she hated lying to him, but what he didn't know wouldn't hurt. For now, anyway. At dinner, he told her that he would be going out of town for a few weeks and asked if she would like to go with him. Vivian was sure he asked because he knew she would say no. Whatever. She had a huge project at work, and she felt she had been mildly neglecting her friends. This would be the perfect time to catch up and get some serious work done. Vivian had been assigned a very high-profile client with a huge home in a very secluded area. He was very private, single, strikingly handsome and ultra-rich. Her commission would be huge at the end of the job, and she had worked several long hours already with much more work to be done. She normally worked alone, but for a project of this proportion, she decided to take on an assistant to help keep them on track. He came highly recommended with glowing credentials and appeared to be just what Vivian was looking for. She would miss Jack, but in a way, she would welcome the alone time. That's how she was, social but a loner and comfortable with it.

That night, she dressed in her sexiest lingerie and gave Jack many things that would remind him of her while he was away. It was early morning, and neither had slept. They were both exhausted from their night of passion, but it was well worth the lack of sleep. She made him breakfast while he showered and, an hour later, was saying goodbye at the door. She had wanted to come clean about snooping through his papers, but she didn't want it to erupt into something right before he left, so she decided to wait. What she really wanted to do was get a better look at those papers! She couldn't help but think there was something more to them, and she had to know.

She showered and dressed for the day, and an hour later, she was parked in front of her client's residence, waiting for her new assistant. He came loaded up with purchases she had asked him to pick up on his way out. Zac was efficient, remembering everything on the list, and they dove into work. He wasn't much for conversation, and Vivian was okay with that. She hated idle chatter. Several hours later, they broke for lunch. It had been catered in as had all their lunches since the start of the project. Vivian rarely saw her client, but later that day, he showed up to take inventory of their progress. He paid zero attention to Zac and directed all of his questions and comments to Vivian. He was impressed with her eye for detail, and on several occasions, she felt his eyes on her when he thought she wasn't looking. When he spoke to her, he looked directly into her eyes, and the look was penetrating. Kind of made her feel like she was standing there naked. He made her feel uncomfortable, but she didn't think much about it. Why did he always feel the need to brush up against her when he walked by? "Miss Edmonds!" "Did you hear what I asked?" Oh God, she had drifted and had not heard one bit of it. She played it off by asking his opinion regarding the sofa. Both he and Zac just looked at her, speechless. Evidently, that was what he had been speaking to her about when she zoned out.

Vivian was slick, however and smoothly went into detail about all aspects of the sofa, and he never knew she was checked out during their conversation. When he had completed his walk-through and was heading for the foyer, he brushed up against Vivian in passing, excusing himself of course. He told Vivian that on the days he did his walk-throughs, he didn't want Zac around. "He makes me anxious with all that running around," he stated. "I'll call you ahead of my visits so that you have them on your schedule." Vivian thought nothing of it and assured him that Zac had plenty of other things to do as well, so it wouldn't be a problem. He left her with a large check for the next portion of the project and, as always, left the amount field blank. She and the girls in the office had secretly dubbed him Daddy Warbucks, and they all got a kick out of it. After a long day, she and Zac headed back to the city, to the office briefly, and then she was ready for a cocktail or two with her besties. They loved hearing all the details of the dark, mysterious client she had, and they sat listening attentively when she told them about his latest request. Several other girls from the office had joined them, and they were equally enthralled by her story. "Girl, Daddy wants those panties!" they all but screamed. She was so not interested and let them know.

Now, they all knew that she was seeing Jack, and it seemed funny to Vivian that they still considered her single. It was their belief that until they both agreed that they would not see other people and lived together, technically, Vivian was still on the market. She didn't disagree. She and Jack had never talked about their relationship, and she wasn't really in a hurry. She liked having fun. She liked flirting. She liked the looks she got when she walked into a bar or restaurant. It made her feel alive. After several drinks, they were all feeling pretty good and talked excitedly about going out to the club on Wednesday for ladies' night. It was agreed upon in minutes. They would all pre-club at Jamie's place because it was the biggest and the closest to the club. Vivian was about to leave and ordered some food to take home because she had just enough of a buzz to know she wasn't doing any cooking. The girls begged her to stay longer, but she had a full day ahead and didn't want to deal with a hangover. She drank the last of her drink, said her goodbyes and her food headed out the door. It was a little chilly, and it helped to sober Vivian just a bit. She arrived home, and she could hear Henry as she put the key in the lock. "Yes, I have a treat for you too, baby," she cooed. He loved it when she spoke softly to him. Animals know when they are loved and respond to affection from their person. Henry was so in tune with Vivian, and the sound of her voice made him purr with delight. She plated some grilled chicken for her furry friend, and they sat together and ate in silence. Until that moment, she had not thought about Jack at all. She had missed her time with just the girls and had fun being out with them again. She was exhausted and knew the morning would come quickly enough, so she turned down the lamps, washed the day away and crawled into bed. It was a chilly night, and the extra blanket was perfect. Henry found his spot close to her, and they settled in. It would be winter soon, her least favorite season. She pulled the covers up close to her chest, and as she drifted off, she thought of another time and place where the cold seeped through her. Cold weather, cold people, ice, frosty relationships. All cold, all seasons of her life that were her least favorite.

Chapter Fourteen

If Dorothy wasn't in Kansas anymore, then Vivian was the new Dorothy, and she sure as hell wasn't in Florida anymore! It was November 1983, and the cold air in Nebraska hit her like a slap in the face as she stepped out into the street to hail a cab. She had landed during the day intentionally in order to get somewhat organized and pick up a few things for her new place, and for obvious reasons, the first thing she would need would be a heavier jacket. She was freezing her ass off, and thankfully the curb was lined with cabs waiting for passengers headed to their destinations. She gave the cabbie her new address, and he sped off like he was on fire, typical of all cab drivers, everywhere. Vivian sat back and took in the first look at her new surroundings. It was not what she had envisioned. There were skyscrapers in the downtown area reminiscent of other cities she had frequented, along with the familiar hustle of the crowds and the noise. At first glance, everything looked cold and gray, along with the weather. They entered the freeway, and it was jammed up. Her driver was swearing, weaving in and out of traffic, and she hoped her first day in Omaha wouldn't be her last. Fortunately, they did not have far to go, and very shortly, they were in front of her new home. It was lovely, in a cute neighborhood on the outskirts of a beautiful park within walking distance from her front door. She was greeted by the real estate agent, who had agreed to meet her at the property instead of the office so she would be able to do a walk-through with Vivian and relinquish the keys. After a short tour of the apartment, she pointed Vivian in the direction of a cute little second-hand store just blocks away, where she was sure Vivian would find a more appropriate jacket.

She offered her new tenant a lift, but Vivian, wanting to familiarize herself with her surroundings, opted to walk the short distance. On her way, she saw a 24-hour mini-mart, a bar, another bar named Andy's and several apartment buildings along tree-lined streets. She took in the aroma of the Mexican bakery/bodega, and she realized she hadn't eaten all day and would stop there on her way back. On the corner across the street from the thrift store was a huge supermarket, an oddly placed strip club and a bank. She could clearly see almost all the way down the cross street, and it looked interesting enough to trip down there to check out what was happening, but her hunger and the freaking sub-zero temperatures convinced her that it could wait another day. She easily found a warm coat, a nice pair of boots, a set of gloves and a soft scarf. She browsed for a bit and eyed a few things she wanted for the apartment, along with a stand-up grocery cart perfect for use while shopping as she had no car yet. The store clerk, finding out she was new to the city, offered several bus schedules that would get her just about anywhere she needed to go. A short while later, back inside her apartment, she ate and, for just a moment, felt lonely. It was the first time in her life that she was in a place where she knew absolutely nobody. A new beginning, and she knew instantly what she needed to calm her fears. She grabbed a newspaper, and while she ate the wonderful tamales with rice and beans she had purchased, she looked through the pet section of the paper. Kittens for Sale! Just what she was looking for. She quickly dialed the number listed, hoping there were still a few available. She was in luck. The lady at the other end of the line had two left, both girls.

Vivian explained that she was new to the city, and the woman agreed to meet her in front of her building in an hour with both the little darlins. Vivian unpacked while she waited, keeping busy to pass the time. She hung a few pics she had found earlier and cleaned the bathroom that was already clean. The apartment came partially furnished with some very cute items that Vivian liked immediately. A vintage sofa, a beautiful hutch and in the kitchen, a retro-style table complete with four chairs, all a different color. She heard a car horn and realized the hour had passed already. She threw on her coat and ran out to the car. Damn, it was cold! When she saw the pair of kittens, she knew immediately that she would not be able to choose. I'll take them both." The lady was thrilled with her decision, stating that the two were very close and it would have been hard to split them up. She gave Vivian a litter box, some toys with a couple of blankets and a huge bag of kitten food. Vivian paid her and threw in a little extra for the supplies. She hurried inside with her new friends and was so excited to not be alone on her first night. They, of course, ran and hid under the sofa. She put their stuff where they could find it and went about her business, not wanting to frighten or force them out until they were ready. She wanted to take a bath in the terrific claw foot tub that came equipped with a shower attachment, so she put on some music, rolled a joint and settled into the tub while the water filled up around her, soothing her tired bones. Did you ever get the feeling that someone was watching you when you were not looking? Vivian opened her eyes, and there sat the two little fluff balls watching her. One was black with a white tip on its tail, and white one had black on the tip of its tail. They were adorable, and she loved them already. It would have been easy to name them something cheesy like Ebony and Ivory or Salt and Pepper, but she just couldn't do that. While she soaked and they stared, she went over names in her head until she settled on Stella and Starla.

Vivian had grabbed a few things to snack on until she could stock her kitchen, so after her bath, she grabbed some chips and a soda and flopped down on the sofa to relax and catch up on some TV. She pulled a blanket around her, and the little darlins tried their hardest to get on the sofa with her, but they were just too small, so she gently lifted them and sat them down near her to allow them to choose how close they wanted to be. They were the cutest little furballs she had ever seen. She must have fallen asleep because she woke to a loud knock on her door, and the morning sun was shining through the window. Her furniture!! The large truck was parked out front, and two burly men were at her door. She propped the double doors to her apartment open, and the men proceeded to unload and put her things where she suggested. The darlins, of course, ran and hid under the sofa. The men were quick and efficient, and a short time later, they had completed the job. She tipped them, got a wink from one of them and then they were gone. Vivian hadn't had a boyfriend since William, and she didn't want one now, but she sure did think a lot about getting laid. Some strange lovin would be nice. She decided she would venture out to the neighborhood bar she had seen the day before, but not before she got busy, and so she did. One lunch break and several hours later, Vivian stepped back and took in her work. Her keen eye for design made it easy to make her mark on the new place. The kittens had made a home in a storage box she used for storing blankets and were napping nicely when she headed out to the store to get some groceries.

The cold air hit her, and she turned around, went back inside and called a cab. Screw walking! It wasn't long before she was at the store shopping for all her favorites. With a full cart, she checked out just as the cab was returning to pick her up. At home, she put all the items away in the cozy kitchen. She stacked the log bundles next to the fireplace, yes, a fireplace and sat down to take a well-deserved break. She rolled a joint and poured a glass of her favorite drink, Moscato. As it neared the time she wanted to head out, she dressed in jeans, a tight-fitting t-shirt and a loose-fitting sweater. She would have to settle on the boots she had bought, but they looked cute with what she was wearing. She decided to wear her hair looser to keep the frigid air off her neck but also because she looked good when it wasn't tied back, and she wanted to make a good first impression.

Vivian wasn't big on makeup, but she loved mascara and eyeliner. Her eyes were her best feature, next to her boobs. She saw the cab before her phone rang, grabbed her coat and was out the door for her very first night out in Omaha. She saw that the bar was packed, and her excitement grew. She found an empty seat at the bar, making sure nobody had already claimed it and waited to order a beer. She nonchalantly scanned the crowd and was not disappointed. There were several good-looking guys who were not coupled up with a chick. It dawned on her why it was so busy on a Monday when she saw the football game on all of the TV. She loved the game, and ironically, her NY Giants were playing the Cowboys. She didn't want to lose her seat but wanted to get in on a game of pool, so she ordered two beers and gave one to the guy sitting next to her as insurance for him to save her seat. He nodded in agreement, and she headed over to put her money down. She wrote her name on the board and went back to her seat, feeling several sets of eyes on her as she did.

A rugged, good-looking blonde pushed his way through the crowd in order to get next to Vivian. "Beat it," he told a young guy sitting next to her. "Hi, I'm Mike," he said in a friendly voice. "Hi Mike, I'm Vivian." Little did she know that Mike would end up being a big part of her life, a friend and an amazing and very fun lover who would be down for sex with her whenever, wherever. They talked a little, flirted a lot and, as a team, ran the pool table pretty much of the night. Mike liked the fact that Vivian could shoot a great game of pool, liked looking at her ass when she leaned in to take a shot and was turned on by her all night. He wanted some of that, and he was pretty sure Vivian wanted some, too. Their chemistry was immediate. Vivian was horny, and Mike was just what she was looking for to quench her sexual thirst. She learned from a girl in the bar that Mike was single and a well-known player at Andy's. "You ain't gonna tie that one down, honey," she stated flatly. Perfect! She wasn't looking for a relationship anyway. She just wanted to be single, have fun and not get hurt. She and Mike talked, and he asked what she was doing after the bar closed, and Vivian told him she would like to be doing him. He damn near spit out his drink at her reply but was turned on immediately and shouted hell yeah!!

Vivian drank a lot played some awesome tunes on the jukebox, and she and Mike, along with a couple of other people, stepped out to smoke some weed. She had a great buzz going and didn't want it to get ahead of her, so she slowed down just enough to keep her head on straight. It was getting late, and she was ready to go and said as much to Mike. He slammed the last of his drink, grabbed a six-pack and shouted, "Let's roll, Viv!" She laughed when she heard him from across the room, and they exited Andy's and headed in the direction of her place. They made out in the cab as if they were teenagers, and both were on fire when they pulled up in front of her place. Mike paid the cab driver, and they helped each other up the steps. Once inside, they were all hands, taking each other's clothes off without ceremony. Vivian did break away long enough to remind him that she had two small kittens and to not step on them. Mike froze momentarily, then proceeded to strip Vivian down to her panties, taking in her full figure in the dimly lit room. He thought she was the most beautiful woman he had ever seen and couldn't keep his hands off her. His kisses landed on her neck, making their way down her stomach to the space between her legs. She took in her breath as he worked his magic.

Vivian ran her hands across his strong shoulders and back, leaving imprints that he would grin about the next day when he left her. They fell onto the bed, and as badly as he wanted her right that moment, he forced himself to take his time with her. He explored every inch of her, and Vivian felt alive for the first time in a very long time. They drank and smoked and had passionate sex until the early hours of the morning. It was just turning daylight when Mike stirred, rolled over and spanked Vivian's ass at the same time he was getting up to leave her bed. "Can you call me a cab, babe?" he asked as he grabbed his pants and made his way to the bathroom. By the time he returned, she had dressed and was sitting with both of the kittens on the sofa. He rubbed their heads, calling them something cute, leaned over, and gave Vivian a kiss that would stay on her lips long after he left. "I had a great time, and I really hope we do this again sometime," he told her as he headed for the door and the waiting cab. She gave him her number, pretty sure she would, in fact, see him again and said goodbye as he left. He had been just what she needed, and as she showered the remains of Mike off her body, she smiled.

In the weeks that followed, Vivian saw Mike several times at the bar and at her place. He showed up unannounced, but she didn't mind. He was fun, their friendship was carefree and open, and she liked it that way. No strings at all, and it made their time together relaxing and fun. She had enrolled in the business college nearby and kept busy with her school work, the kitties and Mike. They didn't really talk about much, but what was there to say when the sex was so good and the rest of the time was spent playing pool and her getting to know the other people around the neighborhood. She was making friends at school, and her social life was on point. She liked the freedom she had away from the past and the people who made her life miserable. Vivian was thriving in school, and she was near the finish of the hours she needed to receive her certification in business management. It had been nearly a year since her move to the city, and so far, it wasn't bad at all. Once you got past the freaking cold, that is. She had settled in nicely, and Springtime was beautiful in the Midwest. She loved Spring. New beginnings, freshness in the air, crisp mornings but warmer afternoons. It was actually pretty perfect. Vivian and Mike had been in a cooling-off period. They were still messing around, but she had seen him with another woman on a regular basis, so she backed off to give him space.

In addition to school, Vivian had picked up a part-time job to help make ends meet, although she was by no means struggling. She felt, for some reason, that everyone was always one step away from being broke and homeless. She feared that, so she worked as much as she could. She woke up late one morning and rushed to catch the number seven downtown. As she made her way out of her apartment, she felt something rain down on her out of nowhere. "What the f***?" she shouted! Had a freaking bird shit on her? Her hair was wet, and her clothing was wet as well, and she knew she could not go to work like that. Vivian believed that bad days turned into worse days, and she was not good at dealing with those kinds of days very well, so she got on her phone and spun a story to her boss and was excused for the day. Vivian was pissed, and that didn't happen very often. Whatever it was had come from one of the apartments overhead, and she meant to find out who had done it and tear into their ass. The window to the attic apartment was open, and she knew whoever lived there did it. What Vivian said next would have made the nuns at the Catholic church blush, but she was beyond pissed, and whatever she did say got the attention of an extremely handsome Latin man and his friend, who poked their heads just above the frame of the window. She challenged the cowards, as she called them, to come down and explain their bullshit face to face. A few moments later, Alberto came out of the building and smack dab into Vivian's life. For years after that meeting, Vivian's world would not be the same. He would be her undoing, and she was ill-equipped to handle it. She would see and do things she had only ever seen on TV, and her life would be a series of twists and turns that, in the end, would leave her desperate for a way out. Vivian didn't know this, but she would be a part of a criminal empire surrounded by narcotics, weapons and some of the seediest people one could only imagine. She should have been frightened, but instead, she was intrigued.

Alberto apologized, and she felt that it was sincere enough to accept it and move on. She should have moved on, right down the street and as far away from him as fast as she could, but his smooth manner kept her a captive audience. He invited her up to his friend's apartment, and she went without even a second thought. A decision she would regret for years to come but too tempting that logic escaped her. He introduced her to Tony, her neighbor, and they offered her a cold beer in an attempt to smooth things over. Why not? A little day of drinking couldn't do any harm. A little harm was the very least of Vivian's worries. Something happened the very moment she entered the attic apartment. Had she been able to foresee what was to become of her, well...if only she had foreseen. For the next few months, Vivian was barely home long enough to care for the darlins. That, in fact, was the only reason she ever went home. Alberto had introduced her to the "new" drug of choice of the eighties, and it was like nothing she had ever experienced. Nothing. She lost all sense of time and what was going on around her, and she trusted no one. She barely slept, but in her mind, she wasn't really that tired anyway. He hung with a crowd of people who were dangerous and unpredictable. She thought little of the hazards of going on drug runs with her new boyfriend, and while he slept, she stood watch over his stash, armed to the nines.

On one occasion, when she was with him, he was to deliver a package to some men in a hotel in another city, but what should have been an easy transaction turned into a nightmare for Vivian. One she would not soon forget. Alberto's supplier had inadvertently given him the wrong package, and what he thought was the product ended up being cut, a material used to stretch the quantity of his packages, which made him more money. The men were angry, and Vivian was afraid. They agreed, however, to ride back to town to make the correct exchange, but not without a hitch. Vivian would stay with his friends until the trade was complete and instructions were given to not let her leave. She was held there by a man who she was sure would kill her if anything went wrong. What seemed like hours later, the phone rang in the hotel, a few words were exchanged, and Vivian was told they were taking a ride. She felt that her legs would not carry her to the door fast enough and thought for a moment that it was a trick and that something had gone wrong and the authorities would find her dead body in the morning. The ride was the longest of her life, but when they arrived at the address given to them, she saw Alberto, who looked as if a ghost had crawled over his back, and she knew this was the end of her nightmare. Well, this nightmare.

Vivian was making her own money and a lot of it, but spent just about all of what she made on her own habit which was growing out of control more as each day passed. After the incident, Vivian grew tired of the constant hustle and the danger that crept around every corner, and she began to stay home more and more each day. Alberto was, in a way, the perfect boyfriend. He was barely there, and she could go about her drug-fueled life without him breathing down her neck. No danger in that! She started sleeping with one of her regular buyers. Brad was her new boy toy. He was fun, carefree and liked getting high as much as she did. He was drop-dead gorgeous, the sex was over the top, and they couldn't get enough of each other for a long time.

He knew to never be around when Alberto was, and he was cool with their relationship. She always felt that he would fade away as soon as the drugs did, so she never worried about falling for him. Mike didn't like to be around Vivian when she was buzzed up, so she didn't see him that often. She missed him, but Brad was a nice replacement.

She and Brad were in the throes of some very heated sex that always went on for hours when she noticed that her vagina was extremely inflamed, and she would later describe it as an acne that covered her down below. She freaked out, knowing it was something very bad, so she immediately went to her MD, who unceremoniously informed her that she was having an allergic reaction to something and the some-thing was dope. Son of a bitch!

"You have got to get cleaned up, Vivian," he stated flatly. You've lost weight, you look like you haven't slept for years, and your vitals are all over the map. You're headed for serious trouble if you don't get a handle on this, and you have to start taking better care of yourself. He prescribed a cream for her use and a handful of reading material about Substance abuse. Vivian went home, and for the first time in months, she stayed home. No drugs, no company, just her and her kitties, who by now pretty much thought she was a guest, but they still loved her and were glad to have this time with her. Alberto never came by, and she was glad he hadn't. She didn't really want to see anyone, especially him. She always worried that he was going to bring someone to the house and had told him that he was not allowed to bring any of his "buddies" there. She was sitting on the sofa drinking some tea when she heard a knock at the door. It was Darla, Alberto's sister. His family didn't like Vivian, so she was surprised to see her. Vivian invited the woman in and was told that it was not a social visit and that Alberto was in trouble. Evidently, he had been caught in a raid and was locked up in the downtown jail. Bond money was needed, and Darla left a large package for Vivian to sell in order to come up with the necessary funds they were putting together to get him out.

Dammit! Why should I have to pull his ass out of the clink, she mumbled to herself, but she got dressed and headed South where many of the strip clubs were, and in a few hours, she had sold all of her packages and returned to Darla's place to give her the cash. Hours later, Vivian still hadn't seen or heard from Alberto, and she was pissed. Screw him. If he comes here now, he'll have some explaining to do, and she fell into a deep sleep waiting for him. When he did arrive days later, he was a mess. He had been busted with a large amount of weed, some crystal, and quite a bit of cash. He was sure he would get time behind this as he was already a felon. It didn't look good for him, and he pleaded with Vivian to wait for him if he did, in fact, go to prison behind his arrest. She was worried more about rent, bills and taking care of things while he was away, and she told him as much. She had long past given up her job because Alberto had given her more than enough money to pay her bills, and she didn't know what she was going to do or how she would manage if he went away. This would be the first of many times that Alberto would be sent away, and after the first few times, Vivian had no other choice but to live at his parent's house, which for her was a jail sentence of her own. His father hated Vivian, and his mother had pledged her alliance to Alberto's ex-girlfriend Diana, who, for some reason yet unknown to Vivian, was still very much a part of their lives. She had to get out of there, and she was willing to do pretty much anything to make that happen. Her family had written her off as usual, assuming the worst as they always did with her. Vivian's sister, Lyla, had not given up on her but would not loan her the money she asked her for out of fear Vivian would use it for drugs. It was difficult for her to see Vivian like this, but she knew she had to stay strong for her until Vivian was strong enough for herself. This was a decision that she made several times and that many years later would save Vivian's life.

Vivian didn't know what she was going to do or how she was going to do it, but she vowed never to give up, and as she sat at the table eating her meal alone, she looked down at the plate in front of her. She saw beef, not chicken and the tortillas on her plate were corn, not flour. As she ate, she wondered if she would ever get what she ordered or if she would always have to settle for what was served.

Chapter Fifteen

Vivian had a full day ahead of her, and if she wanted to meet up with the girls after work, she was going to have to stay focused on the tasks at hand. Zac was waiting for her at her client's home, and they dug in, only taking a break for a quick bite, which again had been delivered to them. Aaron Walters was one of the wealthiest men in town, and yet no one really knew that much about him or how he made his fortune. Vivian didn't much care as one's wealth really meant nothing to her. She had come from very modest means, and she never really cared for the upper class and how most of them lived. Sometime after lunch, she received a call from Aaron, wanting to meet to discuss a new detail of the project with her, and asked if she would meet him in the city for their meeting. She left Zac with orders to finish up what they had been working on, and she headed back to meet up with her client. The address he gave her was very familiar because it happened to be Steve's, her favorite hangout. How odd, she thought as she pulled up in front of the establishment. She would never have dreamed that this man would even know about Steve's, much less choose it for their meeting. He had chosen a table right by the door, and as she sat down, he ordered her a drink and began talking about the plans for the next portion of the redesign. Vivian thought it presumptive of him to order for her, but he had ordered her usual, so she didn't mind and listened tentatively as he spoke. She assured him that they were right on schedule and would be able to move forward by the following week. "You have impeccable taste, Vivian, and I am quite pleased with your work," he said in a low voice.

There was something mysterious about him, maybe even a little dark, but he was her client, and she was not about to get into the personal details of his life. They were just wrapping up when the girls from the office came in, and for the first time, Vivian realized just how late it was. He bid her goodbye after agreeing to meet her later the following week to check on their progress. As he headed for the door, he put his hand on her shoulder for just a moment, leaned in and wished her a good evening. His breath was warm on her neck, and she felt chills rising on her skin, but not in a good way. She blew it off as just a reaction to the closeness and made her way over to her friends. She could tell by the collective look on their faces that they were just as surprised as she had been to see them there. "Its really no big deal," she stated flatly, and they quickly moved on to club night, which was right around the corner. They were all excited at the prospect of letting their hair down, and as they all parted at the door, she noticed a dark town car parked oddly out of place just down the street. They all commented on it and then split off in separate directions, shouting their goodbyes into the evening. No one, not even Vivian, gave the car a second thought, but as she reached her front steps, she glanced back. The car was gone.

During the week, Vivian stayed in town, but she and her furry friend would always make the drive to Jack on the weekend. It had become a ritual that she felt quite warmed by, so when she grabbed her overnight bag from the hallway, Henry got excited because the bag usually meant that it was Jack's time. She felt a little guilty when she left without him but assured him she would spend extra time with him in the morning and be a good boy while she was gone. It's funny how people feel that they have to explain life to their pets, but Henry was her heart, and she treated him not as a pet but as a friend.

Vivian had work to complete at the office, and it was another busy day for her. Derrell wanted updates on her project; orders had to be placed, and calls had to be made to ensure everything was on track with the project.

She was excited about the evening ahead but had no time to think about it with all she had to do. She kept busy all day, not even breaking for lunch when the girls suggested she do so. There was much to do, and it was days like this that she was grateful for the extra help. Vivian's phone rang, and it was Jack. His cheerful voice was just what she needed, and she took a few minutes to catch up. He would be returning on Saturday, and she felt excited at the prospect of seeing him again. They enjoyed a little phone sexting, and the smooth sound of his voice reminded her of why she was interested in him, one of the reasons anyway. She suddenly missed him, a thought she had not entertained much since his departure and as they ended their call, she expressed that she could not wait to see him. After their call, she sat for a few minutes, and of course, the thought of having his place to herself Friday re-sparked her curiosity about the papers she had come across.

At five o'clock sharp, Vivian closed her laptop and headed in the direction of the small crowd of women milling around by the exit. Her excitement grew, and as they hurried out the door, the club was the only thing on their minds. A few hours later, they entered Fat Freddie's, and for a Tuesday, it was popping. Ladies' night brought out not only a lot of women but also its fair share of men. She supposed Ladies Night was really Men's Night in disguise. They were all having a great time dancing and laughing, and the drinks kept coming. Vivian stuck to the beer while the others took shot after shot. She was no good when she drank liquor. It turned her into some crazy lady, and she didn't like who she was when she drank it, so she didn't. Several men asked her to dance, and she did. A couple of them asked her to party after the bar closed, but she backed out of it, claiming she had an early day the next day, although she didn't have to be in the office until eleven. She knew ahead of time that there was no way she would ever be able to swing seven thirty! She needed some air and a cigarette, and she and Stella slipped out and were shocked at what they saw. SNOW!! Holy Crap! It was light but indeed coming down steady. They were happy they had decided not to drive. Vivian hated to drive in the winter and usually opted to take alternate transportation while others tried their hardest to navigate the roads. The South never received a whole bunch, but when it snowed, it created havoc for everyone. The girls rushed to finish their smokes and hurried back into the warmth of the club. They ran into the others and shared what they had seen. They let out celebratory cries, and even the snow couldn't put a damper on their night.

Vivian found a seat and was heavy into a conversation with Lulu when she saw him from across the room. He had seen her first and had watched as she and her friends lit up the dance floor. Should she go over to say hello? "Absolutely under no circumstances should you," Lulu chided. Well, she couldn't be rude. He had seen her, and what would he think of her if she didn't at least say hello. At that very moment, Vivian lost sight of him, and she shrugged it off and joined her friends on the dance floor. Hours later, it was time to head out and get some shut-eye before the morning crept up on them. The car Vivian had ordered must have been delayed by the fresh ground cover, and she encouraged her friends to go, assuring them that she would be alright, but Stella and Devin firmly declined, leaving her by herself, so they huddled together under the canopy to wait. A car pulled up to the curb in front of them, and she saw Aaron as the window slid down. "Can I offer you ladies a lift to your destination?" he asked politely. Before Vivian could think of a kind way to say no, her two friends welcomed the offer, and they all piled into the town car. Damn, it's cold out there, the girls stated in unison. Talk about the weather always seemed to be an ice breaker, pardon the pun, and Vivian was hoping she wouldn't have to say much as the ride made her feel a little uncomfortable, but she did relax in the warmth of the car and the beers she had consumed made her feel warm inside. The conversation was light, and Aaron was the complete gentleman; however, he sat very near to her, and she felt his arm touch hers more than once during the ride. Why? She was the first to be dropped off, and as the driver pulled up in front of her building, Vivian could not recall whether she had given him her address but was thankful that she would not be left to ride alone with Aaron. There was something about him that made her feel uneasy, and as he helped her from the car, she lost her footing on the slick street and damn near fell on her ass but instead fell straight into his arms. She thanked him for catching her and noticed he held on just a little too long before releasing her from his grip. Vivian went straight to bed, tossed and turned and had some hellasious nightmares. She woke up the next morning feeling a little put out for no reason at all and knew it was going to be one of "those" days. She attributed her mood to the feeling she had about her client, Aaron.

She met Zac at the warehouse and plunged into work, hoping it would break her out of the mood she was in. It did. By afternoon, she was her old self. Phase Three of the project was about to begin, and that was what she needed to focus her attention on. She was being paid well, and that alone deserved her full attention, along with the fact that Aaron would put her on the map if she did well. He had connections all over the city, or so he said, and it would be in her best interest to let nothing distract her. She also decided that she would let him know that Zac would be on the job site when she needed him, and she meant it. Zac was her assistant, and secretly, she felt safer with him there. She sent Aaron an email letting him know, and his only reply was, "Fine." For the rest of the week, they worked feverishly to wrap up the second phase and prepare for the following week. She worked late on Friday and went straight to Jack's place after picking up Henry. She contemplated not looking through the files she had seen and did her best to keep busy most of the next morning, but her curiosity took over, and before she knew it, she was back in Jack's office, papers strewn everywhere and no closer to a resolution. She was about to give up when she came across a folder, and as she opened it, she heard a car pull into the driveway. She hurried to put all the papers back, certain that it was Jack, and she sure as hell didn't want him to see his stuff scattered around, all privacy abandoned. He would be furious, and she truly did not want that. Maybe she would talk to him about how she felt. Maybe.

The weekend was amazing. Vivian and Jack lay around, ordered sinful amounts of takeout and had sex every chance they could, just about everywhere they could. He took all of her, and she could barely speak or breathe. He left her wanting more, and he obliged her every desire. His hands were strong, yet very gently he would caress her. The place between her legs was on fire with lust for him. When they were exhausted, they showered and lay together in front of the fireplace. She had missed his touch, his warm embrace, and she let him know in ways he would not soon forget. They talked about her work, and when she spoke of Aaron and the feeling she had about him, she swore she could feel him tense up. He played it off, saying he was tired and that she should not worry too much about Mr. Walters, but his mood had changed, and to her, it was noticeable. She wondered why but let it go, and they relaxed for the rest of the evening. Sunday came too soon for them, and before Vivian knew it, it was time to head back to her place. Jack had told her she could stay on there, but it was twice the drive to work and even farther to the client's home. They agreed to spend time together in the city during the week, and that brightened her mood. She loved it when he was at her place, and so did he. She kissed him at the door, grabbed Henry and headed back home.

For several weeks, Vivian was so busy that she barely had time to socialize at all, and the girls expressed their need for a "Vivian fix" soon. She promised them that she would make time soon, but for now and the near future, her time was all things Aaron's re-design. He had been a little chilly with her after her email about Zac, but his mood had lightened some, and they were back on speaking terms. Zac didn't seem to mind at all and breezed through the day as if Aaron were invisible to him. Vivian was pleased with their accomplishments on Phase Three and looked forward to the next wing of the mansion's makeover. She had noticed that there was one wing not mentioned or drawn up in the plans, and she mentioned it to Aaron one day when they were reviewing what was next. His mood immediately changed, and he became very serious. His eyes were darker, and his voice was but a whisper but firm in the warning he conveyed. "No one and I mean no one, is to step one foot near that area under any circumstances," he all but growled. "Do you understand?" Vivian was taken aback by his demeanor and quickly responded with a salute and a resounding NO PROBLEM, SIR!

In the weeks going forward, their conversation stuck in the back of Vivian's mind even though she knew it wasn't a good idea to let her curiosity get the better of her. One evening, when she and her gal pals were together at Steve's, she shared what had transpired, and the look on their faces was priceless. They warned her to be careful and to not do anything that would jeopardize her job or, more importantly, her safety. "Wouldn't you be at least a little curious, and wouldn't you want to know why he forbid passage to the North Wing?" she asked them. Just saying it out loud made it sound a little ridiculous to her. They looked at each other and then at their friend and simultaneously responded, hell no, and you shouldn't either! After their conversation, Vivian tried to put it out of her mind, but one day, into Phase Four, she found herself alone and tried as she might to ignore the little voice in her head that always got her in trouble. She found herself headed towards the very area she should have stayed far away from. It was like a scary movie where instead of running away from what scared you, you went towards it instead. She laughed to herself. Why in the hell was she scared anyway? This was real life, no late-night movie, and she was not going to be chased down by an ax murderer. So why was she tip-toeing down the hall?

Just as she reached the door that would lead her to the North Wing, she heard voices just beyond it. Vivian stood frozen in place, not daring to breathe for fear she would be heard. Dammit, why had she come here? She turned, wanting to get as far away from there as quickly as she could. The door opened behind her, and Aaron grabbed her by the arm and pulled her into the hallway just beyond the door. Her heart was racing, and she really was afraid. "I thought I made it clear that you were not to come near this area, Vivian." She didn't know what to say, and even if she had, she was unable to speak a word. How dare he frighten her. Who did he think he was anyway? "Take your hands off me right now," Vivian fumed. Aaron hadn't realized he was still holding her arm and immediately released her from his grip. She hurried down the hall into the main part of the home and quickly gathered her belongings, wanting nothing more than to escape the property before he could catch up with her. He caught her in the foyer as she was about to leave and pleaded with her to give him a chance to explain himself.

Vivian was clearly upset even though she was the one who, in fact, had invaded his privacy and had gone against his request. She wasn't sure why, but she stopped and turned. He gave her some song and dance about the type of person he was and how his privacy was so important to him and how she had betrayed the trust he had in her. He apologized for frightening her, and for some reason she wasn't sure of, she believed him and accepted his apology. She left, and on her way back to the city, she was so distracted that she almost drove the car off the road. She pulled over to compose herself and noticed her hands were still shaking. As she sat by the side of the road, she noticed a black town car pulled over behind her near a turnoff. Was it the same car she had seen before? Was she being followed? Okay, Vivian, stop being paranoid. It had been one hell of a day, and all she wanted to do was go home, curl up with Henry, and forget what had happened.

She didn't tell a soul about the incident, but her friends noticed the bruise on her arm, and Lulu, whom she had known the longest, knew something was up right away. She convinced Vivian to break away for just a while, and they met in a little out-of-the-way tavern for a cocktail and some well-needed catching up. They were well into their second drink when Lulu told her friend to spill it, and spill it she did. Vivian knew it would go no further, and she trusted Lulu.

Lulu was speechless by the time Vivian finished her story. She had no words and was afraid for her friend and said as much. "Dammit, you should never be in that house by yourself again, Vivian," she expressed with a tone in her voice that Vivian knew only too well. Vivian had already made the decision to make sure that Zac was always there when she was there, and if he had to leave, she would go with him. Lulu didn't like Aaron, and she had a bad feeling from the first time she ever saw him, but she would never begin to lecture her friend. She knew about Vivian's life, and she had been through and seen things most can only imagine, so she supported her as any good friend would.

They said nothing more about it and enjoyed catching up with each other for the rest of the evening. They grabbed some food and chilled at Vivian's place before Lulu hugged her friend and headed home. Vivian had missed her and felt more relaxed than she had in a while. Lulu had that effect on her. Even Henry relaxed and cuddled on her friend's lap, and he wasn't crazy about many people. The phone rang just as she was about to go to bed and before she answered she knew instinctively that it was Jack. He usually called her to say goodnight and a few other things, and she was happy to hear from him. She did not tell him about "the incident" and would not either. "Dumb, I'm not," she stated to herself. She said her goodnight wishes to Jack and settled in to get some much-needed rest. She was exhausted both mentally and physically. This project had taken a toll on her in more ways than one, and she would be happy when she was done with it. She was ready to move on and ready to be done with Aaron Walters once and for all. Little did she know that she would be far from done with him for a lot longer than she had ever imagined, and as she fell asleep, dreams of the past and leaving another behind crept in and took over what she thought would be a peaceful sleep.

Chapter Sixteen

During the second half of the eighties, Vivian found out she was pregnant, and several months into her pregnancy, she miscarried her twin boys. She was devastated and couldn't stop crying for what might have been. It had been a horrible pregnancy with her being alone most of the time, and Alberto, as she came to discover, was still seeing his supposed ex-girlfriend. The night she went to the hospital writhing in pain, he was laid up in his sister's apartment, making plans for the future not with her but with his ex. When Vivian came back from the hospital alone and in unbearable pain, she knew that it was the final straw. She was done with him and his lying, cheating ass and as soon as she was able to, she left the house in which she had lived for almost seven years and the man she had given the same amount of years of her life to. She had no idea where she would go, but she left anyway. She wandered the streets, grieving and distraught. She had very little money, very few friends and a terrible cocaine habit, which she blamed for the loss of her unborn. She blamed herself even more, beat herself up every day and wanted so badly to forget just for a moment. "Why does this shit keep happening to me," she questioned herself. She spent her days working at a job she was well overqualified for, but on top of being homeless, she didn't want to be destitute. She spent her evenings hooking up with people she met in the bars just so she would have a warm place to sleep.

She never slept well, always afraid if she fell too deeply asleep, something bad would happen. She was afraid all the time, but nobody around her ever knew. They all talked about how strong she was. How brave she was to endure what she had and in awe that she could just keep going. Vivian was broken inside. She didn't care what she did or who she did it with and never considered the consequences of her actions. She ran from South to North Omaha and back, frequenting some of the seediest establishments. She was spiraling and didn't care. She became the party girl. Vivian was partying late one night at the home of a guy named Davey. Everything was available, but nothing was free. It was going to cost you something to partake in the never-ending supply of party favors. Vivian had made some sales for Davey, so she was his guest. They were all having a good time when a chick came into the room loud as all hell, cussing and acting like the badass that she was. The other girls were afraid of her, but Vivian was not. She had earned her stripes many times over, and nobody messed with her much, and if they did, they ended up having a very bad time. She had heard of Vivian and knew she would be at Davey's. Vivian kept an eye on her, watching her. Vivian had become the type of person who just watched. She wasn't loud, she didn't talk much unless she knew you, and she always had her eyes wide open. The days of being naive were long gone, replaced by someone that Vivian didn't know when she looked at herself in the mirror. Her guard was up, and at the very moment Big Deb stepped toward her, Vivian locked on her, keeping her hand in her pocket and on Kenny, her cute .22 pistol.

Vivian wasn't afraid of guns. She had been in the military and shot an M16 with almost expert marksmanship. South O was no stranger to gun violence, so it would not be a surprise if shots rang out at some point during just about any evening or party. For no reason at all, the woman asked Vivian if she had a problem, and Vivian returned with a response Deb did not expect. "Not yet," she stated flatly. Instead of Deb wailing on her as she would have if some other chick had said that, she laughed. "I like your style, Silver." One of the many aliases she would have in her attempt to escape who she really was. They partied for the rest of the night, and when she found out that Vivian didn't have a real place of her own to go, she invited her to stay with her at her place. Vivian cautiously accepted, a decision she would regret but not for many, many years. Vivian felt she might finally have a friend she could rely on and depend on and someone who didn't expect a lot.

She was kind in her own way, and although she was rough around the edges, she was one of the nicest people Vivian had met in a long time. Deb lived in a house on the south side of town that was nice except for the smell of her male cat. Vivian didn't judge her, however. The house was clean, and she gave Vivian the sunroom at the back of the house, out of the way of Bobby, her other roommate, who was also the owner of the house. It was pretty, and it didn't stink. It was her room, and she was grateful. On her first night there, she slept like she hadn't slept for a long time.

Deb was cool. She never told Vivian what to do, never asked where she was going or where she had been. As long as Vivian gave her fifty dollars a week, she could do whatever she wanted. Deb didn't work, but she made her money by other means, and she thought she was good at it. She told Vivian one day that her face may not have been much to look at, but she had a golden pussy, and in the dark, that was all that mattered. Vivian had a pissy ass little job at a second-hand store where she folded clothes all day until the boss, a greasy fat man, decided she was too pretty to hide out in the back, so he promoted her to work the cash register. When it was quitting time, Vivian always felt like she needed a drink and a shower. She told him several times a day to keep his grubby hands off her, but he paid no attention to her words until the day he received a visit from a tall tree of a man who told him Vivian was his girlfriend and that he better be a good boy or he would kick his ass. The tree was a friend of Debs and became a very good friend to Vivian as well. She guessed angels really were everywhere, and he was her very own.

For several years, until the late eighties, Vivian and Deb were inseparable. They went just about everywhere together. Whenever you saw one, you saw the other. They became very close and brought in the nineties as the best of friends. In nineteen ninety, Deb came into Vivian's room and was clearly shaken up. She told Vivian that Bobby, the owner of the house, was selling it, and they would have to prepare to move. Deb was going to be receiving assistance to help her pay rent, and Vivian would not be able to stay with her, so again, Vivian was going to be out on the street. She was hanging out in Dundee one evening when she met a good-looking man who seemed interested in her. His name was John, and he had a place just on the outskirts of the sleepy neighborhood. They went on several dates and became romantically involved a few months in, so John thought it would be cool if she moved in with him and tried living together on for size. Deb was cool with it, not really concerned about much other than securing her new living arrangement, but she was happy that Vivian would have a place to be, and that did matter to her.

Moving day came, and Vivian packed up her belongings and her coke habit and moved in with her man. He was unaware of the latter that she would be moving in along with her things. He smoked a little grass but did not approve of anything harder, and Vivian wasn't about to tell him. It never usually went over well and screwed up many of her plans in the past, so she kept quiet about it. She figured he would never find out if she kept it low-key. She had been high around him before, and he never noticed, so she was pretty sure she could get away with it. She hated keeping things from him, but her whole life had been a series of well-kept secrets, so sadly, it was normal for her. Little did she know her whole world would fall apart around her, and she would escape jail only by leaving John's place.

He had caught her getting high one afternoon in the bathroom when she thought he was at work. He had a little extra time and had decided to take her to lunch when he came upon her and the coke in their bathroom. There was no explaining to be had, no second chance to be given. John was so mad that all rationale went out the window, along with the items belonging to Vivian. Bags of clothing, keepsakes she had collected, all that he could be rid of along with Vivian, he tossed out. When he was through, he took her by the arm and physically removed her from his place and his life, threatening her with the police if she tried to ever return. She lost her footing on the stairs and tumbled into the street. She was mortified and hurt. I mean, it really hurt. She had landed on her knees, and her head hit the stone wall next to the stairs. Had she not caught herself, she would have been seriously injured. As it were, both knees bled from the open wounds, and she had a cut just above her eye. She was certain a shiner would follow. Vivian felt she had sunk to nearly the lowest depth she could, and that evening, with really no place to go, she spent the night on the curb along with her things.

That day should have been enough for Vivian, but what John didn't know was that she had made copies of his outside door key and apartment key, knowing he could not change the locks without notifying his landlord. She knew John wouldn't because he would have to explain, and he just wasn't built that way. As each day passed for her on the streets, she could feel the keys in her pocket. When she washed herself in the gas station bathroom, she felt the keys if she ate, which was so random she felt the keys. The weather had turned bitterly cold, and she could no longer safely stay outside at night, so she took his key to the building and slept under the stairway just until the very early morning when she could go elsewhere in the light of day to keep warm. She did this for months, and the stairwell became a haven for her, but she was always hungry and tired, and she was afraid. She worked but not enough to find a place of her own. She didn't ask for help because she felt she had no one to ask. She was desperate, and she could still feel the keys. Vivian knew John's schedule when he worked and what he did after work. She figured if she sneaked in, ate a small portion of food and maybe catch a quick nap in the warmth of his apartment before he got home, it would be alright. She knew the odds were stacked against her, and she feared if he caught her, she would undoubtedly go to jail, but she was desperate.

Her plan worked until the day it didn't. She hadn't slept soundly for weeks and was freezing her ass off, and John's apartment was so warm and comforting, like an extra blanket on a cold night. She sat down on the edge of the bed just for a minute, and the next sound she heard was John's key in the door. She dove into the closet at the same moment he unlocked the door and entered the apartment. Vivian hadn't had time to remove all traces of being there, and John, having no idea she had a key, thought he had been burglarized. She faintly heard his voice as he called 911 to report the break in and fifteen minutes later, the cops arrived and began their search for clues. She could hear footsteps far away, then close, then closer. She barely breathed. They asked John the routine questions and then delved into the not-so-routine and more along a personal line. Could anyone else have a key? Did he have a recent breakup that had gone bad? One of the officers kept moving around and suddenly opened the closet door where Vivian lay hidden under a huge pile of clothing and boxes. John's weed was stashed on a shelf in the closet, so he diverted attention to the door and the half-eaten food items left on the table. He knew, even if the cops didn't, that it was Vivian. Damn her! The officers finished up and told him they would look into it, but there was really not much they could do. He needed to change the locks immediately. It was so quiet when they left that Vivian thought he had gone as well until he spoke. "Vivian, if you're here, you better come out right now!" Was it a trick? Had the cops really gone? For no reason and every reason, she began to cry softly. He opened the closet door and dug until he felt her body under his clothing. She gave up and crawled out of her hiding spot. She gave him the keys and walked out the door without saying a word. Ten minutes later, a cruiser pulled up behind her as she walked down the sidewalk and turned on their lights. John had called them as soon as she closed the door, and they were placing her under arrest for unlawful entry. At least he had not pressed charges for burglary because that would have been a felony. How kind of him! Fortunately for Vivian, she didn't have a record, so after fingerprints and pics, they wrote her a ticket and escorted her to the door, admonishing her about committing crimes. Vivian was sure they did that because they were pissed that they didn't find her during their search. She secretly wished she had spent the night in jail just so she would have a place to lay her head and a little food in the morning.

She walked from downtown to Dundee, which was a good distance, but she was used to walking. She walked everywhere. When she arrived at Johns, she was terrified. Her stuff was outside, of course, and Vivian was saddened to see the bulk of her life resting on the curb like trash. People had picked through some of her stuff, and she realized she wouldn't be able to take everything with her, so she took what she really needed and a few of her special keepsakes and left the rest behind. She was back in the streets, but at least it was late Spring. She trudged through the summer months, ate when she could and stayed at the women's dorm at the Salvation Army when they had an open room. Fall came and went, and another winter was nearing. She was not about to be out in the cold again, so she took her entire paycheck and got a hotel room and a job at the front desk. The manager felt sorry for her and agreed to let her stay as long as she kept the place in order for him. The hotel was trash and housed some of the worst, but she was in no position to judge anyone, so she kept her head down and did what she had to do every day.

Drugs were everywhere at the hotel. People would be so high that when they couldn't afford to stay any longer, she would go in to clean the room, and many times, she found their remains of the day and their stay. Cash, drugs, clothing etc... She kept it all, never once thinking of turning it into the manager. She got high almost every day and had been shooting up for some time, but thankfully, she had never had a bad high. The tracks were going to start getting out of control, so she got creative with her habit. She used a lot of Vitamin E oil to soften the needle marks, shifted locations so she wouldn't get a runner, kept clean and never ever did she share a needle with anyone. This was her life now. She didn't feel bad anymore because she didn't feel. She didn't cry because she was all cried out. This was the way it was, so she made the best of it. Christmas came, and the only card she got was from the manager. Inside, there was a verse from the Bible and 500.00 dollars. His message was short. Get clean and get back to living. For the first time in forever, someone cared. Nineteen ninety-one was gone. It had been the toughest year of Vivian's life and one she would never forget. It had taught her many things about herself and other people. She felt weak, but her mind was strong. The Bible verse kept turning in her head. "Into the darkness, you Shine. Out of the ashes, you Rise. There's no one like You, None like You." As she welcomed the new year, she had no idea that her life would change and that she would have the life she had longed for. Vivian slept well that night.

Chapter Seventeen

"Dammit, Zac! I thought we agreed that you would always go out to the client's house with me until we wrap up. Shit!" Vivian was a little more than pissed, and Zac's reason for not being able to join her would be a moot point. She stomped her foot indignantly. They were so close to wrapping up the project, and every day counted. "Well, I'm sorry, Viv, but it is customary to attend a funeral when someone you know passes," he stated with just a hint of sarcasm. Had Vivian thought for a moment, she would have realized that there had to be a good reason because Zac never missed work. She felt like a first-class ass and apologized profusely for her premature judgment. He kissed her on the cheek and apology accepted they went their separate ways. Vivian made sure after he left to have flowers sent to the funeral home from her. It was the very least she could do. She headed out to start her day and hours later, as she was deep into patterns, pillows and artwork, Aaron arrived. She wasn't expecting him, and since the incident, he had made himself scarce even though it was his home. He was in a good mood, and she relaxed a little. He really was quite pleasant when he wasn't trying to be so mysterious. She would realize later that it was purposeful and all just a rouse to keep her off guard. They discussed the final phase of the project, and just as he was about to leave, he received a phone call. His mood immediately changed, and he seemed quite upset with whoever was on the other end of the call. Vivian pretended not to listen but heard him bark orders and stated that there could be no mistakes, no errors. "Do you understand?" he stated flatly and ended the call. He handed Vivian a blank check and was gone.

The week flew by, and she and Jack met to have dinner and a quiet weekend at her place. He was spending quite a bit of time out of town, and even though Vivian liked her alone time, she was beginning to feel like the weekend squeeze, and she hated that. Someone from her past had treated her the same way, and she didn't like it at all. Whether it was the long week she had or just her, she let him know how she felt about it, and they had their first argument as a result. He left to clear his head, not wanting to fight with Vivian. If she only knew the reason he was gone so much, she would understand. He couldn't tell her even though he wanted so badly to. She would know soon enough. He went back to her place with a toy for Henry as a peace offering. It was touching, and their argument was over.

Their time together would be much the same in the weeks that followed, but Vivian tried to put that aside and enjoy his company. She was straightening up his place during one of her visits when she came across a phone number in the pocket of his jeans. There was no name on it, and that just about made Vivian crazy, wondering who it belonged to. The next week, while she was at the office, she had Jamie call the number. She hated being sneaky and should have trusted Jack more, but she had been taken advantage of for so long it was almost impossible for her. She sat quietly as Jamie dialed the number. After a few rings, she heard a woman's voice at the other end. Jamie played it cool, stating she must have dialed the wrong number when the woman said her name was not Alice but that it was Donna and hung up the phone. Who the hell was Donna, and why did Jack have her number? She pretended that it didn't matter to her and went back to work, but for the rest of the week, she was in a mood and didn't want to "talk it out" as Stella had mentioned.

For the first time in ages, she and Jack did not spend the weekend together. She told him she had to do some things for work, and he didn't give it a second thought. He did notice that Vivian seemed a little distant but attributed her mood to how busy she was with her work. He would never have imagined it's real reason, not for a million years. Vivian stayed holed up in her apartment with Henry. She needed to be alone to think things out. Should she ask him about Donna, or should she say nothing? Maybe it was nothing at all, and she had read too much into it already. Bullshit. It was never nothing when a man had another woman's phone number and never thought to mention it in conversation. Did it have something to do with the papers she had seen and what the hell was in that folder? She was making herself crazy and decided to get out of the apartment for a little while. She went for a drive downtown. It was quieter on the weekend, and she thought a little window shopping would do her good, maybe even a cup of tea and a snack in a place she liked to frequent whenever she got the chance. Vivian felt her body relax as she took in the gorgeous items in the shoppes windows. She stopped into a few of them and made some purchases, cute little items all wrapped up in an adorable drawstring bag, which added a personal touch that she loved, not for herself but for her friends at the office where she was rarely seen these days.

She did buy herself an assortment of flavored teas suitable for those cold winter nights. Vivian came out of the store and headed in the direction of the cafe. She passed a tavern and, of course, looked through the window to see who was starting happy hour just a little too early. Inside, seated at the bar, was Jack. Next to him was an attractive middle-aged woman. They were immersed in a very heavy conversation, and Vivian went unnoticed. She could do nothing but stare in disbelief at what she saw. Her first thought was to barge in and confront them, but she just couldn't or wouldn't embarrass herself like that, so she did the next best thing, tapping on the window loud enough to get their attention, and when they looked up, she flipped them off then fled down the street. As she hurried away, she could hear Jack calling to her, but she kept on towards the safety of her car and raced away as quickly as she could. She laughed a little as the look on their faces flashed before her. As she was driving, her phone began to ring, and she knew it was Jack. She ignored it, and it went to voicemail. He called again. She let it go to voicemail. Again. She was in no mood to hear what he had to say for himself, and any reasoning he had was of no interest to her.

Vivian was crushed, but she didn't cry. Tears had long since escaped her. She had been through this too many times to count, and it was easier just to block it. Why Jack, though? She was sure he was different. How did she not see it with him? She was a fool for falling for his smooth ways. She didn't know the answers, but what she did know was that she was not about to let this man walk into her life, turn on the sweet stuff, then bullshit her the way she was certain he had. Back in the safety of her apartment, she decided to camp out in her bedroom for the evening so that she could turn the lights in the rest of the apartment off, giving one the illusion that she was not at home. That "one" being Jack. She had plenty to say to him, but it was not going to be on his terms. She would decide if and when she would speak to him. She needed time to process this, and she needed to speak with a friend. Her friend. She called Lulu.

Lulu was as surprised as Vivian had been when she told her what her afternoon had been like. She liked Jack and thought he was crazy about Vivian, but maybe she was wrong. She actually wanted to give Jack a chance to explain. Maybe there was a logical explanation. She, however, was a solid team Vivian member, so whatever she wanted was irrelevant. "So what do you think I should do?" "Lets at least listen to his voicemails," she answered. The moment Vivian heard his voice, she had to bite back the tears that threatened to escape. Damn him! She expected to hear a line of bull, but Jack's only message was asking her to please call him. That was it? Call him? She was in shock. "No, I'm sorry, Vivian. Let me explain, Vivian. It's not what you think, Vivian." "So, are you going to call him," her friend asked. Sure, I'll call him. When I'm good and ready. Well, let me know how it goes, and I'll talk to you in the morning when you have more time to think about how you're going to handle this. Lulu said goodbye to her friend and hung up. Vivian didn't sleep well that night, but in the morning, she knew what she was going to do. She sat down with a cup of coffee and dialed his number, hoping it would go to voicemail, but Jack answered, and she panicked and hung up. He immediately called back. "Jack, good morning. I would like to meet with you so we can have this conversation face-to-face. I'd rather not speak to you on the phone," she said right away. She selected the time and place, and before he could say anything, she ended the call with a crisp goodbye.

Jack was concerned. Should he just tell her the reason he was with Donna? He knew if he did, Vivian would know everything, and he feared for her safety. He had to stick to the plan. He would be glad when this was over, and he hoped their relationship would survive. He hoped the danger would pass and what he had to do would end quietly, without incident. It was a long week for both of them, and by the time the weekend came, they were both on edge. Jack and Vivian were the type of people who were rarely ever angry, and they both had had the time to assess the situation, so when they met at Louie's, neutral ground, they had calmed down, so they were cordial at the very least. Vivian knew if she looked at Jack too long, she would get lost in his eyes. Focus Vivian! He has a lot of explaining to do. She was surprised when Jack did not explain, but he did say that Donna was a friend who was in trouble, and they had met after he agreed to help her. He also said how HE was hurt that she didn't trust him more after the amount of time they had spent together. None of what he said was a lie, but it wasn't the total truth. She was the one that was hurt, but it was now a moot point. She had wanted him to understand how it looked and what she thought, and she wasn't ready for him to express himself as he had. He, of course, listened attentively to everything Vivian said, not once interrupting her and nodding in agreement with statements she made.

Jack wanted to tell her how she could be in danger and that everything he was doing was to protect her from harm, but he couldn't. He wanted to tell her about his job and what he actually did for a living, but he didn't. He wasn't sure how she would react if he did, and he wasn't going to jeopardize their relationship just to find out. It would have to wait, and as they wrapped up, both agreed that the incident could have been handled better and that they had to trust each other, or it just wasn't going to work out for them. He held her hand and told her how much she meant to him and if it had been anyone else she would have thought he was handing her a pile of crap, but it was Jack and she really liked him and was maybe even falling in love with him. They didn't talk anymore about it, and through the weeks ahead, they actually became closer than ever before. Vivian still didn't tell him about going through his papers, a secret she planned on keeping, too. There was something in those papers that would answer her questions, and she was hellbound, determined to get to the bottom of it once and for all.

Their time together was as before, and Vivian found herself looking forward to weekends when they could be together again. She spent time at his place more often, and they had discussed moving in together on a couple of occasions. She liked the idea of waking up next to him every morning, but she thought of the drive and having to give up her place. They settled on her keeping her place in the city so that on the days she felt she was too tired when she worked late, she would still have a place to relax. Jack had even offered to pay her rent but she was having none of that. She paid her own way, and there was to be no negotiating that decision. He loved that about her and knew it would be pointless to insist. He felt a little more at ease, knowing she would be near him. He would be better able to protect her. That was his number one priority, and in the coming months, it would prove to be the very thing that would save her life. He was so close to putting an end to the secrecy, the hidden agendas, the lies he had told so many people. Soon, he would be able to breathe again, relax and enjoy the one person who brought meaning to his life. Vivian.

It was snowing very hard, a rare and unexpected occurrence, the weatherman had said. Vivian had been at Jack's for several days without being able to get back to the city. The highways were closed to most traffic, and people were being advised not to go out unless it was necessary. She was working from his place because it was impossible to travel to her client's home, and he had even warned her not to attempt the trip. Jack was snowed in out of town but was sure he would be able to get back in a few days. She and Henry were relaxing in front of the fireplace as the wind howled outside, and she was glad her phone still worked because she was getting bored having nobody to talk to or see. She spoke with the girls several times and made sure her boss received her daily project updates. She was burned out on television, so she made herself a cup of tea and tried to convince herself that she should stay out of Jack's office and mind her own business. Yeah, that didn't work, and she found herself nestled in his chair, snooping through the endless stack of files. Just as she was sure Jack had taken the folder with him, she found it neatly tucked in the very back of the drawer.

In the folder was a series of conversations with no names identifying who was a part of them. The words "subject" and "victims" were their only identifying markers. The victims had, in essence, been terrorized by the subject and believed to be held captive before being rescued. Rescued by who? It went on and on describing the incidents, which were terribly gruesome, and the plan developed for the recovery of whoever it was that needed rescuing. The subject had disappeared, but there were recent leads to his whereabouts. Each person was described in detail and had Vivian thought about it, she would have known who they were, but she was so intent on the content that she overlooked critical information that probably would save her from imminent danger. There were several dates and times, and she noticed that the latest was as recent as the year that had just passed. Page after page told of a person who, in her mind, was frightening, crafty and needed to be caught. The last pages in the folder documented someone who could possibly be in danger now and the steps that were being taken to protect that person. Wow! She pushed back from the desk and sat in wonder.

What was more of a mystery to her was why Jack had these papers and why he was involved. "Oh my God," was he a covert operative, as she had wondered? Was it not as ridiculous sounding as it had when she first said it? What exactly was his involvement in all of this, and why hadn't he mentioned one word to her about it? "Well, dammit, he was going to come clean when he returned, or else she feared their relationship would be over. He was the one who spoke of honesty, trust and open communication, so he was going to have to prove his words weren't just words. She hoped the roads would be open soon because she really wanted to be back in the city, back with her friends and back in the safety of her apartment where there was no mystery and no secrets. She went to sleep that night with many questions clouding her mind. She didn't sleep for shit, and in the early hours of the morning, she got out of bed and as she sipped her coffee, waiting for the latest weather updates, she thought about that damned folder and its contents.

The road crews had worked hard to get the area back to being passable, and a couple of days later, citizens were once again able to drive the freeways, and the city streets had been cleared as best as they could. It was still messy, but if one was careful, driving was doable. Although Vivian hated driving in the snow, she geared up and hit the road, Henry by her side and with some patience and a lot of slow lane driving, she made it back to the city and was relieved when she pulled up in front of her building. Home sweet home. There really was something to that expression. She unloaded Henry first, and soon, she was settled back in at her place. Her mail had piled up, so she made tea, sat down and went through the stack. She did call Jack and left a voicemail so that he wouldn't worry that she was in a ditch somewhere. As she sat going through her mail, she suddenly froze. Had she put the folder back? Crap! She couldn't remember whether she had or not. Well, tough shit, she was going to put it all on the table anyway, so it really didn't matter at this point.

Jack called later that evening, never mentioning the folder, but was a little disappointed that she hadn't waited for his return. He would have loved to spend some time with her. She blamed her early departure on her work, claiming she was so far behind that she just had to get back in order to recover from the lost time. She noticed every time she mentioned the client or her work there, Jack's mood darkened. He often expressed how he couldn't wait for her to be finished with this project and Aaron Walters. It was so unlike him. Maybe he was jealous of her time with Aaron. No, that was not it. Jack was too put together to be jealous of any man. She always assured him that she would much rather spend her time with him, but that just didn't pay the bills. In the days ahead, she worked in the office until she received word from Aaron that the roads were good for driving and that she should have no problems. He had paid extra money to have a snow removal team come out and clear the roads that led to his place. Of course, he did, she thought to herself. She and Zac headed out the very next morning and were a little surprised to see Aaron when they arrived. He had waited to make sure they got there safely and to go over the final Stages of the project. He gave Vivian two blank checks and announced that he would be out of the country for the remainder of the project and that if they needed anything at all, the number he gave Vivian would be how he could be reached.

The two had so much to do that there was little time to chat, but she had missed Zac, and when they broke for lunch, they had the chance to discuss what his plans would be when the project was complete. She didn't know that much about him as an individual. He was all work when they were together, and that impressed her. She was certain he was gay, but Vivian never cared about things of that nature. She believed one is defined by how they treat others and how they treat themselves. She always said, "It's not where you live but how you live," and she firmly believed that. He had always been kind to her, and she loved working side by side with him. She had spoken with Derrell in one of the few serious conversations they would ever have, and she told him that Zac's work ethic was above reproach and he would be a welcome addition to the company in a floater position and would he consider it. Derrell, never being able to make a decision out right, left it up to her. She wasn't sure if he would accept her offer because he was still very young and seemed uncertain about what his plan was. His plan was far from what Vivian thought, and he was beginning to feel bad about it. She had been the first person to give him an opportunity without hesitation, even if his resume was stacked with fictitious prior employment. She had been in a bind, and he was convincing enough in his interview that he knew she would never check his references, and she hadn't. His employer had made sure that had she checked, she would have found no discrepancies. He had tried not to become friends with her but it was impossible. Once one met Vivian, she would grow on them, and he grew to be very fond of her. He knew what he was supposed to do and why he was there, so he did his best to keep his head down and go along with the plan, no matter how he felt. Once, after he was hired by Vivian, he came close to revealing that plan to her quite by mistake, and his employer rushed to clean it up quickly. After that, Zac was extremely cautious. He had been cautious his whole life.

He grew up in New York. His mother was absent most of the time, and his father was a big shot in the drug world. At a very young age, his father and his uncle had him running slips and packages to shady parts of the city and even to shadier people. In his teens, he got in trouble and was about to enter the system when his Uncle stepped in and made a deal with the prosecutor, and that was that. From that day on, he was in his debt, and once he was an adult, his father came to him and told him he owed a guy and that Zac would do his bidding for him. The next thing he knew, he was in the South meeting his employer and learned of the debt he was to clear. Why Vivian? The details were sketchy, and he was told that the less he knew, the better. How cliche, and how did he think it would be better? Vivian would be devastated if she knew. He wanted desperately to warn her of the danger but knew if he did, his life would, too, be in jeopardy. That had been made clear to him, and there was no doubt that he would keep his word on that.

As they wrapped up lunch and got back to work, he watched Vivian closely, and a feeling of sadness overcame him. He had told her that he was grateful for the job opportunity, but he could not make a decision without thinking it over and could he let her know when they were close to being done. Vivian said of course, and thought nothing else of it. The project would be wrapped up in a few weeks, and he could decide then. The thought of being finished with this project made Vivian feel very happy. She would be away from this place and away from Aaron Walters. She was looking forward to the mini vacation she and Jack had spoken of. She wasn't sure how they would get the time away, but it was a pleasant thought. Had she known what lies ahead, she would have taken that vacation much sooner.

Chapter Eighteen

Vivian got clean. Along with that, she landed a job as Assistant Manager of the Holiday gas station in downtown IA. She really managed the store in every way, and the only time she saw the "real" manager was on paydays. He claimed he was running errands and attending to the financial aspects of the store, but she swore she was the one doing all that, and he was just taking the credit when the owner was around. She didn't care because she and the store clerks were there most of the time by themselves and preferred it that way. She hated being micro-managed and knew the job without him breathing down her neck. Vivian had a lot of responsibility. Anyone with the keys to the kingdom would know what it took to run a full-service gas station/store. She still didn't have a vehicle of her own, but the owner had made her get a driver's license so that she could drive one of the store's trucks. She was proud of herself and did her very best to make sure she kept her nose clean and her mind right. She had met a couple that lived near her job, and the three of them went in on a place together. She liked Denny and Marie, who had three children who were just the sweetest kids she ever met. The couple had their share of demons, but Vivian never judged them, and they got along very well. In the evenings, Vivian hung out at Clem's, a very happening hot spot, with her friend Jules. They hung out nearly every night and had the time of their lives. The bar was nestled in a neighborhood that was familiar to Vivian, and the owners were two drop-dead gorgeous brothers. It was the type of bar that was as busy on Mondays as it was on Fridays. If you didn't arrive at a reasonable time, you would be left to stand until someone moved.

The two women were always dressed to look their best, and there were plenty of good-looking guys to feast their eyes on. They were both single and weren't really looking for a boyfriend, so they just had fun, and on occasion, one or the other hooked up with someone, which was considered a double bonus. Vivian was a crack-shot pool player and hung out in the pool room with the men. She still didn't have many girlfriends, feeling that they always competed and talked about everyone around them. Jules was her closest friend, and they just wanted to catch a good booze high, listen to the music and flirt their asses off. Jules fell for a man in a cowboy hat, but that never got in the way of their fun. There were plenty of mornings after that Vivian was glad she had bank runs to make and orders to pick up so that she could sneak home and catch a little nap just so she could make it through the rest of the day. She didn't always have to stay at the station because her store clerks had been hand-picked by her, were always reliable, and rarely needed time off. She could rely on them to get what was needed done when she wasn't there. Vivian ran a tight ship but was always fair and respectful of the people who worked with her, so they liked her and didn't fuss when she was away for the whole day.

One evening at Clem's, she was sitting with Jules waiting for her turn at one of the tables when she noticed a silver-haired man and his friend playing a game at one of the other tables. He was tall and handsome, and Jules noticed he was checking her friend out. Vivian noticed, too. When it came time for her to play, she headed for the table and turned on the charm. As she walked by him, she whispered, hey, handsome in his direction, and that was all it took. His name was Ray, and for the rest of the evening, they partnered and ran the table. He was impressed at how well she played, but he was more interested in her. A good tune came through the speakers, and she and Jules went to dance. She saw him coming onto the dance floor just as the song ended, and as if by intention, a slow tune by one of her favorite bands began playing. She asked him for a dance, and as he held her around the waist, something came over him, and he knew she was going to be a part of his life for a long time. Sometime later in the evening, a woman came in and went straight to where Ray and Mikey were standing. Vivian learned from a fly that she was someone he had been seeing. Vivian immediately went to their table and pointed the chick out to her friend. He had a girl, but he danced with her, flirted with her. He could not be trusted. As she and Jules were leaving for a blues club where their friend was playing, he walked past her, slipped a piece of paper in her hand and kept going. She and Jules laughed and fell out into the night and on to the next hangout. She added his number to her date bowl and didn't give him another thought even though she saw him alone several times after that at Clem's. She knew he was the type of man that wouldn't come crawling. She could respect that. His friend Mikey came over to their table and asked if they wanted to play a game of doubles, so they grabbed their drinks, leaving their cigarettes and a spare beer on the table as a place marker. Mikey touched Vivian's arm, and when she looked, he told her that Ray had broken up with Kimmy the very same night he had passed her his phone number.

Vivian was impressed and surprised. Had he done that because of her? They never mentioned it and had a great time for the rest of the evening. Vivian was busy for the next few weeks and couldn't hang out as much as she would have liked, and finally, one Friday, she was able to get away for the weekend and didn't have a date. She dug her hand into her date bowl, a bowl of numbers she had gotten and used when she found herself without a date. She pulled out a slip, opened it, and there was her date's name, or so she hoped. She dialed the number and a girl answered the phone. Vivian asked to speak with Ray, and she called him on the phone. Several hours later, in the middle of a tornado warning, he pulled into the driveway to pick her up. From that date on, they were always together. She didn't leave Jules out, and all three of them had a great time whenever they were all together.

Jules broke the news to Vivian one night that she and her family were moving to Missouri, and she would need a truck to drive her and her stuff down after her parents had gone ahead of her. She asked Ray and Vivian if they wanted to go on a road trip, and Ray agreed to drive them down. They all headed out after Vivian made arrangements with the owner, not the manager. Seeing as how she hadn't taken a vacation since she was hired, it was an easy decision. They were only supposed to be gone for a few days anyway, but the owner told her to take her time and enjoy herself, so she did. The 4th of July was approaching, and Jules' parents invited them to stay for the celebration. Ray was all for it, so Vivian said yes as well. She touched base with the owner, and he saw no problem with it. Ray was so easy to get along with, and Vivian felt relaxed in his company. They talked for hours, and for the first time in quite a while, she was happy. I mean, I am really happy. In the coming weeks, she would look forward to meeting up with him, and he always made sure she was okay when they weren't together.

The first time Vivian spent the night with Ray, she never went home. She only kept her job long enough for the owner to find someone as good as she had been to replace her. Having done that, she was released from her duties with a nice bonus added to her final check. She picked up her things from her place and officially moved to his place, which was actually his brother's house, but he had an apartment in the lower half of the split level. She helped him with rent by watching his brother's young daughter while his brother's girlfriend was at work. Ray's brother was very sick with kidney disease, and it was hard for him, so Vivian took over, and Jenny fell in love with her. Many months later, the child would lose her father to his disease. Ray was crushed, and it was a sad time in their lives. He was glad she was there with him and appreciated the way she handled things during that period of their lives.

The only dark spot in the couple's relationship was Ray's mom. She was on the fence as to whether Vivian was suitable for her son. He was a mama's boy, and she let everyone know what was expected of them if they were going to date one of her sons. It went on that way for a long time, maybe throughout their entire relationship. Marcy and Sally had gone through the same thing, and Marcy was the only one who came out of it unscathed. Joan was never outright rude to her when they would go to her home for a meal or the holidays. It was the small things that stuck. It was years later when her true colors would really surface, and although it was meant to be the end of the road for Vivian, it was a blessing in disguise.

Vivian and Ray had the best of times the first few years they were together. They never fought and seemed to always be on the same page until "it" happened. Vivian was chilling one day downstairs when Ray came in with a small package. She didn't have to be a road scholar to know what the contents were. She was concerned. Ray knew she had quit doing drugs, and Vivian was proud of her accomplishments since getting clean. She was terrified to go down that road again, but her addictive personality got the better of her, and it only took a few minutes for her to convince herself that it wouldn't be the same this time. He, of course, never forced her to do anything she didn't want to. He never did. Vivian did a small line, and that old feeling came rushing in. She didn't lie to herself. She loved the way it made her feel. Months went by, and she and Ray dabbled in coke only on the weekends and only as a pre-night out treat. Vivian could see where this was going but was crippled to stop it from happening. A year later, she and Ray were using a lot, and it was beginning to cause a rift in the house.

One day, out of nowhere, they decided it was time to make a move and get their own place. They hunted for an apartment, and Vivian found herself back in her old neighborhood. The rent was cheap, and the apartment was okay. Vivian was working at the W Corporation and was making okay money, but most of it was going towards their party habit. Their friend Andy kept them supplied and sometimes partied with them. Little parties became all-nighters, and when coke wasn't getting the job done anymore, they switched to crystal meth, a very dangerous drug. Ray quit his job and started scrapping, which, if done well, brought in a good amount of cash. Vivian was doing meth before work so she could put in overtime with no problem. They were losing weight and losing sleep. One night, on the way home from a score, Vivian got pulled over. Thankfully she knew the officer as a friend of Ray, and she named dropped her ass off. It worked, but he followed her to the apartment anyway to make sure it was actually Ray that she was hurrying home to. Coming into the apartment and finding him hiding in the closet was all she needed to see to know that their situation was out of control. A short time later, Vivian learned of her father's passing but was too poor to attend, and Babs made sure she couldn't in her own selfish way. Vivian sunk into a state of depression, which resulted in self-destruction and doing drugs to ease her mind.

It was nineteen ninety-five, and they had barely managed to hold on to the apartment. Rent was starting to always get paid late, and the landlord had finally had enough and served her and him with an eviction notice. Vivian was in a panic. She had been here before. With nowhere else to go, they found rooms for rent in a hotel on Dodge Street and moved into a large room with a shared bathroom down the hall. She did her best to make it a home, but she knew she was just compensating for a loss that was about to get even bigger. She came home from work one day, and Ray was stretched out on the bed, not looking well. She thought he had got a hold of a bad batch of dope, but she soon found out that it was much more serious. Ray was having a heart attack and was rushed to the medical center just around the corner. He spent many days in cardiac intensive care and, upon release, was told by his physician that the next time just might be his last time. Ray took it easy for a few months, but as soon as he was back on his feet, they were back at it. Vivian was still going to Clem's after work, and on one of those occasions, she ran into her long-time friend Deb. She was happy to see her friend, and they sat catching up, telling stories of what was going on in their lives. Deb never judged. She was far from perfect and offered to lend her friend a way out. She laughed and told Vivian that all Ray needed was some good old-fashioned down-home cooking to heal his broken heart. As she left, Deb turned to her and added, "tick tock, time is wasting. Get with it, girl or get dead."

Vivian went back to their room with high hopes and a much better frame of mind. She told Ray about Deb's offer, and he was in agreement that it had to be better than where they were, so they packed up their habit and their belongings and moved to Deb's house a little further North. It was a big greenhouse situated on a corner lot, and it had been split into two apartments. Deb lived upstairs, and another couple lived in the basement apartment. One day after they moved in, Deb took Vivian downstairs to introduce her to the neighbors. Vivian didn't have many female friends to speak of, but from the moment she met Shelly, she knew they would be more than friends in the years to come. They would be family. Just about every day after that, Vivian went down to hang out with her new friend and her people. They'd partake in Mother Nature's garden and watch soaps on the tube. Deb was welcome, too, but she was always watched because she felt the need to take what wasn't hers, even from people she called friends. Vivian wasn't like that, and Shelly knew this. When she had places to go, Vivian rode shotgun. She was welcomed into the fold and fit like a glove. Shelly and her man got a kick out of Vivian and Ray and used to peep them from their window at night when the couple was outside high as a kite, working on their vehicle. It didn't matter what time it was to them. It was always daylight in their world. Ray liked Shelly's man right away, and even though they didn't chat that much, he felt that he was a friend.

The two women hung out North and South. It didn't matter, and Vivian felt right at home when she was with her friend. She never had to do anything to impress anybody, and it was easy for her to be herself around Shelly and her friends. Her friend could see through Vivian's eyes the shit she had gone through, and the young woman to her seemed wise for her years. She learned quickly that if Vivian said she had your back, she had your back. She didn't talk much, and Shelly liked that about her. She kept an eye on things, and if she said something, she knew about it. She could read people, and Vivian was a quiet storm, either liked you or didn't. If she didn't, you may as well have been invisible. She never did understand how Vivian and Deb had struck up a friendship. They were polar opposites. Shelly liked the fact that Vivian was down for just about anything. Vivian never hesitated to help them "shop" or divert traffic while a loved one was running from the car, never asking questions. Shelly was fearless, and Vivian loved people like that. Her place was always popping, and Vivian was drawn in by the excitement that seemed to center around the couple downstairs. Ray didn't care because he always knew where to find her if they had shit to do. Sometime later in their friendship, Vivian was a part of the celebration of her friend's first babies, and she was overjoyed by the adorable bundles of love. Vivian liked to spend time with her friends. She felt relaxed and could talk to her about anything. They laughed, cried and raised hell together, and she was so happy to have a friend like Shelly. Even when it was time to move away, it was not unlike Vivian to walk across town, she walked everywhere to see her friend. All she had to do was call her and tell her she was on her way and her friend would be waiting when she got there. That was their friendship.

Vivian's drug problem followed her across town and stayed with her through most all of her travels thru the next year. In nineteen ninety-seven, she and Ray moved into his mother's house, and Vivian hated it. She believed it was the main reason she stayed high almost all the time, and even Ray knew it had become a problem for them but was not in a position with his own habit to deal with to fix anything, so after a close call and a near overdose he and his son left in his son's semi, leaving Vivian behind alone, with no money and a very nasty drug habit. It was the only time that his mother thought it was unfair of him, and she did her best to not be a bitch to the young woman living in her basement. She even gave her money, but Vivian needed more. She went to a friend's house, got a package and in two hours, doubled her money and had a small pile of dope for herself. She got high alone in the basement, all the while worried that if she overdosed, Ray's mom would be the one to find her, and that was worse than the nightmare she was living as each and every day passed. Ray called her, but she wasn't really in a feel-good mood about him leaving, and even though he apologized, she just wouldn't get over the fact that he had left her alone with no money and a drug habit bigger than her. Drugs wouldn't be Vivian's fatal mistake. A rash decision, a store and a strong urge to show the world that she was somebody would cause her to take a step towards a point of no return.

As she pulled up in front of the store, she knew the odds of getting caught or, worse, getting shot, but her need for a high was stronger than her will not to commit robbery. She was getting ready to leave for a friend's house when she heard voices upstairs. She was sure Ray's mom was at work; she never missed work, never, but it was her voice and the voices of men asking where Vivian was. She knew she was caught and gave up with no resistance, and as she was led out of the house, she turned, and the last thing she saw was the small smile on Ray's mom's face. Little did Vivian know at the time that she had been featured on the local television's Crime Stoppers edition of the news, and Ray's mom, not believing who she saw, picked up the phone and called the hotline number.

Vivian was coming down and angry when she was brought into the women's section of the DCCC. Her only call was to Deb, who, of course, didn't judge her but told her not to worry and that she would make calls. Ray didn't help. Her sister wouldn't help. A lawyer came to talk to Vivian and told her she was looking at five to seven because she had given the illusion that she had a weapon when she committed the crime, although she had not. She felt so alone. She actually thought it would be better if she were dead. She had reached the bottom with nowhere to go but up. She screamed into her pillow and cried silent tears. It would take a miracle to fix this screw-up, so Vivian did what she should have done a long time before. She prayed to the Lord and asked for his hand to guide her and help her, and the Lord answered her prayers.

Chapter Nineteen

If you've ever had a bad feeling about something or someone, listen to yourself. If you feel like someone is watching you, look. If you think someone is following you, turn around. Vivian had that feeling but could not put her finger on it, and ignoring it wasn't helping. She was as jumpy as a criminal with a warrant. She grinned at the analogy. "Not on your life, Vivian!" The final phase of the project was underway, and she was buried in fabrics, art pieces and furniture. The snow had melted off, but it never lasted very long, which is one of the reasons Vivian had chosen to live in the South. She had no time for anything or anyone but her work. Although she had officially moved in with Jack, she spent several nights in town, too tired to make the drive to the country. She did, on occasion, stop by Steve's for a drink and to catch up with the girls. They were as happy as she was that her project would soon be wrapped up. For a while, they noticed the difference in her mood. On one of the evenings she decided to hang out, she was pleasantly surprised to turn and see Jack standing behind her chair. Damn, he was handsome. She stood up, and he held her tight. The feeling of his arms around her released all the stress she had felt for weeks. He whispered something in her ear, and she blushed. Vivian never blushed! Their eyes met, and a short time later, they said their goodbyes to their group of friends and headed out the door in the direction of her place.

She and Jack were deep in conversation, so she didn't notice the dark sedan parked up the street from her place. It was too dark to see its occupants, but she knew it was the same car she had seen several times before, and this time she told Jack about it. He told her to stay where she was and went to check out the car, but as soon as he crossed the street, the car sped off before he could get close enough to it. He was worried. He didn't want to frighten Vivian, but he knew or was pretty sure who it was, proving it would be difficult. All in good time, he thought to himself. He had information that the subject was in the South, but where? His only thought at that moment was to make sure Vivian was safe and protected. He hurried back to where she was standing, and they continued to her place. She asked him why he thought the car had sped off, but he brushed it off and told her not to worry. They arrived at her place, and his hands were all over her even before she could close the door. Henry wanted to make friends, but Jack wanted Vivian. It had been too long since he had felt her soft skin against his, and he expertly peeled off her clothing so that he could take all of her beauty in. Henry would have to wait.

Vivian grabbed some drinks, gave her buddy a handful of treats and joined Jack in the bedroom. The lamp gave off a soft glow, and Jack couldn't take his eyes off her. He ran his hands down to the small of her back, and Vivian felt the searing heat of his touch. He kissed her softly at first and then with more urgency. He gripped her close to his body, so close they felt like one. His hand found the place she loved for him to touch, and she moaned with ecstasy. Her body moved in rhythm with his touch, and as he lay her down, his tongue replaced his hand, and she cried out for more. Jack wanted their time together to last, so he backed off just enough to allow her breathing to relax just a little, and then he was inside her, moving, grinding, all thoughts of anything else had evaporated, and he could think of nothing else but pleasing this woman. His woman. He was gentle with her, then rough. He had come to know that she liked for him to be domineering, and he aimed to please her in every way he could. He turned her over and entered her from behind, hearing her soft moans and his arousal was unleashed into explosive passion. Vivian arched her back to feel his body against hers, and he held her there while he went as deep as he could, pushing her to the brink until she screamed out his name and as he felt her warmth around him, he released, holding onto the moment until she was still again. He wanted more of her, all of her, in all ways. They stepped into the shower and made love again. Hours later, they were both famished, so Vivian padded into the kitchen wearing his shirt and nothing else. She put together a plate of snacks for them to share and a couple of Cokes. Henry had sneaked in and was cuddled with Jack. He just smiled and shrugged his shoulders. She crawled into bed, and they ate and watched the late-night or early-morning news. Sometime between the weather and sports, Vivian dozed off. She slept soundly. She always did when Jack was there. She reached for him when she woke up, but there was an empty space where he should have been. She heard voices in the kitchen, and she put on her robe to join him and find out who he was talking to. Jack didn't hear her come into the room, and he continued to speak in a very commanding voice to who-ever was on the other end. He barked out some orders, and she had no idea who he was talking to so rudely. Jack was normally very polite, and to hear him speak like that took her quite by surprise.

When she cleared her throat, he ended his call abruptly. "Good Morning, Doll," he said in a voice much different than the one on the phone. He grabbed her around the waist and kissed her deeply. She kissed him back, and the phone call was forgotten. His hand went up under her robe, and the sweet sexual assault began. An hour later, she was showered, dressed and ready for work. Jack stayed behind, stating he would see her for dinner later. He had calls to make and an appoint-ment in town, so he was in no hurry. He had never been alone in Viv-ian's apartment but was relaxed there, and he settled in and got busy. He used her desk, which was an impressive piece. She must have found this at an antique store, he said to Henry, who just stared at him, won-dering why he was there and not his person. A couple of hours later, he was starting to get hungry and checked the fridge for something to snack on. Not finding anything he was craving, he gave Henry a snack, wrapped up what he was working on and got ready to leave for his ap-pointment. He got up, and a huge stack of papers, plans and what was obviously Vivian's project folder fell to the floor. He began the task of putting them all back when his eyes fell on a page that must have been her client's bio page. He knew from listening to Vivian that she ran backgrounds on every client before she accepted any project.

He would call and ask to see if she had forgotten it, but a moment later, he noticed something that sat him back in his chair, speechless and in shock. The man described in the bio sounded a lot like the subject of his investigation, and his forehead began to sweat. He wrote down everything he could and quickly left Vivian's apartment bound for his downtown office and his meeting. He had to find out more about this, and he could think of nothing else. He was so distracted he barely missed the vehicle stopped ahead of him. He slammed on his brakes just in time. Dammit! At the office, he got down to business, cutting out all the extra "BS" and wrapped up his meeting in record time so that he could focus on the information he had in his briefcase. He didn't want to be right and hoped that the information would be a dead end. What he found was compelling evidence that convinced him that this man that Vivian was doing business with was, in fact, the reason for months of long nights without sleep. His blood ran cold. Now more than ever, he knew what had to be done, and he had to act fast because his love was right in the middle of things and could be in real danger. He would do anything to keep her safe.

Vivian didn't know it, but since they had gotten to know one another and had developed a relationship, he had done a little checking into what made this woman who she was. He couldn't help himself. It was an inherent trait he had developed through the years. She had opened up to him and shared some of her past, and it angered him to hear what she had been through. What really pissed him off was how a man could do what had been done to her and just walk away from it without any consequences for his actions. She had been afraid to go to the authorities. They were not treated as the victims, and as a result, rapists went on to rape again. He had spent his entire life working to make those who committed unspeakable attacks pay for their crimes. He didn't know how personal this really was until it was someone he spent time with, cared about, maybe even loved. Little did he know just how much she would need him, but he would soon find out.

Jack had taken on many cases that involved not only women but children and, through the years, had put many offenders behind bars where they belonged. He combined forces with the DEA and Human Trafficking Division to take down the scourge of the earth. He formed his business as a cover so that he could move around freely and without question. His resume was extensive, and he was damned good at what he did. His employees were hand-picked and served as operatives when the need arose.

Vivian's coming into his life was purely by chance, but once her story was shared, he knew he had chosen the right profession. He had laid next to her when she cried out in her sleep and woke up frightened by her nightmares. When she saw him with Donna, his cover was almost exposed, but he formulated a story that she believed, and he knew in the end that she would understand. He hated using her and was on the verge several times of coming clean with her, but he didn't. He didn't want to put her in harm's way because some of the men he worked to track down were dangerous and had ties to the underworld. What he didn't know was that the man he was seeking out for Donna would be the client who had hired Vivian to re-design his property and so very much more.

When they met for dinner that evening, Vivian thought he was acting a little strange and asked him if everything was alright. "You hiding another woman," she teased. He laughed it off and did his best to stay engaged for the rest of dinner. It had been a long day for both of them, and all he wanted was to hold her in his arms and put his mind at ease. If only it were that simple, that easy, he thought to himself. When they returned to her place, they both worked for a while, and when it was time for bed, they showered to wash off the remains of the day, and Jack relaxed a little. Being this close to Vivian usually always did, and holding her close, touching her soft skin, brought him back to the present. They stayed in each other's arms until the news was over, and they both fell asleep. He always wondered why she moved to the far side of the bed but figured it was for comfort. It was actually because she didn't like feeling crowded or suffocated. She actually feared the feeling more than just not liking it. Damned ghosts.

He woke early enough to catch her still sleeping, and he knew at that moment that he had fallen in love with her.

Chapter Twenty

Vivian had spent her thirty-eighth birthday locked up. She had a lot of time to think about her future and knew she didn't want to continue down the road she had been traveling for so many years. She hated her life and loathed who she had become. When she had stopped feeling sorry for herself because nobody came to bond her out, she got down to the business of living a new life, and for her, it would start behind bars. Vivian learned from one of the guards that there were classes she could join that would help her through her drug rehab, so she signed up for them and took it very seriously for once in her life. The ladies who taught the class came from church, and it was there that she felt her reconnection with her maker. She had felt for a long time that he had turned his back on her and that she was beyond his help when, in all actuality, she had turned her back on him. She didn't find Jesus because he was not the one that was lost. She found herself, and Jesus was there waiting for her.

Vivian's sister not helping her was not because she didn't want to. Lyla hated knowing where she was and, worse, hated knowing her baby sister was going through the worst time in her life, but she also knew if she bailed Vivian out, she just might be helping to send her to her grave. She knew her sister needed time to get her mind right, and if it took tough love to get her there, then that was what she would do and did. As much as Vivian hated being in jail, she appreciated that Lyla had made that decision. It proved to be a life-changing and life-saving choice. Ray didn't visit Vivian and never put money on her books for the entire six months she spent incarcerated. At first, he barely spoke to her on the phone. That was the first time in their relationship that he didn't show up for her when she needed him most, and she was hurt by it. Sadly, it wouldn't be the last. Deb was her only visitor and, in fact, was the one who got Vivian a lawyer. Without one, she would surely have done much more time than she did. She put money on her books and would be the one to provide a place for Vivian to stay when she did get out.

Vivian completed her drug rehab course and was so proud to receive her certificate of achievement. It was the first of many milestones for her, and it was no small thing. Her day in court was coming up, and she was terrified, with nobody to talk to about it. Ray was too busy chasing his own demons among other things she was sure he chased while she was away but would never admit to. When she walked into the courtroom, she was surprised to see him there alongside Deb, who pretended not to know him. Loyalty was paramount in her world. The judge went through all the charges for the record and then wanted to speak with Vivian off-record. He was not convinced that she would have done something like this under normal circumstances, so he wanted to hear it from her. This was no time for Vivian to be insolent, and she decided it was time to be honest with him and everyone else. She did say that had she not been using, she couldn't imagine herself committing a crime of this magnitude. He believed her. He asked her who was with her in court and was not pleased when he discovered Ray had left her alone, thinking only of himself. In the end, what saved her ass was the fact that she had no record to speak of other than a couple of misdemeanors which amounted to nothing at all. He sentenced her to six months, and she had to agree to see a drug counselor to help her stay clean. He advised her to stay out of trouble but assured her that if he saw her name on any court docket, he would make sure she went to prison. She was so relieved she cried right there in the courtroom.

Vivian had already done all but forty-five days of her sentence, so she returned to her cell, ready to ride it out. It was the longest time of her life. She decided to kill a little time and make plans for the immediate future, writing them in her journal as a checklist of sorts. She knew she had a fine to pay before she could be released and asked Ray if he could pay it. He acted as if it was a whole lot of trouble for him, but she didn't give a shit. It was the least he could do, and she made sure he knew it. He still hadn't given her a good enough reason for leaving when he did, and she wanted someone else to feel as bad as she had about it. The night before her release, she didn't sleep at all. She still wasn't sure he had paid her fine, and she tossed and turned until the early hours of the morning. She had lost faith in him, and despite her impending release, something she should have been excited about, she was sad. The guard finally called for breakfast, releasing Vivian from the confines of her cell. She tried her best to put on her game face and joined the other inmates in the day area. Partway through breakfast, a guard opened the door, yelled her name, and told her to roll out. That only came if all was clear for her to go, and she wasted no time gathering up what she had decided to take and left the rest for her bunkmate.

The sun had never felt as good to Vivian as it did when the door was opened, and the ceremonious "don't come back" had been said to her. She knew she would never be back, and that was the only thing she was sure of. She stepped out, and for a moment, she stood in silence, taking in the first feeling of freedom, then chased down the first person she saw and bummed a cigarette. She hadn't smoked in six months, and she wanted one more than anything she could think of at that very moment. She inhaled deeply and fell straight on her ass from the head rush she felt. She laughed it off and picked herself up, resting on the steps for the rest of her smoke. She gingerly stood up, and as soon as she had her sea legs, she took off. Nobody was there to pick her up, so she started walking again in the direction of Deb's house north-side. She didn't bother calling Ray because he hadn't bothered to come get her. Screw him, she said out loud, and it felt liberating.

Staying at Debs was a little like old times, but she had a kid, and her new man was a jerk. He hated Vivian, and the feeling was mutual. He made Vivian's skin crawl, and she swore he was putting drugs in her Pepsi but couldn't prove it. Because of him, she knew she couldn't stay there long, so she worked every day and extra hours to save enough money to get her own place. She had been re-hired at W Corp and was still seeing Ray, but he seemed comfortable living at his mom's, and Vivian was not welcome there. For the next year or so, she worked, went to outpatient treatment and hung out as much as she could with Shelly and her new family. When she heard about Vivian being arrested, she was in shock. She figured Vivian was a badass, but this was over the top, even for her friend. She knew her friend was quiet, always watching, and she wondered what had caused her to be like that or whether she was always. Further into their friendship, she would come to know and understand.

Vivian finally had enough money saved to move, and it couldn't have come at a better time because Deb's bipolar episodes were getting worse. They had a huge blowout, and Deb, her friend for years, broke all the rules and called the cops on Vivian. She told them when they arrived that she wanted her out, and to make it all even worse, she told them that Vivian was running a prostitution ring out of her house and that Ray was slinging dope, which couldn't have been farther from the truth. She couldn't believe what she was hearing. She had put in the time to be friends with this woman, and now, looking at her, she didn't know who she was. She knew they would never be friends again. That's how Vivian was. She loved madly, but if she was betrayed, there was no opportunity for a second chance. To Vivian, it was just one more person that took advantage of her trust. The police let Vivian in to get her things, and Ray, not knowing what else to do, took her to his mother's house, pleading with her to give Vivian a second chance. Vivian only needed a long enough time to find an apartment, and even though she was back with Ray, she felt alone. Nobody talked to her, never acknowledged that she was even in the room, and she hustled to get the hell out of there as quickly as possible. Thankfully, it didn't take long, and she and Ray moved into a place on the north side of town. Ray was not working because of his heart condition but was collecting govt funds for his disability. Vivian went to work every day, and life seemed to get better for the two until it wasn't. She had sworn off drugs of any kind and was serious about getting her life together, but Ray, as she found out one day when she came home from work early, was not. She caught him and some trick chick getting high in her bedroom, of all places, while her child sat in the living room alone. Vivian didn't know which one pissed her off more, but the next thing she knew, she was tossing the chick out of the apartment and told Ray that if this was what he wanted for his life, he could go with her. He stayed.

Hours of conversation ensued, and she explained what her goal was and that she wanted him to be a serious part of her future. She told him she loved him, but if he continued to use drugs, she would go it on her own. Jail had made her realize she didn't really need anyone. She had been alone there, and she could be alone again. It didn't matter. Ray loved Vivian, although he never said it, so he promised to quit, and he did. Life got good for them, and she could see a real future with him. In Two Thousand, they moved into a cute house on the south side and were happy there. Even his mother was being a little kinder to her, and although Vivian didn't care, it helped in her relationship with Ray. His health was the same, and he spent a lot of time at the doctor. So did Vivian. She had gotten sick and wasn't getting much better. Vivian woke up one day and knew something was seriously wrong. She felt like she was being poisoned, and it wasn't by Deb's boyfriend as she had thought before. Her liver was sick, and her doctors were concerned. They biopsied and found bad things. Vivian was frightened but kept a stiff upper lip. Her sister Lyla worked at Mayo and gave her all the information she needed to help her. She was a blessing, the one member of her family who never gave up on her because she knew Vivian would never give up on herself. Vivian knew before they told her what it actually was, and for the next two years, she fought to stay above ground. Through the treatments, shots, meds and sickness, Vivian stayed at work. Her friend Shelly knew and watched as her friend worked it out day after day. She never doubted that Vivian would handle it. She knew her friend was tough, and if anyone could do it, it was her. Vivian drew strength from her friend's encouraging words and was grateful to have her in her life, always there to lend her opinion, give her the hard truths without hurting their relationship and offer spiritual guidance along the way. Shelly's faith in God renewed Vivian's faith as well, and she was a better person for it. She was grateful that she had a friend like her.

In the end, she had kicked its ass, and when it was over, life finally went back to normal. Just about a year later, it reared its ugly head again, and Vivian wondered, after all she had done to herself and survived, would be what took her to meet Jesus. It would not be. She kicked its ass again, for good this time. Her last treatment day was one of the happiest times of her life, if you can imagine. Her boss and her co-workers sneaked around and planned a celebratory luncheon for her, and when she arrived with her manager to have a "working lunch," they were all there. Someone was missing, though and as happy as she was, she felt the void. She was busy chatting it up with her friends when she looked up and saw Ray. It was perfect, and she was the happiest she had been in a very long time.

Vivian and Ray had made the house they lived in a home, but she wanted more. She wanted to buy a house, and although her credit was in the crapper, they agreed to start looking. They enlisted the help of a banker who walked them through the process, and for a while, it didn't look promising, but she never gave up. By chance, one day, their friend Justin came by and heard that the two were looking for a house and, out of nowhere, said, "I'll sell you mine." At first, Vivian thought he was bullshitting, but he wasn't, and in Two Thousand and Three, right before Thanksgiving, Vivian signed the paperwork, collected the keys and became a first-time homeowner. She sat in the car and cried. She had done it.

She had managed her whole life by the seat of her pants and realized as she was leaving the bank that she had bought the house sight unseen, but it was her house. She had never been inside, never done a walk-through, nothing. She had taken Ray's word for it that the house was a good investment, so when it was time for Justin to go and for them to move in, she was shocked. It would take over a year of very hard work to make the house move-in ready, and they were already moved in, but that was her life. Nothing had ever come easy for Vivian, so she didn't complain, and she and Ray made it their home together. It wasn't perfect, but Vivian didn't care. It was hers, yes, hers. She never let Ray know she felt that way. She always made sure he was secure, thinking of his needs over hers because she felt that was truly what a relationship was. He never knew just how much he would come to rely on her, but he was about to find out.

Two years after they bought the house, Royal got really sick. He was diagnosed with polycystic kidney disease. Tumors had taken over his working kidneys, and he had to go on dialysis to keep him from going into renal failure. It was a very challenging time for the couple, and Vivian was afraid she would lose him to his disease. It ran in his family, and his older brother had died from it. He entered into home treatment, and Vivian researched and learned everything there was to know so she could stay prepared and assist him. She worked and came home and did what she had to do to get him through to the next day. The drive home each day was the worst for her. She never knew if she was going to walk into the house and find him dead, and it played havoc on her emotionally. The treatments worked until they didn't, and the transplant was the only option for survival. Through it all, Vivian never faltered. She put her faith where it needed to be and prayed every day for a miracle. She ran the household, kept up on possible donors, and talked to everyone she could to find a way to help her partner. She was exhausted all the time, but it didn't matter to her. This was just one more thing she would have to figure out.

Ray had a lifelong friend named Donald, who was secretly being tested to see if he was a match for his friend. He came by every day and never said a word about it until he did. He called in May of 2007 and gave Ray the news that he was a match. It was a very good day. It was prayers to God answered. Years later, his friendship with Donald would not stand the test of time, and they would go their separate ways. Ray didn't take as much stock in his friendships as Vivian did, and he would lose many friends as a result. In the end, Vivian would prove to be his only friend.

Ray's transplant was a success, and Vivian never left his side for days after the surgery. She nursed him back to health, not knowing it would be something she would do for the rest of their time together through many other illnesses. They had the best of times in the coming years, and by all appearances, everyone was happy. Everyone except Vivian. Over time, she started to feel that she was the only one working on everything. The relationship, the finances, the home, everything. Ray was taking meds to relieve his headaches from the anti-rejection drugs, and they were a problem that only she could see. He had become complacent about the two of them, always trying to tell her what they were going to do without considering her opinions at all. She started to dislike the way he treated her, and she noticed she was drinking a little bit more at after-work events, holidays and the sort. She was feeling very unappreciated, and she knew deep down that if there wasn't a change, she and Ray would not survive the fallout. She tried to talk to him about how she felt, but he got defensive right away, and it ended up being her fault that she felt the way she did. He was in no way going to accept responsibility for his part in their failing relationship. Vivian didn't know if he loved her and felt she loved him more than he ever would her. It was a painful realization, and she wondered just how long she could hold on.

Six months later, Vivian moved out. She didn't want to end her relationship with Ray. She loved him too much to do that, but she did want him to really feel how important she was to him and wanted her to be in his life. He didn't have to move out of the house because that's just how Vivian was. She couldn't and wouldn't be a bitch about it and tried to be fair. It was his home, too, and she knew she had done the right thing. She had become friends with a lady at work and was told that there was a vacancy where she lived. When the ink dried on the lease, Ray and his friend helped her move, actually surprising her with the offer. Vivian knew he was saddened by her leaving, but she knew it was what they needed if they were going to make it together. It was Two Thousand and Ten. This was the time for Vivian's rebirth. A chance to show who she really was and how she wanted her life to be without reservation.

Chapter Twenty-One

Vivian, Lulu and Jamie were sitting at the table in her apartment, eating pizza and drinking a few beers. Work had been a madhouse for all of them, so they decided to take a well-deserved night off. Derrell had been working them to death, and they saw no end in sight. Thankfully, Vivian was wrapping up the client's project, so she escaped the onslaught of work her boss liked to dump on them. They all knew it was because he couldn't do it himself or wouldn't was more like it. "What a jackass," Lulu said, shaking her head. Jamie mimicked Derrell, and they all burst into laughter at their friend's imitation of him. Vivian had missed these two women and the time they spent together. It was so nice to just kick back and enjoy each other's company. "So, where's the hunk," Jamie asked. They liked Jack and wondered why he was away so often but felt it wasn't their place to pry. Their friend was happy, and Jack was good to her, and that was all that mattered to them. Lulu watched her friend when she spoke of Jack and could see she was in love with him. Jack was the first person she actually trusted, and for some reason, she knew Vivian would be safe with him.

The three of them talked a little about work, and Vivian expressed how glad she would be when this project was over. She told the girls that she always felt like something was about to happen whenever she was at Aaron's home and that as beautiful as it was, there was something unsettling about it. She told the girls about the sedan she kept seeing and how, at first, she thought Jack was checking up on her, but he was ruled out when they saw it together. "Do you think someone is following you, Viv," her young friend asked. "I don't know, but I get the feeling someone is watching me, and that creeps me out." Let's change the subject, Vivian said, and they all agreed. Tonight is all about relaxing and having a good time. They listened to music, drank a little too much and ate snacks that were normally "no bueno." Henry was in heaven, getting all the attention from three of his favorite people. Vivian invited the girls to spend the night and promised a yummy breakfast if they did. She loved to cook and didn't get to very often these days. "It's a deal," they chimed in unison. They stayed up late, caught an old classic movie and were bleary-eyed by the time it was over. Empty bottles were strewn everywhere, and they all knew it was going to be hell if they didn't get some sleep. Vivian took two aspirin, drank a bottle of water, and gave the same to her friends. She swore by it, and sure enough, in the morning, she didn't feel so bad and neither did they. Breakfast was amazing, and Vivian pulled out all the stops. The Bloody Marys were heaven, and by the time they headed their separate ways, they were feeling pretty good. Little did Vivian's friends know as they hugged her and said their goodbyes that by week's end, all hell would break loose, and their friend's life would be turned upside down.

Zac was distracted, and Vivian was getting annoyed with him more and more as the week went on. She finally had had enough and confronted him in the family room. "Zac, I don't know what is eating you, but you really had better snap out of it. Mr. Walters is paying a lot of money to make sure things are exactly as he asked, and if we keep having to do things over, it's going to be a problem. Zac turned and looked at his employer, his friend and for just a moment, he wanted to tell her, but he was frightened of what would happen if he did. He told her he had not slept much the night before, which wasn't a lie and promised her that he would get his shit together. Two days, just two more days. Dammit, how did I get myself into this mess? What if something went wrong? His employer's plan was foolproof, and he shouldn't have been worried, but there was a lot at stake. He thought less and less about the money he was being paid and more about his life. Vivian's life.

When they were ready to leave for the day, for some reason unknown to Vivian, he hugged her. He never hugged her, and she knew something was terribly wrong. He released her and ran to his car, taking off like a bat out of hell. She stood in the driveway, perplexed. What the hell was that, she thought. She figured the project had him on edge, and things would return to normal Friday when she picked up their last check and rid themselves of Mr. Walters. Zac had never given her an answer to the offer she had posed weeks earlier so she figured he was not interested. As she drove back to the city, she had Jack on her mind and planned to call him when she got home. She missed him and needed to hear his voice. As she exited the freeway, she saw the black sedan again at a roadside store. She pulled over so that she could get a glimpse of who got into the waiting car. Who she saw stopped her breath. Aaron Walters. He was supposed to be out of the country, so why was he here? Did he come back early? Did he ever leave? She ducked out of sight as the car sped past, hoping he didn't see her, which was pointless because he had seen her car several times before and knew what she drove.

She hurried home and called Jack right away. For some unknown reason, she didn't tell him about the sedan, figuring he would tell her she was worried about nothing and that it wouldn't be unusual for someone to return from a trip unannounced. When she thought about it for a minute, she saw the legitimacy of that theory. Aaron was a man of mystery, so it wouldn't be a reach for him. She and Jack had a good conversation, and he promised to be home in time for the weekend and that he missed her as well. She was to meet him at their place as she would be finished with the project and would no longer have to stay in the city all the time. As they were about to hang up, she said it. He had never said it before, and it warmed her heart, and she replied in kind. "I love you too, Jack." After the call, she relaxed, making a small meal for herself and one for Henry. She was catching up on some long overdue emails and mail when the telephone rang. She heard Zac's voice on the other end and was a little surprised that he would be calling after hours, something he had never done. "Hey Zac, what's up?" There was a pause at the other end until Zac responded. "Did you get a message from Mr. Walters," he asked. Vivian hadn't checked her phone and quickly looked to see. There was a message, and it stated that there was a problem at the house that needed to be addressed immediately. She thought it odd that he knew there was a problem because he was supposed to be out of the country, and she had not reported anything to him regarding any type of situation.

Vivian was a little put out that he expected her to drive all the way out to the location at this time of the night. "I'm going to wait until morning Zac. I'm not driving all the way out there when we have to be there first thing anyway." Zac panicked for a moment, then quickly reminded his employer that if they waited, that would add an additional day to the project. He knew Vivian would not want that. Vivian hated to admit it, but Zac was right. "Fine, we'll go out there, but dammit, there had better be a real problem or else!" She told Zac she would meet him there in about an hour, and she hurried to get dressed for the ride. She was pissed and wove a string of cuss words that had Henry peering out from behind the chair. She grabbed her coat and keys and was out the door, slamming it as she left. An hour later, she pulled onto the property, seeing Zac's car as she drove up. The lights were on, and as she entered, she had a feeling she couldn't explain. She felt fear, and instinctively, she turned in an effort to leave, but her feet wouldn't carry her to the door. She was shaking and knew the telltale signs of a panic attack coming on. She hadn't had one in years, and she knew right away that something bad would happen if she stayed there. "Run, Vivian," the voice in her head screamed out, but it was too late. Just as she reached for the door, she felt a sting in her neck as if she were bitten by a bee or something, and at that moment, Vivian's whole world became liquid. Her last thought before she passed out was of Jack.

Vivian woke in a dimly lit room with a small window, a bed and a bathroom. A wardrobe stood in the corner of the room and, oddly enough, a television, but there was not much else. She let out a scream, but it bounced off the walls and echoed, frightening her. She tried to get up from the bed, but her head felt heavy, and she knew she had been drugged. Questions spun in her head. "Where the hell am I," she thought. The last thing she remembered was walking into Aaron's house. Was she still there? Had she been taken somewhere else? What the hell was happening? She got up and went to one of the two doors to the room. She pounded on it, calling out for someone, anyone, to answer. It was of no use. Nobody heard her, and nobody came. She began to cry, then she got mad. Usually, when the tears stopped, she would have a plan formulated, but in this case, she was at a loss. She went into the bathroom, splashing cold water on her face. She looked around and could see it was well stocked, as if it had been prepared just for her. A chill ran up her back when she saw that all of the items were what she would purchase and use at home. Aaron was involved in this and must have been watching her for a long time to know what she liked. Her worst fears had come to light, and she knew that he was in this to harm her, but why? What had she done to deserve this? She couldn't begin to reason the logic in all that was happening, but she did know that it was bad. Very bad.

She looked out the window and could see what she was sure was the outline of trees. It was still dark, and she wondered what time it was. She reached for her phone in her pocket, but it had been removed, of course. She knew she had to do something, but what? He had tricked her into returning, and she felt like a fool for having believed him. Where was Zac? She hoped he had not been injured and prayed he had been able to escape before he became a captive as well. Someone had to eventually come to check on her, but in the meantime, with nothing to do but worry, she lay down to try to rid her head of the terrible pounding. The only bright spot in all of this is Jack. She knew he would find her, and she had no doubt that Aaron would be on the receiving end of his anger. Vivian fell into a restless sleep, and a short time later, she awoke to keys being put in the lock of the door. She stood, ready to attack whoever came through it if she had to die trying. Zac came through the door carrying a tray, and Vivian felt like she had been punched in the stomach. "You son of a bitch, you're a part of this? What the hell is going on? Zac stepped back for a moment, not saying a word, but when he did, she wished he had remained silent.

Vivian, you have to do everything I say, or he is going to hurt both of us. Zac looked at her and felt so terribly guilty that he was a part of all this as soon as he saw the fear in her eyes. "I don't give a shit what the hell he does to you, but nobody is going to hurt me, and you can bet your ass on that," she spat at him like a viper. "He's very dangerous, Vivian, and if you disobey it, it will not be good for you." He's done terrible things to people, and he WILL NOT care what he does to you. Vivian just looked at him as if he were a stranger. I trusted you, Zac. How could you do this to me? I don't even know who you are right now. Please just leave me alone. Zac realized he was still holding the tray and sat down, telling her she should eat something. "Shove it up your ass," she replied vehemently. He left the tray on the table and turned to leave. "Vivian, remember what I said, do everything he tells you." It's the only way you might have a chance to survive, and then he left her alone with the words he had just said. She looked at the tray of food, and in a mixture of anger and fear, she hurled it across the room. She would rather die than accept anything from either of them. She was exhausted, but as terrified as she was to sleep, she lay down and closed her eyes, praying that this was just a dream and that in the light of day, she would awake and all the bad would be gone. Sadly, it would not.

Vivian opened her eyes, and Aaron was in the room. She sat up, startled by him, and although she had worked with this man for months, who she now saw was someone quite different. He had a menacing look on his face, and his eyes were darkened by the evil inside him. When he spoke, his voice was deep and almost a whisper. It frightened her; he saw it in her eyes, and he was pleased by her fear. She started to speak, but he ordered her to stay quiet and not ask questions. She didn't care and defiantly made it clear to him that she was not afraid of him and that if she had the chance, she would escape and make sure he was sent to prison, that is, if Jack didn't get a hold of him first. He let forth a sinister laugh and told her she should be very afraid and that nobody would ever find her until it was too late. "What did I ever do to you, Aaron? I just work for you." I don't even know you. He sat down, looking right into her eyes and what he said next made her die just a little inside. "Ah, Vivian, you have no idea how valuable you are to me, but you will, and you will do everything I tell you, or life will be very bad for you." He grabbed her tightly and kissed her. She felt sickened by his touch and stood lifeless as he attempted to seduce her. He placed his hand on her breast and squeezed so hard that it hurt, but she never reacted. This enraged him, and he drew back and slapped her hard in the face. "I said you WILL do what I want, Vivian." She tried very hard to hold back her tears. She would never give him the satisfaction he was looking for. She relaxed a little, and he let his guard down for a moment too long and felt her rage as she landed a knee on his crotch.

Aaron let go of her in pain, and for a moment, she thought he would hit her again, but he just laughed and said, "If you want a fight, we'll do it that way, you bitch. You'll learn." He was out the door before she had a chance to say another word, but she knew what he meant, and she knew he would be back, and she was afraid. Her face stung from the slap, and she saw the red welt as she looked in the mirror. Bastard! Her hands were shaking, and she tried her best to calm down. She thought of Jack and wanted to be in his arms, away from this place and away from this man. "Oh, Jack, I know you won't give up until you find me." Please find me. Little did Vivian know at that very moment Jack was indeed looking for her.

He had come home to find the house empty. It wasn't unusual because Vivian was wrapping up the project, and she had been working late hours, so it was more convenient for her. What was odd was that he had been trying to call her, and her phone kept going straight to voicemail. That never happened. Vivian always had her phone turned on, and it was rare that she would let her battery run down completely. Jack went to her apartment, and Henry was the only one home, and he was not happy. He had no food, and his water bowl was not only empty but very dry, as if it had been sitting for a while. Jack took care of his furry friend and looked around for telltale signs of her being there recently but came up short. There were small things, however, that struck him as curious and a bit unsettling because he knew Vivian and knew her habits. He looked for an address book. "Do people still keep address books," he asked Henry, who ignored him as he ate what Jack had put down for him. On the table that housed her phone, he spotted one. Of course, she would have one. It was the weekend, so he didn't bother to call her office, knowing nobody would answer. Jack didn't want to worry Vivian's friends, but he knew that if anyone had spoken to her, it would be them. She always touched base with them and made it a point to never be too busy for a chat with her girls. He dialed Lulu, and when she answered, he added Jamie to the call. Their first question before he even had a chance to say anything was if Vivian was alright. They thought it was odd that Jack would be calling for any other reason, and they were instantly concerned for their friend. He asked if either of them had spoken with her and if they knew what her final plans for the house design were. Neither of them had spoken to her, and they assumed she was on her last day, the Friday that just passed. They were unaware of the call from Zac and the unscheduled trip to the house.

Lulu, who never usually panicked, panicked. She had never really trusted Aaron, and even though Vivian had assured her that she would be fine and that it was just work, she was still worried. She felt that it was him in the sedan that they had seen on several occasions, although nobody could prove it. Jack asked the girls if they knew the location of the house or the address at least. Neither girl knew but told him that Derrell would have that information. Dammit! He couldn't wait until Monday for it and asked the girls if there was a way for him to be contacted after hours. Derrell didn't like Jack, and Jack was afraid he would be difficult when approached or asked anything that had anything to do with Vivian. He didn't like the way Derrell looked at Vivian, and some of the stories the girls thought were gross and stupid worried him. Derrell fit the profile of a predator, always around, always conveniently showing up uninvited. Vivian had said he was harmless, but Jack was not as sure. Jack told the girls he would keep them updated and that if they heard from her, they should have her call him immediately. He hung up, knowing they would worry until they saw their friend again and knew she was alright. He dialed the number Lulu had given him for Derrell, but there was no answer. He left a message that it was urgent that he call back as soon as he received it.

In the meantime, he called on his partners and began working from his end, tracking her whereabouts. Cell phones could be tracked if the location feature was on, but he really wasn't sure if Vivian used it or not. She didn't like the idea of the whole world knowing where she was and what she was doing. One of his guys found some information that would have brought a weaker man to his knees, but what Jack read only infuriated him, and he knew in his heart that Vivian's disappearance was no small matter. He directed his men to keep looking. He called Derrell again, but no answer. Dammit! Where the hell is this guy? He left message after message for him, but Derrell never called back, and by the afternoon, Jack was no closer to finding out where she was. He rifled through all the paperwork she had on her desk, hoping to find a shred of information that would be helpful. Nothing. He knew he couldn't just sit there. He had to leave, had to do something. He found Derrell's address on his social media page, fed the cat and grabbed his coat. "Don't worry, buddy, I'll bring her back. I promise."

Twenty minutes later, he pulled in front of Derrell's place. No car was in the drive, but he went to the door anyway. He knocked, but nobody answered. He knocked again, and an elderly lady opened the door. He asked to speak to Derrell, but she said he wasn't home and she hadn't seen him for a few days. He left a message with his number for her and asked her to make sure he got it as soon as he arrived. She assured him that she would and closed the door, leaving him no better off than he had been before. Driving down the road, he went over everything he did have in his head. Nothing fit, nothing made sense. This was what he did all the time, and yet he could not piece this together and find her. He had hoped that Derrell would be able to give him an address, phone number, or anything that would help. He knew Vivian had an assistant. Dammit, why hadn't he remembered that sooner! He worked with Vivian every day and knew her schedule, but most importantly, he knew the address of Aaron Walter's place. If he found Zac, he would find Vivian. Little did he know how true that thought would be. He called Lulu and asked her what she knew about him that might help. She told him Zac was hired through a temp agency, gave him the name and didn't have time to say much more before he hung up and was on the phone to the agency. The after-hours service answered, and after explaining that it was an emergency and that he needed to reach Zac right away, she gave him the phone number and address.

Jack dialed the number as he sped down the road toward the address. Nobody answered, and his voicemail was not set up. He got to Zac's place and was greeted with the same empty space where a car should have been, and no answer when he knocked on the door. What the hell is going on here? He's not here; Derrell is not there. No phone calls. Where the hell is everybody? All of a sudden, it clicked. The two people who should know everything about Vivian's whereabouts were nowhere to be found. Something about that set-off alarms. His phone rang, jolting him back to the present. The call was coming from an unknown number, but he plugged in his tracker anyway. He answered and knew immediately that it was Derrell finally calling back. Jack couldn't stand the guy, but this was about Vivian, so he was going to be as decent as he could be. Hey man, thanks for calling back. This is Jack, and I was wondering if you've heard from Vivian at all. He went on to say that he knew she was finishing up the project at the Walters mansion, but nobody had heard from her or seen her in a couple of days, and he was worried she may have had an accident or something, so could he give him the address so that he could run out there and check on her. There was silence at the other, and Jack thought for a minute that he had lost the call, but what he heard next would cut him to the core.

"Well, Jack, that little bitch didn't have an accident, but when we're through with her, she will wish she were dead, " he stated with a laugh that chilled even Jack. "You will never find her, and if, just if, you do manage to, it will be too late because if anyone comes near here, she's as good as dead." He continued. "She's gonna pay for every shitty thing she ever did or said when she thought I wasn't looking, and she will regret the day she ever messed with me. We'll just see who thinks they're better, and trust me, it won't be her." Jack's blood boiled, and when he spoke, his words resonated in a tone that would strike fear in most men and definitely in a cowardly scumbag like Derrell. No threats, no ultimatums, no deals. Just one sentence. "If you do anything to hurt her, I'll kill you with my bare hands." Derrell just laughed, and the call ended, leaving Jack to hope he had not just sealed Vivian's fate. When he arrived at Vivian's place, he saw a vehicle that he knew to be one of his partners'. Tim had a serious look on his face, and when Jack walked up to where he stood, his friend said calmly, "We have to talk."

Chapter Twenty-Two

For the first time in Vivian's life, she was free. Free from controlling relationships, free from always having to share a space in her square with someone else. She was free to breathe, and as she exhaled the toxic past, she smelled the sweet scent of pure bliss. She loved her apartment, which was complete with the two furry friends she had just added, Lilly and Lola. They ran the home while she worked at a company she had been at since she got out of jail. She had a nice nest egg that she had saved while living with Ray, so she relaxed and reveled in her newfound surroundings. Vivian had recently reunited with her friend Shelly and her family after having lost contact with her for quite some time. She had missed their friendship, and when she heard the all too familiar voice of her friend while shopping one day, she was overjoyed. God works in mysterious ways, and she knew that it was he who had brought them back together. She felt that there were people who were meant to be in her life, and it was her friend. Vivian fell right back into the fold as if she never left. Vivian's friend Cari was also a coworker who lived in the same complex as she did, and they had a blast. Cari had lost her husband, and in a way, she was going through the same change as Vivian, just in a different way.

She was the opposite of Vivian in every way, and they learned new things from each other. Cari loved Vivian's carefree attitude and wished she had the courage to stand up for herself like Vivian did. She wanted to be tough and strong like her friend, but it just wasn't natural for her, so she let it go. They were sitting poolside one-day drinking margaritas when Cari said something that stuck in Vivian's mind long after their conversation. She knew friendship meant everything to her friend, but in that one moment, she doubted Vivian's loyalty to her, and right then, Vivian knew it was the beginning of the end of them.

She went home that day wondering if she was just another person in her life that she had to prove something. "I'm done with that shit," she muttered, but she was still hurt by the discovery.

Vivian had very few friends. Those friends had stood the test of time and understood what it meant to be a friend. She was never good at meeting new people and had a hard time opening up, but with good reason. She trusted her friends and knew that they would be there for her, and they knew the same about her. Her friends didn't judge her, didn't expect anything from her other than her friendship, and gave that one hundred percent, so when someone like Cari assumed that she was not loyal, it spoke volumes. In the coming months, Vivian tried her best to work on the friendship because it was important to her, but she felt that she was the only one putting in the work. On one occasion, when they were thrifting together, Vivian found some clothing she would never have dared to wear before, but because she had lost a significant amount of weight, she felt confident in her new skin, so she bought some very short skirts and tops that revealed more than she ever showed off before. When they got back to the apartment, Vivian tried them on and modeled them for Cari to get her opinion. They had had a great day, and she hoped it would continue. Cari had a dog named Tug, and when Vivian came out of the room with her new outfit on, she held up the damn dog and stated, "Look at your Aunt dressed up like a slut, Tug!" Vivian was crushed but would be damned to let this woman know just how much she had hurt her feelings.

After Cari left, Vivian showered and got ready to go out for the evening. She had discovered a corner bar right down the street that didn't look like much but was always busy. She liked holes in the wall. Some of the best people came out of those types of places, and she felt she would try it on to see how it fit for her. By the time she was done getting ready, she looked and felt like a million bucks, and she was ready for some fun, something that had been lost to Vivian, and she planned to do something about it. Cari called, probably to apologize like she always did after hurting Vivian's feelings, but she let it go to voicemail, not really wanting to hear another empty "I'm sorry" from her. Plus, she was in too good of a mood to have a wet rag dampen her spirits. She checked her handbag, grabbed a jacket, said something cute to her furry roommates and was out the door headed to Harry's Place.

The crowd was pretty good for a weeknight, and Vivian(Veronica) was having a blast. She introduced herself as Veronica, a name she had chosen long ago as her bar name. She didn't like people to know her real name unless they were solid friends, so Veronica it was. She had caught the eye of many of the men, and she flirted a little too much, but it was harmless and all in good fun. Harry, the bar owner, kept asking her all night where Betty and Scooby were, and Vivian swore she saw Brad Pitt, but not really. In the months ahead, Vivian would meet people there who would become her friends, and some would be in her life for many years as well. A few would hate her, some would like her, and only a handful would love her, and she would carry them in her heart until the end of days.

It didn't take Vivian long to become a regular customer at Harry's. She liked it there. She could be herself, well sort of, and she was in charge for the first time, and that meant everything to her. She was having fun, but her mind took her to Ray every day. She spoke with him a lot and went to see him as well. She missed him more than she thought she would, but he seemed to be feeling just fine with his newfound freedom. She wished he would tell her that he missed her, but she knew that it wasn't his style, unfortunately. She still felt the need to make sure he was alright and probably always would. It was who she was.

Vivian wasn't a slut by any means, but she was getting her fill of male suitors never less. She didn't want a boyfriend. She already had one, kind of, but it had been years since she and Ray had any intimate interaction. It wasn't because he didn't want to, it was the meds. Always the meds. It seemed as if the damn meds always got in the way of everything and were the basis, she believed, for the bulk of their problems. "I'm still young and should be getting it on a regular," she told her friend one day. "I mean, sex isn't the basis for a relationship, but it is necessary!" she added. Shelly agreed. She couldn't believe the number of years it had been for her friend. "Girl! You're doin better than me cuz there's no way I'm goin without for that long!" Hell no! They laughed about it, but there was truth in it just the same.

Harry's girlfriend Jeanni and Vivian had formed a friendship that years later would still be a topic of many conversations. They never knew how they met or when they met, but after they did, they were inseparable. If they saw one, they saw the other. Vivian liked her, although many of the patrons at Harry's did not. They say you're judged by the company you keep, but Vivian doesn't care. She liked her company. They partied their asses off, and Jeanni was always down, no matter when to party. They drank in the morning when Vivian was off work and drank throughout the day until Jeanni would leave to go home. She never stayed out too late unless something extra was happening at Harry's. Vivian, however, started closing the bar, and it would end up being a problem for her.

Vivian met a man who was a lawyer until he wasn't, and they liked each other immediately. MD was a great guy, one of a kind, and they became the very best of friends. He called her Ronnie most days and Vivian only when he was upset with her. He came into Harry's often, and when she was there, they would hang out together. Vivian hung out at his place, and he came to hers. They talked about everything, and it was a comfortable feeling for her when she was around him. Vivian liked to cook Italian food, and he liked to eat Italian food, so they started having get-togethers with other friends from Harry's, where Vivian would show off her talent. It became a regular thing for them. They all drank their asses off, smoked a little weed and enjoyed each other's company, hanging out on the patio with great music playing. It was the best of times, and Vivian loved her relationship with him. MD was the only one that Vivian came clean with, and he knew things about her life, her real life, that nobody did. They were that close. She trusted him with her heart and soul. He would have been the perfect boyfriend had they not been as close as they were as friends. One night, when they were hanging out at his place, they tried to mess around but ended up laughing so hard that both of them knew it was not meant to be, so they relaxed and enjoyed what they had together. She had never felt that close to someone before, and he meant the world to her. He was her best friend, her confidant and her sleepover buddy.

Life was good for Vivian, and she was happy until she wasn't. One night, she took one of the guys from the bar that she had her eye on and his friend back to her place to smoke some weed and play some foozeball. To her, it was harmless, but Joe's friend had other things on his mind, and after hours of partying, they all laid down to sleep it off. The guys rode bikes and didn't want to drive home, and Vivian had plenty of room, so they all split up and crashed. In the morning, before Vivian could even see, the smell of stale alcohol permeated her senses, and she felt something or someone lying heavy on her chest. She thought it was Joe at first, but as her vision cleared, she was appalled and sickened to see his friend groping her. She pushed him off her and jumped up, pissed as hell, and was cussing his ass out when Joe woke up. Sadly, he didn't say anything, and she asked the two of them to leave. It wouldn't be until months later that Vivian would approach them at Harry's, and she would let him have it. After the two left, she felt dirty, violated and disgusted that he would have done that, but she was more pissed at herself for letting them in, assuming they had the same intentions as she had. She got in the shower, and as she was scrubbing him off her, she cried. Later that day, she would confide in MD because he would understand, console her and give his opinion without hurting her feelings. He was like that. Another of the many reasons she loved him.

One snowy night about a year into Vivian's new adventure, she was leaving the bar after a couple of cocktails when she slipped on the ice and landed flat on her back. "Son of a bitch!" she cried out. She felt immediate pain in her back and knew she had hurt it, but she didn't know just how serious it was until days later when she went to the doctor, had X-rays and received the diagnosis. She could barely walk and knew it was serious before he even told her that she had a hair-line fracture and she would need to take time off work to heal. "How much time off," she asked. Six to eight weeks was not what she wanted to hear. She needed to work. Her rent and car payments took up a lot of her checks, and she was barely making it. LOA with short-term disability only paid so much, and she knew she wouldn't be able to stretch it to make ends meet. She sought out Shelly's advice, and she said something that made sense, but Vivian dreaded it. "Girl, you own that house, so you will never be out on the streets again. If you have to, you might have to move back in for a while until you get back on your feet, literally." Vivian knew her friend was right, but she dreaded the thought of it. She had tucked her tail many times before, and she hated the idea of moving back into the house and having to see the smug "I told you so" look on Ray's face.

In the Spring of Two Thousand and Eleven, moving day came without fanfare, and the silence in the house was palpable. Vivian was back where she had started, and she felt defeated. She fell into a state of depression and stayed holed up in her room, feeling like a stranger in the rest of the house. Her friends from Harry's kept in touch, but that just made her feel worse. She missed them. She missed her time alone. She missed her freedom. "Why is this happening to me again," she asked herself over and over. She was pissy towards Ray, and he treated her the same way. The tension was so thick it could be cut with a knife. For some reason, he thought she was back for good, which was so far from being true, so he decided to set ground rules. Ground Rules? Seriously? Hello! It was her freaking house, but she was in too much pain to fight, and so she submitted. Again.

Five weeks into a grueling physical therapy schedule, which was helping some, Vivian felt a replenished strength from within. Screw him and his rules. I'm doing this and getting the hell outta here she repeated over and over until it was ingrained in her psyche, and that was exactly what she did in the Spring of Two Thousand and Twelve.

Vivian told Ray that their living situation was not working and that she was moving out. Again. He was pissed as hell and had the nerve to try to give her an ultimatum. "If you freaking leave this time, don't try to come back again," he growled through his teeth. She told him that she didn't want to fight and that they should be able to work things out like adults, but he was beyond all logic and refused to lift a finger to help her move her things to the Fredricks apartments across town. She had been returned to active status at her job, and as luck would have it, the building was located a stone's throw away from Vivian's apartment. "Well, there won't be any snow days for me," Vivian joked.

She moved just about everything she owned in her car and finally convinced Ray to let her use his truck for the furniture. It cost her, though, but she really didn't care. She was out! "Yes, Virginia, there is a Santa Claus!" she shouted as she pulled out of the drive with the last of her belongings. Once in her apartment and back to work, she felt at peace again. She loved her alone time, and her apartment was very comfortable. Jeanni dubbed the huge tree in the backyard "her tree" because it stood alone, and that was reason enough. Something was different this time, however, but Vivian was blind to see what lay ahead. Although she was back at Harry's and surrounded by her friends, something happened, and she went wild. Partying every night, waking up just in time to go to work, messing around where she shouldn't have and being careless. It was as if she was trying to fit everything she had missed her whole life into a small space of time. She met a biker who had no inhibitions and expected her to react the same. He gave handcuffs a new meaning, and he spent hours with Vivian until she begged him to leave. They did things she would never talk about and never do again, and she couldn't get enough of him. They used each other for sex and didn't feel guilty about it. She knew it would end one day, but she didn't care. She wanted him, and she wanted him to do bad things to her just as long as he wanted to. For the rest of her life, if she smelled Polo Black, she felt a little something down there. Damn, biker.

Her job relocated her to a new building where she met Kitty and Charlie. They both loved the party circuit, and they hung out quite often. They would still be very close friends of Vivian's(Jane) many years later. Now Charlie was a crazy, fun party girl who, like Vivian, liked hanging out, staying out late and drinking like there was no tomorrow. They fit like a glove. Their friendship was easy, and many nights, they bar-hopped till the wee hours of the morning. She hung out with Charlie more than she did Kitty because there was never a plan, just a let's go and then going. Kitty was a planner and liked a good venue. They hung out with his people because Vivian made him relax and laugh. They were good for each other, and the time she spent with him was what memories are made of. Kitty and Charlie came over one day to see Vivian's new kitty. He was a precious boy kitty named Big Boy who loved Vivian immediately. He was a one in a million, and Vivian adored him. Vivian and Kitty sat around getting stoned (Charlie was in the Army Reserves, so she couldn't), playing with the cat and chatting around, and then the funniest, most ridiculous thing happened to Charlie. At first, they thought she was getting sick because she had her hand over her mouth, but she wasn't. She had a tongue piercing, and the ball got stuck between two of her teeth, and she couldn't get it unstuck. Vivian and Kitty fell out laughing so hard that Vivian almost peed on her new sofa. Whether it was the weed or the situation, they couldn't stop laughing. Years later, they would reminisce about that day and laugh every time. It's funny what sticks and doesn't. Pardon the pun.

Chapter Twenty-Three

Things were going along fine until they weren't. After about a year or so, Vivian and Karl (MD renamed him) moved into Kitty's basement apartment to save money. Times were tough for her, but she was not going to let it get her down. She had formed a bond with Kitty, and they were very close friends. He was willing to help her out and didn't mind her being there because he loved her company. He told her several times she was like a mother figure to him as well as a friend, and she felt good inside. She was still seeing the biker, and he didn't care where she was. He followed her there. MD didn't like him, so Vivian did her best to keep that part of her personal life separate from their friendship. Her back was getting worse every day, but she laughed it off, telling Kitty it was because of all the wild sex she and the biker were having. It wasn't far from the truth, but some things are better left untold. One day, while she was chilling at the house, she got a call from Ray. By then, they were back on speaking terms, so she wasn't surprised to hear his voice on the other end of the line.

"I've got cancer, and I need your help," he said softly into the phone. She didn't blink an eye, and for the next few months, Vivian drove back and forth, helping him get through the radiation treatments and the sickness and just be there for him so he wouldn't have to do it on his own. Sadly, he would forget that when she needed him the most, but it didn't matter to her. She would have helped him anyway. That's the person she was.

Her friend Shelly reminded her one day and many times after that Vivian and Ray were always going to be in each other's lives, and she was meant to be the one to help him when he needed her. She made sense of things when Vivian's faith faltered, and she always felt better after speaking with her.

Vivian was sitting by herself one night when the tall, cool drink of water walked in and sat down beside her. She had been trying forever to see what he was all about, but it hadn't happened, so she stopped trying. They proceeded to drink the night away, and near closing time, he got up to leave. As he walked by her, he whispered an invitation to his place in her ear. He then left, leaving her to wonder if she should or shouldn't. "Yes, you should, Vivian," and she did. It was delicious and well worth the wait. It was the best one-night stand she had ever had, and she would never forget it or him. He would cross her mind many years later, and she would always smile.

Vivian's finances were in a better place, and she decided it was time to move out again. She and Kitty talked about it, and he supported her, although he would be sad to see her go. He was used to her being there, and he would miss their morning coffee and nap on her giant chaise lounge chair. Charlie was already living in the complex where Vivian was moving, and she was happy to have her in the building next door to hers. She didn't like being alone, so she wasn't there much, but they still worked together, drank together, and saw each other a lot. They would walk to the gas station and feast on Jumbo hot dogs with Cheese and a big fountain pop. It was those days that Vivian was the happiest. Her back was still bothering her, and it was making it harder every day for her to move around without pain. She was back and forth to the doctors on a regular and had even talked with him about a breast reduction to help relieve her pain. She was missing more and more time at work and was in fear of being fired if she didn't do something. Very few people knew exactly how much pain she was in because Vivian never complained. Charlie was also going through some things and decided that she wanted to leave Nebraska and move to Kansas. Vivian was saddened by the news, but she supported her friend's decision and was there to see her off in the morning. She packed her things, hungover and all and loaded them onto her relative's trailer for the drive out of town. She knew that no matter how far away Charlie went, they would always be friends. Always. Even so, as she watched her friend drive away, she shed a tear. After she left, Vivian went to meet up with MD. He always made her feel better, and she needed him to cheer her up. She felt a storm brewing, and in the days and weeks ahead, Vivian's resolve would be put to the test, and she would need more than cheering up. She would need a miracle.

She lay flat on her back in her apartment, and not for any good reason. It was the only position she could handle without pain. She hadn't been out in weeks and only moved when she really had to. MD came over every day, bringing her food and cigarettes. "I have to get up," she stated flatly to him, so he did his best to help her to her feet, knowing she wasn't going to get far but wanted to help his friend in any way he could. At her last visit, the doctor had said she had the back of an eighty-year-old and without intervention, it would only get worse. He also would not sign a release for her to return to work. "Under no circumstances are you to go back any time soon and not at all if it were up to me." Her landlord had given her her last extension and was on the verge of giving her an eviction notice. Ray was being a jerk and was of no help to her at all. He acted like her back problem was her own undoing for moving out, like some sick karma for wanting to keep her sanity intact. She knew she was out of options and time was running out. "Why does this shit keep happening to me? Why is my life so messed up? When do I get a break?" she screamed out through tears of frustration. MD could only tell her that it would pass and that she could handle it. Maybe Ray was right. Maybe she had messed up so many times that this was her punishment. She knew that it wasn't true. God knew her heart and knew his plan for her. Well, it could hurt a little less along the way, dammit.

In July of Twenty Fourteen, Vivian walked into the company she had worked at for sixteen years and walked out with no gold watch, no cake or parting gifts, nothing but her medical resignation with the ink still wet. She sat in MD's Wagoneer and cried. He knew his friend's world was crumbling and was helpless to make it all go away. The movers were coming the next morning, and everything she was taking with her was ready to go. Some of her favorite things were being dragged to the apartment across the hall, along with the memories they held. Vivian had grown used to it. She had given a lifetime of things away, and to her, it was normal. She hadn't asked Ray if she could move back in. Hello no! She informed him she was coming back, slammed down the phone, and that was the end of it. MD was going to drive her to the house because there was no way she would survive a ride across the city in a U-Haul. He wanted so badly to chew Ray's ass out, but he knew it would just make things worse for Vivian, so he promised her that he wouldn't. He spent her last night in the apartment with her, a bottle of Moscato and take-out pizza, all her favorites.

The truck arrived on the south side bright and early (on purpose), and her belongings were divided between the garage and the front bedroom, which thankfully had its own entrance. There was no way she taking that walk of shame in front of him. Screw that! MD said his goodbyes, and as she sat down on her bed, she was keenly aware of the dark days ahead. She had met with a lawyer and had filed for SSDI, so it was all just a waiting game that would last two and a half years in pure hell. During this time, Vivian would endure heartache, pain, and a loss she never could have imagined, and she would do it all alone with only the comfort of words from her friends to keep her from losing her mind.

Vivian didn't know what kind of shit Ray was trying to pull, but it was some shit! He labeled things. Yes, labeled them. Food, pantry items, hygiene products, you name it, he put his name on it. It was pretty childish, but Vivian didn't let it get to her. She just laughed it off, which just served to piss him off even more. She had to order public transportation because he refused to drive her anywhere. Doctor's appointments had to be arranged around a ride, and her back was failing as a result. He just didn't care. The only thing he did care about was the nursery he had and the money he was making from his garden.

He gave her no money, and she had to rely on her family and friends for any help she needed to support herself until her case was settled and she could start getting a check on a regular basis. If she spent any time with friends, he acted like an ass when she got home.

Vivian drank to forget. He called her names when she would come to the house with a buzz, but she didn't care. She prayed every day for strength and cried herself to sleep at night. One night after she had returned from spending time at Harry's, she and Ray had a major blow-out of a fight, and she kicked his dope friends out and then proceeded to throw his shit out the front door as well. She had had enough. "Get the hell out and don't come back," she fired at him. "I'm tired of your shit and your friends. I'm tired of you treating me like something you scraped off your shoe! Where were your buddies when you needed someone to wipe your ass?" Ray had never seen her that mad, and although he knew she had a temper, it had never come to this before. She was furious. When she woke up the next day to find him still there, she flipped out again. "What are you still doing here?" He looked like one of the lost boys because he knew he had no place to go. "Where are your friends now?" she said belligerently.

Things changed after that. Ray tiptoed around for a while and hoped Vivian would cool off. He really had pushed her too far, and for once, he felt bad for a minute. He still didn't voluntarily support her financially, but she had to have money to live on, so she made a deal with him that whatever money she needed, he would give it to her, and she would pay it back when she got her settlement. Pretty shitty that she had to do that for him to help her, but she was trapped and had no other alternative but to negotiate. It was a shame after all the help and support she had given him when he was laid up and was in the same boat as her. Vivian reminded him that she was the one who had supported the household while he was waiting for his disability. She wiped his ass and stayed by his side through his transplant and recovery. She nursed him back to health when he had a second heart attack, but he didn't seem to think any of that was relevant. She would owe him, and she would pay him. "Bastard," she said as he left the room and hoped he heard her.

Vivian loved the holidays, especially Christmas. Not so much for the gifts, but she loved to decorate, watch holiday movies and sing along (a little too loud) with the festive songs on the radio. Ray's mom must have told him to lighten up a little because when she put up the tree, he said nothing. Ray went to his mom's for Christmas dinner, but Vivian was not invited, so she made some food at the house for herself, sat in the kitchen by herself and ate by herself. The end of Twenty Fourteen would come and go quietly, and she hoped the New Year would be better. Sadly, it would not.

Vivian looked out the window and prayed for Spring. It had been predictably frigid, and they had seen more than their fair share of snow for the year. She was eating herself into a stupor and had put on what she called her "winter weight." Most would say she had just got fat. Screw them, she thought to herself as she squeezed into a pair of sweatpants thinking they really weren't meant for everyone, something she thought she would never say. Her sister Lyla reminded her regularly that she was always welcome in Arizona and all she had to do was ask. Vivian was tempted but knew she had to stay in Nebraska if she ever wanted to get her disability. She listened to the weather report as Bill read off the numbers for the next week. An unusually warm spell was ahead, and they could expect temperatures in the 40s for a few days. That lifted Vivian's spirits, and she formulated a get-out-of-the-house plan immediately. She just had to get out and see her friends, and this was her window to climb out of.

January Fourteenth started with sunshine and a warm breeze. Thank you, God, and thank you, Bill! Around one pm, she headed for the bus stop. She didn't dare ask Ray for a ride. It was too nice of a day, and she didn't want him to ruin it for her. She was used to taking the bus and knew the schedule to get across town to Harry's. Three transfers later, she was in front of her stomping grounds, and she was happy. She met Jeannie there, and together they spent much of the afternoon catching up and agreeing whole hardheartedly that Ray was an ass. Harry treated Jeanni much the same as Ray, but in her eyes, he could do no wrong. He was the love of her life, crappy as it was. All of the regulars were there, and it was like old times. Vivian told Jeanni she couldn't stay too late because she had to travel back across town, and the later it got, the less the bus traveled in that direction. Harry heard her and offered to pay for a cab if she wanted to stay longer. She took the money, knowing she would still take the bus, but needed the cash. She always needed the cash. She stayed for a while longer, and just as she was about to leave, MD walked in wearing his paint clothes. Hey Ronnie! He said, happy to see her. He had missed her and was glad she was there. She had a beer with him and talked about getting together for a feast at his place and whether she would cook. She accepted, and they made plans for the next weekend. He would pick her up, go grocery shopping and then go to his place. Already, several people were on board with it. It was always a good time and they all loved Vivian's cooking. It was settled, and she got ready to leave, hugging him deeply and holding on for dear life as he hugged her back. She got to the door, turned, and the last thing she said was the last thing she would ever say to him.

She fell asleep that night happier than she had been for quite a while. Ray had even eaten some of the pizza she picked up on the way back. She had missed her friends terribly and was so happy about the upcoming weekend at MDs. She slept so well that she hadn't heard the phone ring. Whoever it was would call back, she thought as she lay there for a few minutes longer before getting up to start her day. She needed coffee, and the aroma of it brewing drew her from under the covers. She was on her way back to her room when the phone rang again. She saw that it was Jeanni and picked up, greeting her friend warmly. Jeanni's voice cracked a bit on the other end, and it sounded as if she had been crying.

Vivian, (Veronica) I have to tell you something, and it's bad. She was crying. She told her friend to sit down and listen, and then she began.

By the time she was finished, it felt as if Vivian had fallen into a pit, and it was dark all around her. There was a noise, and as she refocused, she realized the noise was her screaming out in horror and pain. MD had been seriously injured at Harry's and had been rushed to the hospital, where he lay in a coma. The rest of the call was all a blur to her. She remembered Jeanni telling her to pray, and then she hung up the phone. She could no longer speak and knew Vivian couldn't either. Vivian's soul was crushed. "No, God, please, No!" This couldn't be happening. She felt faint and lay down on the bed, curling into a fetal position and crying. The phone kept ringing, but she couldn't talk. She knew friends were calling to tell her the same thing she already knew. She had to get out of the house. She had to get near MD. She had to. Vivian knew he was at a hospital very close to her, so she packed an overnight bag, dug out her emergency credit card, and for nearly a week, she stayed in a hotel and was at the hospital every minute of every day. She wasn't allowed to see him, but if she had, she would never have recovered. She just wanted to support his family and be there if anything was needed or anything changed. Vivian barely slept, couldn't eat, and she was very afraid for her friend. When she did go back to the house, the first thing Ray asked was if she had a good time running around like a slut. Vivian never blinked an eye. She went straight to her room and stayed there. She slept like she had never slept one day in her life. She cried all the time and prayed. She could barely breathe and felt like the weight of the world had found its place on her chest.

When she finally told Ray what had really happened, he was cruel. "You're crying over a drunk in the bar?" He walked away laughing. Ray knew who MD was and knew the friendship he and Vivian had, and she believed he was jealous of their relationship. He assumed they had a thing, and she would never tell him what they really had. He wouldn't have understood anyway, so it would be a waste of time. It hurt her to her very core to hear him say that, and she would never forgive him. She ordered some food and sat alone in the dark. Her only solace was Karl. He never left her side. He was her saving grace in the long days ahead. She opened the bag of food and looked in. It was someone else's food because it sure as hell wasn't what she ordered, but just like everything else in her life, she ate it and didn't complain. The days went by, and Vivian stayed in a daze. She only talked to those close to her and close to MD. She shut just about everyone out. She didn't know what to do, so she cooked. Not for herself, definitely not for Ray, but for MD's family. She sent several meals with them and hoped it would. Well, she wasn't sure what it would do, but she hoped anyway.

On January Thirty First Twenty Fifteen, Vivian received a call from Jeanni. MD had passed away that morning after being removed from life support with his family by his side. It was the worst possible news she had ever had, and there was no way for her to deal with it. She cried for him, his family, his friends. She had to go to Harry's to be with the people he loved and those who loved him. That was where she needed to be, so she went. She knew what had caused his injuries and death, and she wanted to lash out at the bartender who had served him more than he needed that fateful night, but it wouldn't bring him back, so she refrained even when she approached her to convey her sorrow and sympathy for the loss of Vivian's friend. It was the beginning of the end of her time at Harry's. Years later, she would not go there at all.

On February Third Twenty Fifteen she went to the funeral of her friend alone. Ray refused to take her to the funeral home. She begged him to take her, but he refused. She got on the bus and rode the distance to the funeral home, walking through the snow and cold to get there. She met MD's daughter for the first time, and they would become close, as Vivian had promised her. For months afterward, Vivian grieved. Years afterward, she still grieved. She felt she would grieve his loss forever, and it became normal for her to think of him whenever she saw a blue jay or heard a song when she was cooking Italian food. There was always something there to remind her of him. He had given her a Lily for Easter one year, and it grew too big for her apartment, so she took it to the house and planted it in hopes it would thrive there. Year after year, it grew, and every Spring, she would look at it and think of him.

By Two Thousand and Sixteen, something had changed in Vivian. Her path was clear, and she was hyper-focused on what lies ahead. She had gone to court for her hearing and had been approved for full disability. She was waiting patiently for her back pay. Ray was waiting, too. Selfish prick! After all he had put her through, he still expected her to take care of him first. It was the only reason he started being nice to her. He knew his payday was coming.

Months later, Vivian was busy planning her next move. She wanted her own place, and she felt that she would never be happy until she was out from under Ray and his ass hat ways. As much as she loved him, she hated him. She had found a place in Dundee, ironically just a block away from John's place. She had everything in place and was ready until the bottom fell out of the barrel. Ray ended up having a quadruple bypass and needed help, so of course, Vivian stepped up to the plate regardless of his behavior and helped him get back on his feet. As soon as the dust began to settle, his mother took sick and shortly after, she passed. Ray fell apart and asked Vivian to make sure her funeral was handled properly. He was only a few weeks out of the hospital himself, and even though Vivian did help him, she couldn't help thinking of how he treated her when MD passed, and she needed his support, but she never said a word, and as a result, she made calls to the landlord and told him she would have to put off moving. A year later, she moved. It wasn't her first pick, but in her haste to get the hell down the road, she took the apartment against her better judgment and hated it from Day One. "Oh well, it's just one more thing'" she thought. She and Ray were in a different place, and one day, when she was talking to Shelly, she confided that she thought he had gained a new respect for her after his mom passed and maybe, just maybe, things would be different. A year later, Vivian moved right down the street and into a lovely apartment full of light, and she loved it. She stayed there for several years, and she was the happiest she had been in a very long time.

Vivian started spending a lot of time with Ray again, and surprisingly, he came to her place often. It was a good period of time for them, and she was able to take a breath. She was doing her own thing, working part-time for Shelly and just enjoying life. She had a new kitty (RIP Karl) she called Lucy whom she loved because she had come from a bad place and had been mistreated and Vivian could relate, so on a cold and snowy night she took her home, and she fit like a glove.

She noticed one day that Ray was acting funny, and she asked him if he was alright. He never told her the truth, but he actually sat down and began to tell her things that were happening to him, and he was afraid. He had a roommate, but he was hardly ever there, and it began to concern Vivian. She knew his health was failing. He had carcinoma, and she had helped him on several occasions with his treatment and recovery. He was falling a lot, and she feared for his safety, with good reason. He had always been a neat freak and kept the house in excellent condition, but she had started noticing things that were disturbing to her. She had known this guy for thirty-two years and knew instinctively when something was not right. Her instincts were probably what saved his life. He contracted a virus that put him in ICU for over a month, and he was near death. Vivian was by his side every day, and she endured the abuse she received from a man who was suffering from delirium and didn't know her from a can of paint. He wouldn't remember any of that, and he had barely recovered when, in March of Twenty-Two, she got a call from his roommate saying Ray had fallen and he needed her help. "When does this shit ever end," she asked herself. She was all in on helping him because, sadly, he discovered that he had no one except Vivian. "I'm so exhausted," she told her friend one day when she had a brief reprieve from the madness. Vivian drove to the house, and what she saw had her on the phone to the rescue squad. He had peed on himself, and there was vomit everywhere. The stench in the house was the smell of death. Three hours later, Ray underwent brain surgery and another two days later. It was determined that he could not be home alone safely, and the hospital staff pointed a proverbial finger in Vivian's direction. There was no doubt what needed to be done, but she honestly didn't want to do it at first. She had selfish thoughts of her freedom, her apartment and having to give all that up to be a full-time caregiver for someone who had not stepped up to the plate through the years when she had needed him most and had treated her like shit, too many times to count.

She was sitting in his room, and it became crystal clear as she looked at him lying in the hospital bed, confused and not able to remember normal things. He looked old; the man she had spent over half her life with was but a shell of himself, and her sense of human kindness got the better of her. Vivian moved for the last time, and as she undertook what was to be the most challenging part of her life, she reflected on all of the men who had found her and left her, mistreated her and controlled her, and treated her like she was nothing and even as she entered the next phase of her life, she knew that it still Wasn't What She Ordered.

Chapter Twenty-Four

Vivian wasn't sure how long she had been in the room, but she knew if she didn't get out somehow, she would be dead soon. She had been subjected to an onslaught of beatings and torture at the hands of a coward who hid behind a mask. He never spoke, and had he been able to get it up, she would have been raped as well. As it was, she had been stripped of her clothing, and she was beyond cold. She could shed no more tears and only felt despair. Zac stood by, helpless to intervene. "You freaking coward," she spat at him each time he opened the door to bring her a tray of food. He could no longer look at her and felt sick at his involvement. "Vivian, don't fight him. You're only making it worse." "Worse, you bastard? Screw you, Zac. You are going to prison, I hope you know." He knew if he wasn't killed to protect his employer's identity, he would most certainly get locked up for his role. He had no idea who the other man was, but he knew he wanted no part of it.

Vivian had figured out that the man behind the mask was not Aaron Walters. He was much larger than Aaron, and he had an odor that if Vivian lived to be eighty, she would always smell it. Besides, Aaron always entered the room from the adjoining door with no mask on. He had done what he wanted to do to her, and he must have felt hiding his face was pointless because Vivian knew she was in his house and thought that he was the mastermind behind her abduction and imprisonment. What she didn't know was that he wasn't but had been paid a ridiculous amount of money by the masked man to allow him to also be there. He didn't particularly like what the man had done to Vivian, and he told him if he didn't watch himself, there would be a problem. Aaron had had his way with her several times, and the only reason he was concerned at all was that he would never be able to sell her for the hefty sum he had been promised by his international client if she was damaged goods. That was the only way he agreed to be involved with Derrell's plot at all. The dude made him sick, actually, and he would be glad when he was rid of him.

One night, after Vivian had endured yet another round of torture at the hands of the masked man, Aaron came to see her. She was treating her wounds in the small bathroom when he came through the door. "Vivian, I want you to be clear about your future and to make no mistake about it. You will be leaving here very soon, but how you leave is up to you." Vivian just stared at him, wondering what his plans for her entailed. "You filthy pig. Do you think you're really going to get away with this? There are people looking for me as we speak, and the only place you will be going is to prison!" She laughed and continued. "You and that fat bastard are gonna share a cell, and maybe if you're nice, he won't turn you out and make you his bitch!" The anger in Aaron's eyes was evident, but she didn't care. She hated him, and she wanted him in hell. He looked at her, and what he said next made her sit down hard on the bed, speechless. "You have very little time left here, Vivian. "We, you and I, will be leaving, and once we do, no one will be able to rescue you. Not even Jack." Oh my God, did he say Jack? How did he know Jack? Surely, Jack had no business with him, yet he said Jack's name as if he knew him personally. Vivian didn't know that Aaron had been on Jack's radar for over a year and had been the reason he had always felt so protective of Vivian, but Aaron knew. He knew Jack had him under surveillance, and it had made moving around difficult but not impossible. She looked at Aaron, and in a calm voice, she said, "he will kill you."

At that very moment, Jack was working tirelessly to find Vivian. Once he knew Derrell was involved, he pulled out all the stops, went to his office and ransacked it, looking for one shred of evidence that would lead him to where she was being held. Lulu and Jamie were frantic, and the office was buzzing with the news that Derrell, their lousy loser of a manager, actually doubled as a criminal and that he was partly responsible for Vivian's disappearance. "That bastard hurts our girl. There will be no place he can hide from us," Lulu announced to Jack, and he knew she meant it. He looked at her and felt the love she had for Vivian. Jamie was in tears and had a difficult time holding it together, but it was understandable, and their friends tried their best to console her. They knew Derrell had it bad for Vivian, but never in a million years had they imagined this. They blamed themselves for not pushing Vivian harder for details when she took on this client, but they couldn't go back now and wanted to help Jack in every way they could. One of Jack's partners had traced the call from Derrell, but it came back to a burner phone. They were unsuccessful in pinging the location. It seemed like one dead end after another, and Jack knew he was dealing with a professional and that he would have to be very careful or he would tip him off, and that, he was afraid, would have serious consequences for Vivian.

He took a step back briefly to re-group, and then he was back at it again. He had to find her. She depended on him not to give up. She didn't know to what ends he could go that would lead him to her. He and his partner Tom drove to the place Derrell and his mother shared, and after some convincing, she allowed them to search his living area in the bottom half of the house. On the surface, they could see nothing out of the ordinary, but Tom saw a room with a padlock on the door, and he quickly destroyed it with a hammer. He called out to Jack, and when they entered the room, Vivian was everywhere. Photos of her in different settings, some with the girls, some alone and at work, covered the walls like wallpaper. There had to be thousands of them. He must have been stalking her for quite a long time to have that many, and a chill ran up the back of Jack's neck. "This man is even more dangerous than I thought," he said to Tom. In one corner of the room, he found a stack of notebooks, page after page, dedicated to Vivian. He found personal items that Derrell must have taken from her office taped to the pages. Sick bastard.

In one of the pictures, he saw a man, not just any man, however. It was Aaron. He knew that face anywhere, and he was beginning to put it together. They were in this together, but why? Aaron's crimes were more sophisticated, and he always worked alone, so Jack figured it had to do with money, a lot of money. He found some of Derrell's bank statements and was surprised to see the amount of money he had in his accounts. Derrell had money. A lot of it. They took everything they could back upstairs and questioned his mother. She pretended not to know anything, but they were sure she was hiding something, so while Jack kept her busy in one room, Tom placed a tap on the phone and a bug in the room just in case Derrell came to the house. Even a madman would check on his mother, and Derrell was not that smart. He would be back. They made a call from the car, and Jack ordered one of his men to post up outside of the house and gave orders that the position should never be abandoned for any reason. His man had worked long enough with Jack to know what that meant. He would be there until he heard otherwise. He packed a bag, and shortly after Jack's call, he pulled up just out of sight at Derrell's place and settled in for what could be a very long stakeout.

Derrell had grown up in the same city he currently lived in, never moving away for any long period of time. His childhood had been plagued with abuse, and as a teen, he was bullied by his schoolmates. His mother was an alcoholic, and his father had skipped out on them when he was a small child. He was always on the outside looking in at everyone else, and the only comfort he ever had was from his grandfather, who treated him as if he were the most important person in the world. After he passed away, the bullying and verbal abuse got worse, and he dreaded each day he had to go to school. The girls were especially cruel, teasing him about his weight and calling him names like pimple face, fatty and all the names the unfortunate kids got called. The girls played pranks on him all the time, but there was one prank that was the reason he snapped and became what he was as an adult. The annual Fall dance was a big deal, and the preparation for it took time. Formal invitations were mailed, and the boys and girls began the process of choosing who they would attend the event with. Derrell knew he was not going, and even if he had, there was nobody who would accept an invitation from him. As the event grew near, he was surprised to see a note attached to his locker from one of the girls who had made his life hell, asking him to be her date. The note had started with an apology for her behavior, and she hoped he would forgive her. It went on to say that she also had a life of hell at home, and that was the reason for her lashing out at him. She was going solo to the dance because she had had a fight with her boyfriend and she had no date. She asked if he would be sweet enough to meet her there and be her escort. Derrell could not believe what he was reading. This had to be a trick, he thought. She was too pretty and popular to want him to be her date, and she hated him. All of the warning signs that someone else would have seen went unnoticed by Derrell. He was so desperate for acceptance that he ignored them and was filled with excitement. He swelled up like a pufferfish. She wanted him, Derrell Patterson.

The night of the dance, he looked in the mirror and liked what he saw. His mother didn't tell him that his pants were too short and nobody wore a tuxedo jacket anymore. He had even taken a shower and slicked down his hair. He left with the corsage he had picked out just for her and headed to the school. For just a moment, the movie Carrie flashed through his mind, but he laughed it off, reminding himself that shit didn't happen in real life. She met him at the door of the gym, and everything seemed normal for once. Nobody called him names or played any tricks on him. He guessed that being with the popular girl had its advantages. He was the only one who didn't notice how awkward he was in a social setting. He danced out of step and spilled a drink down the front of his shirt. She was very nice to him, holding him by the arm and dancing only with him. Little did he know that the shit was about to get real. She told him she was too hot and needed some air, so he walked her to the door, and they stepped out into the cool evening. She pretended to be cold, and he gave her his jacket. Suddenly out of nowhere, a group of jocks rushed him and herded him toward the football field. He tried to break free but was no match for them. He was out of shape and flabby for his age, huffing and puffing when he walked most of the time. The boys got him to the field and proceeded to strip off his clothing. He was down to his underwear and t-shirt when one of the boys produced a rope. He struggled to free himself from their grasp, but it was no use. They tied him to the goalpost.

The girl took her lipstick out of her purse and wrote on his body. He couldn't see what it said, but he didn't have to. She laughed in his face and told him she would never be seen in public with someone like him and told him how pitiful he looked. "You look like a pig, so maybe you should smell like one too." Someone dumped shit and pissed on him, smearing it all over, and then they left, snorting and laughing as they went. Derrell was still tied to the goal post-Monday when the first PE class hit the field. By then, he was almost comatose, bruised and chilled by the night air. Nobody had found him because it was the weekend and his mother had been on a bender, so she hadn't even noticed his absence. He was mortified when the gym teacher cut the ropes, and as he fell to the ground, he changed. He never went back to school and stayed in his room all the time. He told his mother he was not going back, so when the school called to report the incident and ask where Derrell was, she simply told them he would no longer be attending high school there and to never call again. He lay on his bed, and that horrible night replayed in his head over and over until he thought he would go mad. He had gone quite mad, but that wouldn't be determined for years. He saw HER face when his eyes were closed and heard HER voice not only in his ears but inside his head. "That bitch will get hers, mark my words," he said to himself. Many years later, that bitch did get hers. Donna was walking home from work when she was dragged into a car and taken to a dead-end road, where she was brutally assaulted and left for dead. He had had an accomplice, and together, they brutalized her before throwing her out of the car on a dirt road just outside the city. The police had been called to the hospital to document the incident. She wasn't able to tell them much, but she felt he might not have been a stranger. He had said something that had a familiar ring to it, but for the life of her, she couldn't remember what it was. The perpetrators had gotten away, no one was ever charged, and nothing was done. Nothing until she met Jack. He and his team stepped in where the detectives left off and have been investigating the crime ever since. It had led them to Aaron, but they had no idea that the other person would be someone nobody ever expected.

Now, as Jack and Tom sifted through Darrell's papers and note-books, the whole awful truth came together, and they knew Vivian's abduction had been mapped out and seen through intentionally by Darrell. Aaron was not innocent by any means, but it was crystal clear who the mastermind was. Among the papers was a timeline from the beginning to its last entry, the day Vivian went missing. The project had been a rouse to put Vivian and Aaron together. Dammit, why didn't I see this? Was I too personally involved with her and missed all the signs I've been trained for?" He had thought Derrell was creepy but thought he was harmless. He even recalled telling Vivian not to sweat him when she was worried and talked about leaving the job because he got under her skin. He was deep in thought when his phone rang. It was Steve at the stake-out location, and the bird had come home to the nest. And if he left, did Jack want him tailed? Jack gave him instructions to move when Derrell moved, but by no means was he to intervene. They listened to Derrell and his mother as she screamed that he had some nerve getting her involved in his shit. She told him about them being there, and when she told him they had been downstairs, he came unglued. It was quiet for a time, and they figured he must have gone down to see if anything had been disturbed. "You stupid bitch! You had to let them in. You couldn't just for once have my back," he shouted at her. "Because of you, this changes everything."

A moment later, Rod was on the phone to Jack. "He just lit outta here like he was on fire. I'm behind him and will call back when I have a location." Jack warned him again not to be spotted. Rob was the best at his job, and Derrell would never know he was being followed. "Call me the second you have the house on the site, and be careful. Vivian's in that house." Rob was about fifteen minutes into the tail when Derrell pulled off the road, stopping at a dive bar. He drove past, tucked his vehicle out of sight and waited for him to leave. It wasn't long before Derrell was back on the road. Thankfully, the traffic was heavier, and Rob's car went unnoticed. Another fifteen minutes passed, and Derrell signaled his exit. Rob drove on, not wanting to alert him. He watched in his rear-view as Derrell exited the interstate, then whipped around as soon as he knew it was clear and Derrell was out of his vision. He exited where Derrell was last seen and traveled the secluded road slowly, not knowing where his mark was. There were very few homes, and all of them were surrounded by gates and hidden by trees. For a moment, he thought he had lost him, but then he barely saw Derrell's car turning off the road. He stopped and waited for what seemed like hours but wasn't. He drove by and saw the rear end of the car disappearing through a set of gates and up a steep hill, then out of sight. Rob called Jack immediately and gave him his coordinates. "Do not move, and no matter what, DO NOT let anyone leave that property." Then silence. He knew his boss was on his way. Nothing else had to be said. Rob had met Vivian, and he knew how Jack felt about her. He also knew how ruthless Jack could be and had seen him in action many times before. Jack got the job done and was not afraid to take someone down to do it. "This guy gonna get his ass whooped. Glad it's not me!"

Back at the house, Derrell spat out what he had learned to Aaron. Aaron hurried to initiate his plan and made calls to let his buyer know that plans had changed and the trade would have to be done sooner than they had planned. Derrell had disappeared, and he knew immediately where he had gone. He didn't have time to deal with him at that moment, and he busied himself with packing, emptying his safe and arming himself in case things went south.

The door opened, and Vivian jumped up from where she lay. The masked man was on her before she could move and she knew something was wrong. She felt his rage as he landed blow after blow, and she felt the end was near for her. She must have blacked out for a moment, but when she came to, he was still there, waiting. He stood in the corner catching his breath, and when she got up, he grabbed her by the throat and began squeezing the life from her. She fought for her life like never before and, in the midst of the may-lay, grabbed at his mask, pulling it from his face. His hands went to his face, but it was too late. She had seen him. Vivian was still dizzy, but as her vision cleared, there was Derrell standing there with the look of someone whose ghost had just walked up his back. "You bitch! You ruined it, and he was on her again, unloading blow after blow. She thought he was going to kill her, and she pleaded for her life. She could taste the blood in her mouth and was afraid.

Suddenly, the door flew open, and Aaron appeared, pointing a gun at Derrell, warning him to stop or he would finish him. He had Zac with him and ordered him to clean Vivian up and get her dressed and ready to go. Vivian could barely walk, and as he took her to the bathroom, she looked at him and pleaded in almost a whisper for him to help her. Aaron heard her, pulled Zac away from her, said something to him, and then let him go. Zac came back into the room and silently washed the blood from Vivian as best as he could and started dressing her, his hands shaking violently. "Be quiet, Vivian. We won't make it out of here if you don't." Derrell stood outside the bathroom spewing profanities at her and reminded Aaron that he was paying him a lot of money and he shouldn't have gotten in his way. "I wasn't going to kill the bitch, just wanted her to have a parting gift," he said and laughed wickedly. He looked at Vivian and spat in her face before he began. "You don't remember me, do you, Vivian. She looked dumbfounded by the question, so he continued. Let me refresh your memory." High school, your friend Donna. The football field. Oh my God, this was him! Vivian had only heard what happened to Derrell, and he never knew she had severed her ties with Donna when she found out what they had done. She had never liked Derrell, but she was never involved in the cruelty they had subjected him to. However, she didn't stop them from doing it and never said a word when asked what had happened. She had laughed along with them each time, but she was just trying to fit in and didn't know better. When he was finished talking, she could only say how sorry she was that they had done those things to him but that she wasn't involved and had no idea what had happened the night of the Fall event. It wasn't her fault. She was young and stupid. He raised his hand to strike her, but Aaron grabbed it before he could hit her. "I said enough." It's bad enough that I'm going to have to keep her with me until she heals up without you making it worse than it already is.

The room's only cameras were set up to watch Vivian and were not programmed for the rest of the house and property. Nobody even knew the room was there, so Aaron felt it wasn't necessary. That was a mistake he would live to regret. He was unable to see Jack, Tom and Rob scale the gate, enter the property on foot and breach the door of the mansion. Rob had disarmed the security devices, and they were in, searching the rooms for any sign of its inhabitants. When they were all cleared, the three men moved with stealth-like ease. Jack was about to open the door to the wing that Vivian had tried to enter months earlier, but Tom stopped him. He pointed to a line that ran across the top and disappeared. Dammit! Jack could feel Vivian's presence, and he had to get to her. Just as they were about to turn and look for another entry point, they heard footsteps coming quickly in their direction from the other side of the door. They each moved into position to attack, and as the door opened, Jack was floored to see Zac come through it. Before Zac could react, Tom closed his hand over his mouth and dragged him out, but not before the door was jammed open. "Shit, that was close," Jack whispered. At first, he didn't know if Zac was a friend or enemy, but he soon realized he was part of it, and it took seconds for Zac to point out where they were holding Vivian. "She hurt Jack," he said and hung his head. "I'll deal with you later, you son of a bitch." Zac knew he was done, so he told them what Aaron had planned and that he had better get to her before it was too late. "There's another door. It's an exit that leads to the helipad. Take Rob to it from outside you piece of shit! No tricks either, or you're dead."

Rob went with Zac while Jack and Tom headed down the long hallway to a set of stairs leading to a door. They could hear voices inside and knew it was Derrell and Aaron. They waited until Rob sent a signal to his phone that he was in place. If the door was unlocked and they caught the men off guard, then it would be over within minutes. There was no escape for them, but he was still apprehensive because he knew Vivian was also in that room. He didn't know for a fact but was pretty sure at least one of them would have a weapon. It was a chance he would have to take. He turned the handle, and as luck would have it, the door was unlocked. On his three count, they stormed the room. The men tried to flee but were met by Rob as they opened the exit door to escape. There was nowhere for them to go. Jack ran to Vivian, who was stretched out on the bed. She was very still, and for a moment, he thought the worst, but upon checking for a pulse, she stirred and turned to face him. "Jack!" was all she could say before she gave in to whatever they had given her for the journey. Jack couldn't believe the condition she was in and was furious. He turned on the two men, and before his partners could restrain him, he dealt blows to each of her captures until they crumbled in a heap at his feet. Tom pulled out the zip ties and restrained the two men while Jack lifted Vivian into his arms, carrying her out of the room and to the safety of his vehicle. Tom and Rob followed behind, with Aaron, Derrell and Zac. They were shoved into the Hummer, and Vivian's horrible nightmare was over. But was it? He rushed her to the hospital, where she was treated for her injuries, and the doctors told him that she would be staying. She had several broken ribs, a collapsed lung and multiple abrasions, and he felt she needed to be monitored. "Is she going to be alright," Jack asked with concern. Physically, she should heal quickly. She's strong and healthy, but she is going to need to undergo some therapy to help her cope with this ordeal. Jack didn't leave her side. He knew Tom and Rob could take care of business, so he focused his energy on Vivian. The first call he made was to the girls. "I've got her," he said, breathing a sigh of relief. They wanted and deserved details, and he was not about to cross these women, so he gave them a rundown of her condition. Lulu hung up the phone mid-sentence, and she and Jamie were in the car and on their way before he ever had a chance to say goodbye.

The room was barely lit, and for a minute, Vivian thought she had been dreaming when she saw Jack standing over her in Aaron's house and that her nightmare wasn't over. That was until she was able to focus better, and she saw her favorite people in the whole world catching some well needed Z's by her bedside. The feeling that she felt at that moment in time was indescribable, and her eyes welled with tears of pure joy. He had rescued her. Her knight in Shining Armour had come to her when she needed him most, and she would forever be grateful to him. Days later, when she was allowed to go home, Henry greeted her as he always did, heading for the kitchen for some well-deserved treats. Jack took care of his needs, and Henry satisfied that he had not been snubbed, climbed up next to his person and never left her side. Jack didn't either until he absolutely had to leave and file his statement at the police station where Aaron, Derrell and Zac were being held without bail on several felony charges. The police needed Vivian's account as well, but Jack firmly rejected their request, letting the detectives know she would do so when she felt better. He didn't want her to have to re-live her ordeal until she was ready. The doctors had given her pain medication to help, and she slept most of her first week back at home. Jack waited on her hand and foot. Whatever she wanted, he produced. He had moved the remainder of her belongings to his place, their place, and she was happy to see her favorite things spread throughout the house. Of course, the designer in her knew adjustments would have to be made, but she loved him for trying.

Lulu and Jamie were by her side as well, grateful their friend was back home and safe from those bastards down at the city lock-up. She would need them in the coming months, and they would never hesitate to give her all the support she needed. "I keep having the same dream, she told them one day. I am in a hole, and someone keeps trying to bury me. I can't see a face, but the voice keeps shouting for me to lie down, and the dirt is piling up around me, and there's no way out." The girls never tried to analyze it; they just sat and listened. Vivian would have many nightmares but would work through them with the help of her therapist, who was shocked to hear what she had been through.

A month or so later, she kept feeling sick and thought at first that it was all the meds she had been taking, but the feeling didn't go away when she stopped taking them, so she told Jack she needed to see her doctor just to make sure those bastards hadn't done any permanent damage. Concern was etched on his face, but he remained fearless for his girl, never showing how exhausted and blessed he was that she was alright. The doctor examined her and had some labs drawn on her. It would be a few days until the results came in, and he sent her home with some anti-nausea meds and told her to continue to rest. Vivian was tired of lying down and wanted to start doing things, but her ribs reminded her of her limitations, so she took baby steps in completing tasks around the house. A few days later, the results were in, and when she took the call, her doctor asked her if Jack was there. She started to worry but said, "Of course, he's here," and so the doctor continued. We have the results, Vivian, but I would like you and Jack to come to my office as soon as you can. "Oh my God, Jack, somethings wrong. Why is this happening? Whenever something good happens to me, the freaking bad is right behind it, letting me know that happiness is not for me." Jack tried his best to convince her that what she said was just not true and that everything was going to be alright.

Chapter Twenty-Five

The silence on the ride home the day the doctor gave Vivian and Jack his diagnosis was intense. Vivian sat staring out the window, and Jack was left alone with shock and confusion. What should have been possibly the best news she had lately had left them speechless, neither of them wanting to begin the conversation that was inevitable. What should have been the best news of their lives was overshadowed by the deadly calm.

Vivian went over it in her mind again and again. She was on the verge of tears, thinking the worst but praying she was wrong. She remembered the attacks she had been subjected to at the hands of Aaron Walters, and now she was frightened that she would have to carry this with her for the rest of her life.

Jack wanted to tell her how happy he was, but he was left to think Vivian was upset by the news and that it really wasn't about him, but to him, it was.

"Vivian, are we going to talk about this? You have to know that whatever you say to me will not change the way I feel about you. You, of all people, should know that. You can say anything, but please say something, babe, he pleaded with her." She felt like a first-class asshead for not saying anything, leaving him alone with his thoughts.

When Vivian's doctor told her what he did, she ran from the room, claiming to have to use the bathroom, but what she really did was the only thing she knew was right at the time. She called her dearest friend and told her the news, swearing her to secrecy. Until her friend spit it out, Lulu was scared to death. It was something terribly awful, so she had silently prepped herself to be supportive of her friend no matter what. I mean, shit, after what she had just been through, everything else would almost be a drop in the bucket. Once Vivian spilled it, she explained why she was afraid, and it all became clear.

Sitting in the car now, she looked over at Jack and finally said something. A big something. "What if it isn't yours, Jack. Yes, Vivian had been told she was pregnant, but due to her reaction hadn't stayed around to find out how far along she was, and she feared it was a pregnancy out of a rape. She shared her fear with Jack, and he remained calm, although he was fuming inside. That bastard had touched her, and he wanted to kill him. "Babe, we should just call the doctor tomorrow and ask? Let's not make it something until it's something, okay?" She looked at her man and was so glad he was in her life. It made perfect sense, and she relaxed a little. She would sleep like shit that night, but the next morning, she was out of bed and waiting by the phone for the doctor's office to open. Her hands were shaking a little when she dialed his office, but when he came on the line, she calmly asked him.

He laughed a little and teased her just a bit for running out on him the day before but then got serious when he heard her strained laughter. He knew what she had been through and had treated her from the night she was brought in. He apologized to her for making light of her situation. "Vivian, there is no need to worry. You are at least four months pregnant!" he remarked joyfully.

"Oh, thank you, doctor. Thank you, and then she was gone." He chuckled, knowing she was probably running to tell Jack the good news.

Vivian ran into the bedroom where Jack was still sleeping, and she screamed with joy! "We're having a baby, Jack!" she exclaimed. Jack jumped up, startled by her scream, but when he saw the look of pure bliss on her face, he knew they were going to be alright. Better than alright, they were having a baby! As the months passed and Vivian settled into her pregnancy, she pondered what she would do now that she no longer worked for the design firm. It had shut its doors in the wake of everything that had happened, and she really missed working. Jack would have loved nothing better than for Vivian to stay home, but he knew that would not last. She had to work hard her entire life for every little thing she got, and she was not about to sit around and watch as it passed by her. "Pregnant women work all the time, she reminded him. We don't live in the dark ages, you know!" She had always wanted to have her own interior design business, but life was real for her, and she never was able to swing it. Jack wanted to help her, and she agreed to let him just this one time. Accepting someone else's help was still something she had to work on. She had been let down so many times by so many people and was used to doing everything herself, but she was trying. They found a building that had good bones but needed some TLC and a lot of paint. He provided the man hours, and she put her touch on it, and *VIVIANS VISIONS* were born. Months later, her business had taken off, and she needed extra help. Vivian was painfully aware of what had happened the last time she needed extra help, and she shuddered from the memory.

She decided on a senior lady to handle her books, and it took no convincing when she hired the other two to work beside her, not for her. Lulu and Jamie didn't even blink when asked, and along with them, she brought in Stella, another one of their friends. She was quite pleased with her new crew. Vivian sat in her office and reflected on all the tough times she had overcome in her life, and it brought tears to her eyes when she thought of all she had sacrificed to become who she was now. It had taken many years for her to take care of herself first. The days of being an afterthought were long gone. She no longer needed a man but wanted the man she was with. Jack had given her more in the short amount of time they had been together than any man had ever given her, and she loved him for that.

Several months later, Veronica Jane Wilson was born on a beautiful Spring morning, and she was the apple of Vivian's eye. She had dark curly hair and was a whopping eight pounds. Jack was mesmerized by his daughter, and he knew immediately that he would move mountains for her if she asked. Even before Vivian suggested it, Jack knew he was going to have to scale back on assignments. His number one priority was to protect and care for the two women in his life, and he could think of nothing better to do than that. He moved his office to the house and passed down the more risky jobs to his partners, Tom and Rob. They had proven their loyalty to him, and he trusted them without question.

The day they brought Veronica home, Vivian was surprised at her room, which was located adjacent to theirs. Jack had taken out part of the wall, and a glass door stood in its place. He grinned at Vivian. "We have to be able to hear her if she needs us." Vivian never said a word. Even Henry, who didn't like anyone that took up Vivian's time, loved the baby. For practical reasons, he was not allowed in her bedroom, but he was the first one at her door in the mornings, waiting for her to be brought out to amuse him.

Several months later, while Vivian was going through a stack of mail, she came upon a letter from the courthouse. She knew this day was coming, and she dreaded it. She was still having nightmares, and at times, she was afraid to be alone, something that disturbed her more than anything. She was still a little jumpy when she heard a noise, and she refused to allow any men in their home unless Jack was there. Maybe she would always feel like this. Some demons never fade. The trial was scheduled to begin on the following Monday, so she and Jack met with their attorneys to make sure they were prepared. It was going to be cut and dry, and Vivian would probably not even be called to the stand to testify. There was just too much evidence, and their attorneys figured it was just a formality for the record books even to have a trial. Still, Vivian was afraid. She didn't want to see them, re-live the nightmare she was working so hard to forget. Stella volunteered to take care of Veronica, aptly nicknamed "V" by her Uncles.

The trial was in session, and everything about it was ordinary until it wasn't. Vivian had come face to face with her abductors, and as tough as it was to see them, she was no longer afraid. The prosecution laid out to the jury what they had in their arsenal, and by all appearances, there was to be no doubt of their guilt. It was the defense's turn, and Vivian and everyone around her were shocked to hear what they had to say. They painted a picture so unlike what was true and somehow made it sound believable. They made it seem that Vivian was not abducted but had gotten in over her head. They displayed the photos of Vivian and Aaron at Steve's, claiming something that was quite the opposite. They had also obtained photos of the night the girls were clubbing, and a shot of Aaron was taken. A witness was called to the stand who would testify that Vivian had gotten into a car occupied by Aaron that same evening. Aaron's driver would also testify that he had driven the car that evening, and Vivian was indeed in the car. She was not a victim but a willing participant. Derrells attorneys were trying to plead him out as not mentally fit to stand trial and were asking for a not guilty verdict on the grounds that he was, well, a freaking lunatic who had been abused his whole life and wasn't aware of the consequences of his behavior. All bullshit, of course. And then there was Zac. Poor Zac, who had no defense and nobody to argue anything for him. He would more than likely be found guilty and sentenced without a doubt. He had no money, and the others did, and as it always was and will be, money speaks volumes.

Vivian and Jack could not believe what they were hearing. Vivian's attorney countered with one after another photo that had been taken at the hospital of Vivian's injuries, and her physician testified to the extent of her injuries. Her therapist was called to the stand to educate the jury on the effects of what Vivian had endured and the months of therapy to get her mind in a good place again. Lulu was called to the stand, and as she stared vehemently at Aaron and Derrell, she told the jury about Derrell's unwanted advances, him always insinuating himself wherever she was, showing up wherever she was. Thankfully, Vivian was not called to the stand. Closing statements were made, and the decision was then in the hands of the jury. Vivian and the others left the courthouse, ready to wait for the jury to come back. They sat in the cafe, and her attorneys assured her that it would end in her favor, but secretly, they were not convinced one hundred percent. It only took one juror to change the course of events. Several hours later, they were called back to the courtroom because the jury had come to a decision. As they filed in, Vivian was shaking so bad that Jack had to help her get to her seat. As the judge read the legal stuff, the foreman answered, Guilty on all counts for Aaron Walters. Everyone breathed a collective sigh of relief, and then Derrell's verdict was next. It was the same. The jury had not bought the insanity defense at all. Then it happened. Out of nowhere, Derrell lunged at Vivian and shouted, "I'll kill you, you bitch!" The deputies were able to intervene before he reached her, but Vivian was visibly shaken. Jack escorted her from the courtroom before they read Zac's verdict, which was obviously the same. "Oh my God, Jack, he scared the crap out of me," she exclaimed. Vivian looked as if she had seen a ghost. Both men had been given twenty years, and Zac had ten for his role. Jack reminded Vivian that they could no longer hurt her and that she was safe. She knew he was right and relaxed. It was over, and they could finally get on with their lives.

"Let's celebrate. We deserve that much, and we have so many things to be thankful for," she said. They all thought that was a great idea, and the girls went into party-planning mode. A couple of weeks later, all of their closest friends were at Jack and Vivian's home celebrating life and the new addition to the family, Veronica.

As the months passed and life went back to normal, the past became a distant memory. Vivian and Jack had a small courthouse wedding and a large reception afterward, and they couldn't have been happier. After a lifetime of tragedy and loss, through all the pain and rejection, the men who waltzed in and out, through everything, Vivian had survived. She looked down at her plate of food, and tears came to her eyes. "Is everything alright, babe," Jack asked, noticing her tears.

She looked up at him and replied, "Oh yes, Jack! Everything is perfect and Exactly What I Ordered."

About the Author

Jane Edwards is a new and exciting fiction writer who resides in Omaha Nebraska. In 2016 she retired after twenty years from the corporate world where she was an Account Manager for a telecommunications company after working for several years prior with other Fortune 500 companies. She was certified in Corporate Management as well as Trainer in Standard Operating Procedures. She received her security clearance during her tenure with Boeing where she held a Supervisory position.

When she is not writing she spends some of her spare time working with 3Sisters, a non-profit organization that focuses on empowering girls and women and plays an active administrative role as well as volunteering during their fundraisers. Jane loves to garden and is an avid tomato sauce connoisseur.

She has now shifted her focus to her first love, writing. Her debut fiction, This Isn't What I Ordered, is a sultry, exciting tale of a young woman's rise above the lowest points in her life with many dramatic, exciting twists and turns that will keep you turning page after page wanting more!

Most days you will find Jane under the shade of the canopy in her backyard enjoying a good book, thinking of new story lines for a second novel. When it's not snowing of course!

Jane chose her pen name V V Edwards in honor of a dear departed friend.